SANCTIONED

SANCTIONED

THE ASCENSION MYTH™ BOOK 4

ELL LEIGH CLARKE

MICHAEL ANDERLE

DISRUPTIVE IMAGINATION

LMBPN Publishing
PMB 196, 2540 South Maryland Pkwy
Las Vegas, NV 89109

First US edition, July 2017
Version 1.07 January 2024

SANCTIONED TEAM

JIT Beta Readers

Kelly ODonnell
James Caplan
Keith Verret
Alex Wilson
Micky Cocker
Paul Westman
Erika Daly
Joshua Ahles
John Findlay
Kimberly Boyer
Erika Daly
Thomas Ogden

If I missed anyone, please let me know!

Editor
Jen McDonnell

To everyone who ever dreamed of making a dent in the universe.

— Ellie

To Family, Friends and
Those Who Love
To Read.
May We All Enjoy Grace
To Live The Life We Are
Called.

— Michael

PROLOGUE

Dear Bethany Anne,

I can't quite believe that the General has given me the opportunity to be in touch with you.

This may not come as a surprise, but you've been an inspiration to me my whole life. Growing up as a geek I was isolated and alone. I would spend my hours researching the dark recesses of the XtraNET to access information about you, your missions and what you've done to bring together the Etheric Empire.

I've realised in recent weeks though that the information available in the Sark System was incredibly limited. And probably inaccurate. Your name is whispered as a warning to kids who won't eat their vegetables, and amongst criminals who tempt vengeance.

I found it hard to believe that someone who was so driven by justice would be quite so ruthless.

Since meeting your father my suspicions have been justified. I'm starting to understand the sheer scale of the Etheric Empire and what you've had to do to create it. You inspire people to follow you, without even being in the same galaxy, for time scales longer than a single life time. You've inspired people to lay down their lives in service to the cause.

No monster can do that.

Just catching the glimpses that I have about what the Etheric Empire is, I've been inspired. Inspired to do more. To make more of a difference in the world. To take on bigger challenges.

And still, when I look at all you've achieved, and all the lives you have touched and transformed, I can't believe that I could do anything like this. I have a small team: a handful of good people right now, and honestly I'm struggling.

I don't know how to be the leader they need right now, never mind the leader I will need to be for what may be to come.

And besides, who am I to lead them as broken as I am?

I don't know if there is an answer to this question, but given the opportunity to write you, I thought that if anyone had any wisdom to share on this topic, it would be you.

Forever in your service.

Ad Aeternitatem.

Molly Bates

Gaitune-67, Sark System

SPHINX

THE KURTHERIAN GAMBIT (TM)

ESTARIANS

THE KURTHERIAN GAMBIT(TM)

OGGS

THE KURTHERIAN GAMBIT(TM)

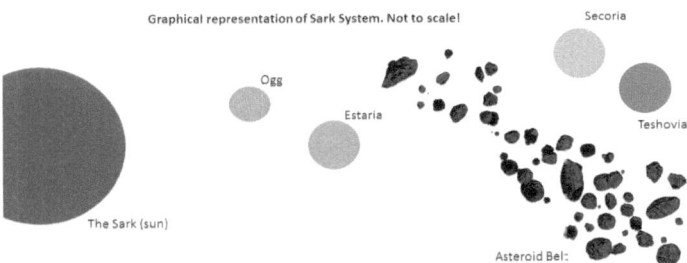

Graphical representation of Sark System. Not to scale!

The Sark (sun)

Ogg

Estaria

Secoria

Teshovia

Asteroid Belt

CHAPTER ONE

Gaitune-67, base conference room

Captain Jack Nolan sat awkwardly on the other side of the conference room table. All her years in the field had made her adept at combat, strategy, and commanding troops. She was a decorated officer, and knew how to rain hell on her enemy. She had the strength to rival even the bigger Estarians on her teams, and had kicked the ass of many a superior rank in her military training, literally - and figuratively -in, well, everything.

She also had a reputation for taking no bullshit.

Or prisoners.

Nothing had prepared her for this, though.

The woman they called "the boss" sat across the conference table, watching her. Every now and then she would make a facial expression like she was having a conversation that no one else could hear. She was geeky, that was for sure; but it seemed like she'd been transplanted into the body of... a cheerleader, and just forgotten.

The commanding officer who had recruited her from Estaria and brought her up to this secret asteroid base sat beside the woman, asking the questions. That was strange in itself, since she was told she already had the job.

If she wanted it.

"What would you say is your biggest weakness?" the officer known as Joel Dunham asked her.

The woman held up her hand to interrupt him. "Actually, I need to ask something." The geeky-cheerleader hybrid glanced over at Dunham. "Sorry - do you mind?"

Dunham waved his hand obligingly, granting her the stage.

The boss looked at her, a small frown across her eyes and forehead. "I'm sorry. I have to ask," she began. "But why do you call yourself by a man's name?"

Jack had been wondering how long it was going to take before someone asked her that. She took a deep breath.

The boss looked a little uncomfortable asking her own question. "I mean," she continued quickly, "it's okay and all. We accept people exactly as they are, for *who* they are, here. But you, er... you seem female."

Jack smiled in acknowledgment. "I am. But my father wanted a boy, so he raised me as a Sarkian would raise a boy - with martial arts, gun training, and hand-to-hand combat. And he called me Jack. My mother had planned to call me Jacqueline."

The woman sat back, her face relaxing. "Ah. I see. That makes sense." She looked at her colleague, and was about to let him continue. Then she did the face like she was talking to someone else.

She seemed to change her mind, and glanced back at Jack, and stood up. "Okay, so the job's yours, if you want it. We'd be glad to have you on the team." The strange woman walked around the conference table to shake her hand.

Jack stood up, bewildered, and took the handshake. She glanced at Joel, who still had holo screens out and was mid-interview or mid-conversation... or mid-whatever this was - and looked equally thrown by his colleague's behavior.

The boss woman turned towards the door and started heading out. "You can manage from here, right Joel?"

Joel turned to watch her leave. "Er, yeah. Sure thing, Molly," he agreed.

The woman left.

Jack, unsure as to whether she should speak her mind, decided to anyway. "Wow. Ghosted!" she exclaimed, a little humor in her voice, as she tentatively sat back down.

Joel grinned. "Yeah. You'll get used to that. She er... struggles with the social element sometimes." He chuckled a little. "Don't worry, she's *great* when you get to know her. She was probably juggling a few things at once, just then."

Jack frowned a little. "Juggling? What do you mean?"

Joel relaxed a little and leaned forward on the enormous conference table, as if letting Jack in on the joke. "Ah, she has an AI in her head. She may have been given intel, or something she needed to act on right away."

Jack looked like she understood. "Ohhhh" she mouthed softly, smiling in appreciation at being let into the fold.

The door to the conference room whooshed open, and a huge muscular guy walked in, making even Dunham look weedy in comparison. "Molly said you guys were ready to start orientation?" he said to Joel.

He glanced over and smiled at Jack.

Joel swiveled around in his chair and sat forward, leaning his arms on his knees. He glanced back at Jack, then back at the muscle guy. "Yeah. We're good, I guess. That is..." he turned back to Jack. "You want the job, right?" he asked.

Jack shook her head, confusing Joel for a second. "Hell yeah," she smiled. "I'm in." She smiled to herself. "Heck, if you guys are even half as crazy as the rumors say you are, and with even a fraction of what I've seen in the last few hours getting here, and all..." she motioned to where Molly had been sitting. "I'm in for anything!"

Joel stood up as the new guy walked around to the other side of the table to introduce himself. "Well, in that case, I'm Sean Royale. I'll be your liaison between normality and crazy."

Sean held out his hand. It was huge. Jack, who had been known to put a large number of marines on their ass in various forms of arm wrestling, took his hand, and made the smart move to not try and prove anything. "I'm Jack," she told him, shaking gently.

Sean grinned. "Good to meet you, Jack."

The pair looked over to Joel. Joel closed out his holos. "Okay, so if you guys are good, I'll go catch up with the lady boss. Squad training in two hours, yeah?"

Sean nodded. "We'll be there."

Joel smiled and left the room, leaving Sean and Jack alone.

"So," Sean reflected, looking at Jack. "You don't seem the normal commanding officer type. How did you end up getting selected for this crazy house?"

Jack shrugged. "Long story. But yes, not your normal CO. I had a knack of winning in the military; they had no choice other than to promote me. That's where I discovered I'm not the natural administrator." She cocked her head contemplatively. "So I think this level of crazy mixed with field work is going to suit me just fine. As for how I got selected..." she gestured towards the door, "You'll have to ask Captain Dunham."

Sean motioned for her to lead the way around the conference table. "Well, in that case, let's introduce you to your team, and the base of magical adventures!"

The two headed out of the conference room.

Jack allowed herself to grin broadly only once his back was turned. She followed Sean out of the conference room.

Gaitune-67, Safe house, Kitchen

Joel found Molly in the safe house kitchen, doing battle with the mocha machine.

Again.

"Þöngulhaus Kaffivél," Molly cussed. "I swear this machine can see me coming. Oz? Help."

Joel stood in the doorway, watching her press buttons and rattle at panels and levers that didn't want to budge. "Stressful day, dear?" he asked.

Molly looked up and glared. "It would be fine if I could get this fucking heap of trash to cooperate."

She turned back to the machine.

Oz?

You're trying to process a fresh cup, but there is already an empty pod in there.

Fuck my life.

Molly grappled with another panel on the machine, and managed to pull it open. She peered into the little compartment that had popped out and dug out a crinkled piece of plastic. Dumping it in the trash, she turned back to Joel.

"Well, that couldn't have gone much worse," she said.

Joel watched her, amused. "You're talking about making a first impression on your new team member?" he clarified.

She scowled at him.

Joel grinned. "I think you did perfectly. She now knows exactly what she's getting herself into…" He couldn't help but chuckle silently, his shoulders and chest bouncing in amusement.

Molly slammed the panel shut and put the mug back under the machine. "I'm glad *you're* amused," she retorted, poking at the button on the machine again.

Joel, still grinning, pulled out a chair at the kitchen table and plunked down. "Okay, let's see what we can do about this leadership thing. I mean, you were doing so well! What, with finding a way to keep Crash from going crazy, and listening to the others about what they need to be motivated and engaged on this isolated rock."

Molly turned and leaned against the counter while the machine whirred and did its thing. "Yeah, really great... You know that Crash hasn't been using the pods just to get his cabin fever ya-yas out?"

Joel cocked his head. "Huh?"

Molly folded her arms. "Yeah, he's using his pod time to go and see some chick he's been talking to on the other side of the asteroid."

Joel looked confused. "But Paige said he's been more relaxed since he had pod time."

Molly raised her eyebrows knowingly. "Well..." she paused, waiting to see if the penny would drop. When Joel showed no signs of putting it together, she moved on. "The point is, this 'motivating the troops,' or, more precisely, training and managing them, *bites*."

The machine fell silent and she picked up her mug. "You want one?" she asked Joel, indicating at the machine.

He shook his head. "No thanks. But this management thing is just something you need to work on. No one - well, very few people - are able to just do it naturally. Why do you think the military invests so much in leadership training, and personnel development?"

Molly sat down on the other side of the corner where Joel had placed himself. She hugged her mug with two hands and shrugged. "Dunno. I can see it's important. But I just don't know where to start."

Joel leaned forward, resting his arms on the desk. "You've already started. Now we just have to keep refining," he told her. "So, why don't we talk about finding out what really motivates them?"

Molly shrugged again. "Okay," she said flatly.

Joel took that as a sign to continue. "Alright, so let's take

Pieter. He's an odd one. He's not a soldier. He doesn't do this for the pride. Or for justice. But he does care about his team. What do you think he struggles with most, though?"

Molly wracked her brains. Her eyes fell on the rim of her mocha cup. "Not gambling?" she guessed.

Joel shook his head. "No. The gambling was a symptom. His biggest challenge is being able to connect and bond with people."

Molly frowned again, and moved her gaze forward to the wooden table, still not looking at him. "How do you know that?"

Joel tilted his head. "You remember when we had that post-op pizza fest, where you announced Maya was joining the team?"

Molly nodded.

Joel sat back in the chair and crossed his legs in a four shape. "You remember how Pieter lit up when Sean ruffled him, and bear hugged him?"

Molly took a sip of mocha. "Yeah, vaguely," she said after swallowing.

"Well," Joel continued slowly, "that was a breakthrough moment for Pieter. He suddenly felt accepted." He tried to catch Molly's eye. "Haven't you noticed how since then, he's been hanging out with the others more, and coming out of his shell?"

Molly glanced up at Joel. "Yeah, he's become more of a smart arse too!"

Joel grinned. "Exactly. Cuz he's comfortable with the team now. He feels accepted, like he can be himself."

Molly started to smile a little. "I see. That's... great." Her eyes developed a distant look for a moment. "So, how does that help me manage him?"

Joel nodded his head and started waving his hands in explanation. "What it means is that he craves connection. So your job as his leader is to make sure he finds opportunities to keep developing that. That's why on the training exercises, I keep pairing him with either Paige or Brock. They've bonded already - so I keep giving them the opportunity to make that bond deeper.

17

Eventually, he'll start naturally spending time with the others, too... But to force him out of his comfort zone before he feels ready to, will just keep him struggling and feeling like an outsider."

Molly pushed her mocha cup forward and let her head hit her arms in front of her. "I don't know how I'm ever going to do this voodoo you do," she exclaimed.

Joel put a hand on her arm. "It's okay. You'll get it. It just takes time. And practice. How about you have a conversation with Maya next, and see if you can work out what's important to her? You know - what she hopes to get out of being on the team. What she wants to do with her life. That kind of thing."

Molly lifted her head, stray hairs flopping over her face and into her eyes. "Yeah. I can do that. I guess."

Joel took a breath. "Good. That's the next thing then." He stood up. "Okay, we're due in training in a couple of hours, and I have some case files to go through. See you down there?"

Molly had put her head back into her arms. "Yeah..." she said, muffled through the table and sweatshirt arms.

Joel shook his head, and tucked his chair back under the table. He patted her head gently. "It'll be okay. Promise."

He left.

Molly?

Yeah?

You have a meeting with the General in ten minutes.

Oh, shit. Right.

Molly lifted her head and pulled her mocha closer. She examined the contents of the cup, her nose wrinkled.

What the fuck is wrong with this mocha, Oz?

I don't know. Take another sip.

Molly took another sip. She paused.

Oz?

Yeah?

What's up with it?

Erm. You might not want to drink the rest.

Why not?

You don't need to know. Just throw it out.

Why?

It's not good. Just throw it.

Molly's head hit the desk again, in exhaustion and exasperation.

Bloody hell. Just shoot me now...

Gaitune-67, Base conference room

Molly sat like a schoolgirl in the head master's office, dwarfed by the size of the empty conference room. The holo in front of her illuminated her skin, making her look blue.

Wish I'd managed to drink even half a mocha before this meeting.

Well, you had time. If you hadn't wasted eight minutes with your head on the desk, you would have been able to.

The hologram of the General leaned forward, as he continued speaking.

"... and that means you need to wrap up your escapades with The Syndicate as soon as possible," the General concluded.

Molly suddenly started paying attention, and rewound in her mind what the General was saying.

"Hang on," she said, "are you... Did you just? How did you know about our plan to go after The Syndicate?"

The General leaned back in his anti-grav chair, sucking on the cigar thing he always seemed to have handy.

Molly kept talking. "Are you bugging the safe house, still? I thought you weren't listening, out of respect for our privacy?"

The General seemed genuinely amused. "I'm not. Nor is ADAM," he added, seeing her next question formulating in her open mouth.

Molly's brow furrowed, her frustrations for the day only

increasing. "Well, what then?" she asked her impatience bleeding through.

The General smiled. "It's not rocket science, my dear," he told her. "You have an AI in your head. Your AI simply mentioned it to my AI."

Molly couldn't contain her disbelief. "What?" she almost screeched, before remembering who she was talking to. "You mean your AI and my AI are having some kind of frickin' bromance-slash-secret-liaison behind my back? And *then* landing me in it?"

The General grinned and nodded. "Seems so," he concluded, taking the cigar out of his mouth.

Oz, you fucking traitor.

Oz didn't respond. Molly couldn't even feel him.

The General leaned in on his desk. "So, anyway, this is how it's going to play out..." he continued.

Joel and Sean stood waiting outside the conference room casually, or not so casually, peering in to see what was going down.

"She looks pissed," Sean said, wandering away from the door and leaning against the corridor wall out of view.

Joel nodded. "Yup," he agreed. "She wasn't in the best mood going in."

Sean sighed. "What do you think they're talking about?" he probed.

Joel was still watching stealthily through the window. "Dunno," he shrugged. "It was meant to be a planning meeting... which was why I thought I should be here when she came out." He paused a moment, and then carefully stepped away from the window. "Come to think of it... how come you're here?"

Sean grinned. "It's alright, cowboy; I'm just here to give her a

rundown of some of the toys you guys haven't cracked into yet."
He gestured off to the hangar deck down the corridor.

"Ohhh," Joel said. "I see. So... official business, then."

Sean nodded. "Right." He had his arms crossed, and he now
flexed his muscles, demonstrating his enhanced prowess. Joel
resisted the urge to roll his eyes. He'd been working out extra
hard since getting to Gaitune, but Paige wasn't wrong when she
noticed that he upped his game again when Sean joined the team.

Joel glanced back into the conference room. "Well, I suppose I
should leave you guys to it then," he concluded.

Sean started to say something, and then changed his mind.
His expression softened. "Well... You know, if you want, I can
show you how to use some of the bigger artillery later. After
squad training." He unfolded his arms and put his hands on his
hips, before reaching up and scratching his head. "If you want,
that is..."

Joel wasn't looking, so he missed Sean going a little red and
awkward about his extension of friendship. "Yeah, sure..." Joel
responded, peering back into the conference room, distracted.

The meeting seemed to be wrapping up. The General gave
one last instruction, and then the holo closed off. "Oh, hang on.
They're finishing," he told Sean.

Sean pushed up off the corridor wall, and stood straight.

Joel paused a moment, and then waved his hand in front of
the conference room access pad. The door whooshed open.
Molly turned from her seat, making no immediate effort to get
up. "All okay?" Joel asked, hovering at the door.

Molly nodded, and leaned back in her chair, swiveling round
to see him better. "Yeah," she sighed. "I can make it work."

Joel ambled into the room, pulled a chair away from the table,
and perched his butt against the table's edge. "'Make it work'?
That doesn't sound like the same girl who attacked the mocha
machine earlier," he smiled.

She grinned. "Yeah, that girl got her arse kicked by two AIs and the General of the Etheric Empire. It's time she got her shit together and showed them who they're fucking with." Her face lit up as she talked herself up. A hint of the devil emerged in her eye.

Joel smirked. "I know that look. That's the look you get just before I get hauled into one of your diabolical plans!"

She smiled innocently, her eyes wide. "I'm sure I have no idea what you're talking about, Mr. Dunham," she exclaimed.

Sean appeared at the door. "Did I hear there was a diabolical plan afoot?" he asked.

Molly glanced over at him, bringing him into the conversation. "You did. Turns out my bitch of an AI has been in bed with ADAM, and let slip that we decided to take down The Syndicate between now and starting on the General's official missions."

I said I'm sorry.

It's okay, Oz. It's better he knows.

"Anyway, the General basically said to get it cleaned away and done, because he wants 110% of our attention. And that works for me."

Joel looked a little surprised. "You mean he basically just gave you his blessing?"

Molly nodded. "Indeed. And he gave us time scales and a training plan to get to in between and after. Oz is going through and scheduling us as we speak."

Sean looked impressed. "Must say, the General has the right idea. The Estarian situation has been a low-level pain in our brains for a while now. It will be good to see that regime topple."

Molly clocked Sean's comment. "Hmm. Sounds like you have even more intel you haven't shared yet." She looked at him like a teacher would look at a naughty schoolboy.

Sean grinned. "Yeah, yeah. I'll fill you in on whatever is relevant when we put our battle plan together. Don't you worry."

Joel cut in. "So we're going to take down the whole Syndicate once and for all?" His voice was a little more surprised than Molly had expected.

She nodded. "Every piece. We have permission, and his blessing, to take the whole thing apart. Right down to the companies and subsidiaries, and any law that we need to alter to keep these dodgy mechanisms in place."

Joel whistled. "Wow. This is going to be one heck of an op." He shook his head. "How long do we have?"

Molly took a deep breath and stood up, stretching out her back. "About a week."

Sean and Joel's mouths dropped open.

"Well, come on, boys," she said straightening up. "No time to stand around gawking. We have work to do." She turned to Sean. "How about we get going with that weapon rundown after training later? I could do with some research time right now."

Sean managed to bob his head. "Er... yeah. Sure."

Joel looked concerned. "How about we switch the training session to a general briefing to get the team up to speed on this latest development?"

Molly thought for a moment, her eyes up at the ceiling.

Can we be ready for a general meeting by then, Oz?

Yes. I think we can do some of the planning with the team's input.

Molly looked back at Joel. "Great idea. How about we involve the team, and pull together any information they might have to help us come up with a plan?"

Joel nodded, smiling a little, despite the elevated stress level. "Someone's learning team management," he told her, impressed.

Molly grinned. "Girl's got to try!" she replied as she strode out of the room.

Both guys turned and followed her out. Sean started walking along side her. Joel hung back, typing into his holo as he walked.

OZ. ANY CHANCE WE CAN CHAT?

CHAPTER TWO

Gaitune-67, Base conference room

Joel sat in a pod on the hangar deck, having carefully selected one that was turned away from the main walkway.

He'd wanted a quiet word with Oz, and the small space, coupled with the audio integration, meant that he could easily have a two-way conversation with Oz here; better than anywhere else on the base or in the safe house.

Joel waited until the pod door was firmly closed. "Heard you accidentally let ADAM know what the plan was?"

Oz's audio channel cracked open. "Yeah. Won't be making that mistake again. She was not pleased."

Joel's voice was sympathetic. "Yeah. She'll get over it. I don't think it was a big secret, anyway."

Oz's voice didn't convey that he was overly concerned. "Yes. I think I'd agree with you. My Molly mood-heuristic has her being completely back to normal with me by the time the group meeting is over."

Joel's tone was incredulous and amused. "You're kidding! You model her moods?"

"And behavior," Oz added.

Joel thought for a moment and leaned back in his seat, leaning one elbow against the side of the capsule. "Wow. But what for?" he asked.

Oz's tone was matter-of-fact. "Wouldn't you like to have a heads up on how she is going to react to something, instead of sitting around and waiting?"

Joel chuckled, hardly believing his ears. "You mean you can make predictions that are accurate?"

Oz's voice conveyed that he had realized that Joel was impressed by his operation. "Yes; within a certain tolerance, of course," he answered, a little pleased with himself.

Joel shook his head, and whistled a little through his teeth. "You'll have to tell me more about that some time."

"Sure," Oz promised. "So, what's on your mind?"

"Well..." Joel started slowly. "It's Sean." He paused a moment. "Well, it's not Sean," he corrected himself. "It's me. I mean, I'm used to being surrounded by competitive jackasses; but normally I can hold my own. But Sean," he sighed, "he just has too much over me."

Oz's voice revealed he would have been smiling. "Ah yes, his *enhanced capabilities*," he confirmed sympathetically.

"Right," Joel agreed, glumly.

"And you're wondering what I might be able to do to help?" Oz checked.

Joel nodded, shifting his elbow, which had been slipping down the side of the pod. "You read my mind, Oz."

Oz chuckled. "No - just your heuristic."

Joel frowned, and sat up straighter. "You're kidding?" he asked, half impressed, half disbelieving he warranted that much trouble.

"Yes, I am kidding," Oz confessed. "I haven't modeled your behavior formally. But, to be fair, you're not as erratic or complex as Molly, so..."

Joel laughed to himself. "Yeah. I hear you,' he agreed, his

attention drifting off as he remembered some of her infuriating complexities. He shook his head, bringing himself back to the conversation. "So, what do you think you can do for me?" he asked.

"Well," Oz conceded, "nothing from your current installations... But," he continued, "if we could acquire some additional implants and tech, we could do a heap of stuff."

Oz paused.

"What exactly are you looking for?" he clarified.

Joel hesitated. "Faster reflexes. For ops," he added quickly.

Oz couldn't see, but Joel's face flushed a little pink.

Oz chuckled. Joel could feel the slight vibration of his laughter through the seat of the pod.

"What's so funny?" Joel asked.

Oz's voice was still bouncing with humor a little. "Nothing. Just funny how male humans compete!"

Joel dropped his arm from where he had wedged himself and was almost up out of the seat in protest. "I'm not competing. I'm... I'm..."

The vibrations of Oz's laughter paused. "Yes?" Oz prompted.

Joel deflated, and slumped back into the chair. "Okay. I'm competing," he admitted, flushing an even deeper shade of pink. "But it will also be good for the team," he added weakly.

Oz chuckled again. "This is true," he concurred. "Which is why I'm going to help."

Oz went quiet for a few moments. Joel shifted awkwardly in the pod, still feeling a bit hot around the face.

Finally Oz spoke again. "We're going to need a set of implants, which I'll have ordered up on the next shipment. And you're going to have to bring Brock in on this."

Joel nearly shot out of his seat again. "Whaaaa?" he blurted. "Brock? Why him?"

Oz's voice was steady, with a hint of irony. "He's the only one of us with a body who might have the necessary skills to implant the devices we're going to need."

Joel settled a little, huffed, and wedged his arm back onto the side of the pod for comfort. Then suddenly, he looked suspicious. "Hang on," he stalled. "Where exactly are these devices going?"

Oz sounded more clinical now. "We should have a stimulator-cum-relay at the bottom of your brainstem, and then one on the outside of the cortex."

Joel did a double-take, glaring at the heads-up display in front of him, as if he could eyeball Oz. "You what-what?! You're talking about Brock doing brain surgery on me?"

Oz sighed. "Well, yes. Technically. But no need to be so melodramatic!" he exclaimed. "The one in the brainstem can be injected, and it will settle in place. The one in the cortex will go in around your temple, where the bone is thin anyway," he explained somewhat flippantly.

Joel went pale, the effects of any blushing completely neutralized.

Oz continued. "It will be fine. Brock has more than enough dexterity to take out a tiny slice of bone, put the implant in, and then replace the bone and let it heal up," he reassured Joel. "You'll hardly feel a difference once it's in…" He paused, and then qualified his statement. "Unless it overheats."

Joel's voice jumped a few octaves. "What do you mean, 'unless it overheats'?" He suddenly remembered himself, that he was trying to keep his presence in the pod a secret.

Oz pulled up a simple diagram from the product page of the device he had located on the XtraNET. "It's a slight risk. If the chip doesn't go into precisely the right amount of tissue, it won't be able to run the signal, and so it might heat up."

The area around Joel's eyes rumpled in confusion and frustration. "In which case?" he pushed.

Oz remained clinical. "In which case, we simply remove it and try again."

Joel shook his head in disbelief. "Oh, right, so no big deal, then."

"Right," Oz agreed plainly.

Joel looked out onto the hangar deck, away from the brain diagram. "I was being ironic," he told him.

"Yeah, I got that," confirmed Oz.

Joel was silent for a moment, thinking through his options. He could always not have the procedure and just keep working out. But then he'd never have Sean's reactions. Or speed. Or strength.

He sighed. "Okay, so I need to have a word with Brock at some point, then?"

Oz's channel had gone quiet. Hearing Joel's response, the audio opened up again. "Yes. I'll let you know when we might expect these parts though."

Joel leaned forward to grab the handrail and pull himself out of his seat as the door opened up again. "Okay, great. And thanks, Oz. I appreciate you helping me."

"Of course," Oz replied. "Got to help a brother out."

Joel grinned and hopped out of the pod quietly.

Before closing the door, he peeked around the hangar, just to make sure no one was around. Satisfied, he waved his hand in front of the access panel, and the transparent door slid quietly down.

Joel crept for a few strides, and then stood up straight and walked casually back to the main thoroughfare around the outside of the hangar deck.

Sean Royale, you cocky son of a bitch. I'm going to show you and your cyborg ass who can shoot, he thought as he climbed the stairs two at a time back towards the demon door corridor. He had another meeting to get to shortly, and a few things to organize before then.

. . .

Gaitune-67, base conference room

Just over an hour later, the team was assembled in the conference room for the briefing. Jack had been introduced to everyone, and sat between Sean and Molly.

Joel was the last person to arrive. Since he and Jack were already acquainted, he waved to her and pulled out a chair around the corner of the table from Pieter. He noticed Pieter tracking his movement and leaned over to punch him gently on the shoulder before sitting down.

Molly was standing up, ready to begin. As soon as Joel was seated, everyone spontaneously gave her their full attention.

She ran through the order of proceedings in her head, as the manual for briefings had suggested. *First, welcome them and acknowledge anything new or different,* Molly recalled. *Jack is new,* Molly told herself.

"Greetings, everyone," she began. "Thanks for being here. I know you were looking forward to squad training, but we'll schedule that for a little later on."

There was a rumble of chuckling throughout the room. Squad training was the bane of their existence; but, like eating vegetables, they knew it was vital to their survival - in a very real and immediate way.

Molly continued. "As you may already know, we have a new team member. Her name is Jack Nolan. She is a decorated former officer, and has run operations and teams bigger and badder than you can even imagine. She's tough as nails, and is probably going to give our boys Sean, Crash, and Joel a run for their money." She paused and glanced around at her GIs. "No offense lads," she winked.

Jack blushed a little. She was far more used to having to prove her toughness than having team leaders pre-warn their guys about her.

This was going to be a refreshing change.

Molly went back to her mental notes. *Tell them the purpose or outcome you want from this meeting.*

She took a breath, organizing her thoughts. "The reason we called this meeting over squad training is because I had a conversation with the General earlier. As a result of what we discussed, we're going to have to shift our plans."

She waited for a reaction in the group. Not a single person flinched.

Relieved, she continued. "What we'd originally scheduled was to go full-tilt into training for the General's mission in three weeks' time. In the interim, Joel, myself, Oz, Sean, and Maya have realized that there was a pattern behind our latest missions; The Syndicate was behind them, trying to set us up." She paused, glancing at her more senior team members briefly. "We finally have enough data and resources to commit to taking them out, once and for all. When the General found out about this, he not only sanctioned it, but insisted we clean it up before we join the mission they have planned."

She took a deep breath. "So, in effect," she concluded, "we've doubled, or maybe tripled, our workload."

Brock grinned, his hands on the table, leaning into the discussion. "Nothing new there, then, eh?" The team erupted into chuckles. Paige clapped her hands, and Crash slapped on the desk to make more ruckus.

Molly grinned at him. "Knew you'd be up for it!" she said, her shoulders relaxing a little.

Pieter leaned forward and crumpled up his face a little, like Sean does. He sat a little askew on his chair, too. As Sean does. "So, who are we to kill, and how dead can I kill them?" he asked, mimicking Sean's intonation.

That was it. The conference room erupted into another bout of laughter that could be heard all the way through to the hangar deck. Molly put her hands on her waist and hunched over laughing.

Finally she composed herself. "You can kill them very dead, Pieter." She glanced over at Sean, who was doing his shoulder-and-chest-bouncing silent laugh. "Perhaps the real Mr. Royale can help us out? You have new intel about the Syndicate? Namely, how we can find them?"

Sean sat up and leaned forward, careful to not screw his face up, or shift his weight sideways. He glanced at Pieter coyly, his eyes narrowed, before turning his attention to the group and responding. "Right," he confirmed. "Our contact, Garet Beaufort, has been posing as a member of The Syndicate for the last several months…"

He paused, noticing Joel's eyes widen. Molly didn't show any signs of it being new information to her.

Sean continued. "… Ever since he went back to Estaria, after you first extracted him. He'll be able to tell us when all the members will next be in a room together. They'll have layers of security we'll need to handle, but once we know where and when, we just need to decide what to do when we get there. Snatch and grab. Point and shoot. Or something else."

Sean glanced over to Molly for her decision.

Molly shrugged. "I'm more concerned with breaking up the systems they have implemented and represent. Sure, we can kill them; but then we need to do the work to dismantle what they've put in place… which will come afterwards, I guess."

Sean held her gaze, waiting for a definitive.

She hesitated a moment, thinking, then shrugged again. "Okay. Take them out."

Sean grinned.

Joel took a breath and inserted himself into the conversation, as the rest of the team watched carefully for their orders. "I think the reality is that unless these people are forcibly removed from influence, they're going to keep that system in play; a system that is costing lives, and causing suffering for generations of civilians. We have a moral duty to intervene."

Molly's face relaxed a little. She nodded, moving onto the last point she needed to cover in her meeting plan. "Okay, so strike team will consist of myself, Crash, who will guard the pods, Sean, Joel, and Jack."

She then indicated to the remaining team members by pointing a finger at each of them, as if selecting them on a dashboard. "Pieter, Brock, Paige, and Maya; I need you here, working to gather anything you can find that will tell us the weaknesses in their organizations, that will pull them down once they are dealt with. Paige, I wonder if you can also get with Garet after the takedown, and find out how to change the legislation which is allowing this kind of regime to thrive?"

Paige nodded and made a note. She seemed more focused on the job in hand than the prospect of having to speak to her ex. Molly noticed, and made a mental note to keep tabs on that situation. And possibly confer with Joel about it in their next management training pow-wow.

"Maya, Joel can hook you up with our police contacts on the surface. They will no doubt want to help any way they can. They've been trying to take these guys down for years. Especially the female detective we met... She sounded like she'd been immersed in tracking down the group for several years. Her name... Chaakwa?"

Molly looked at Joel for confirmation, and he nodded in agreement. She glanced back at Maya who was taking a note. "Okay, got it," responded Maya.

Molly glanced around the table. "Anyone have any questions?"

Brock raised his hand. "Do we still have training today?"

The mood in the room lifted a little. Molly sat down, waving her open hand to Joel.

Joel considered it for a moment. "Yes, training in half an hour. We'll keep it tight, and then you can get on with prep for the mission." He glanced over at Sean. "I guess we wait for you to give us our window?"

Sean nodded silently, but definitively.

Brock sat back in his chair and Pieter glanced over at him with a glare. "Way to go, reminding them of training," Pieter huffed comically.

Molly remembered there were other items. "Ah, one second, people."

She looked over at Maya. "Maya, you need to close the loop on your life on the surface. You can't let anyone know where you're going to be, but you probably want to let the people who care about you know that you're safe and well. And better give your boss a heads up so he can disappear for a little while. Don't want him getting caught up in any backlash, since he was one of their pawns."

Maya nodded.

Joel had a suggestion, and leaned in a little again. "We could always go do that today, so that it's out of the way before we strike? Make sure we're not missing anything, or leaving her boss vulnerable in our efforts."

Molly agreed. "Good thinking. Okay, perhaps you want to do that after training."

Joel nodded. Maya looked down at her notes. Molly couldn't see her face, but she needed to wrap up the meeting. "Okay," Molly announced, "the rest of you can go get ready for physical training."

The room became a hub of activity as the team stood up and started chatting.

Molly called over to Maya. "Maya, can I have a word?"

Maya got up and tucked her chair out of the way as the rest of the team emptied out of the meeting room.

She ambled round to Molly's side of the table. "Hey…"

Molly smiled, and perched on the table's edge. "Hey. You okay? You seemed… well… *something*, about having to go down to surface."

Molly waited for Maya to speak.

Maya nodded her head quickly and smiled weakly. "Yeah, I'm fine. I just... I know we agreed that I'd stay up here. And this is truly what I want. I'm just... I didn't think I'd have to say goodbye to my friends so soon."

Molly looked down at her feet as she processed. She looked up. "Ah, I see. I can understand that. Your boss?"

Maya had a hint of sadness in her eye. "Yes. He's been like a father to me."

Molly felt her sadness. She tried to contain her emotions, though. "I get it," she said sympathetically. Molly hesitated, trying to figure out how to handle the situation. She imagined what Joel would say, and then just repeated it as she heard it in her head. "Just know that you've found a new family now. We'll take care of you..." She hesitated, and then made an effort to pat Maya's upper arm, awkwardly. Then she smiled. Equally awkwardly.

Maya wasn't quite sure what was happening. She shuffled a tiny step backwards. "Er... Thanks," she said.

Molly suddenly looked more rigid. "Erm. So. Why did you decide to come to Gaitune to work with us in the first place?" she asked stiffly.

Fuck, this social crap is hard.

You're doing great. Remember Joel says practice, practice, practice...

Maya looked at Molly a little stunned. "Er. Well, Sean brought me up here, and you offered me a job."

Molly felt flustered. "Yes, yes, I get that. But what gets you *excited* about it? I mean, is it your teammates? Or a certain teammate...?"

Dudette, you are so crashing and burning on this.

Thanks, Oz. Now fuck off.

"Erm," Maya took another half step backwards. "Yes...? I guess? The opportunity to work in a team..."

Maya had started blushing uncomfortably. "So. I. I should

probably go and get ready for training..." she said gesturing towards the door.

Molly nodded in relief. "Yes, of course!" she said as brightly, with as much manufactured team spirit as she could artificially muster. "See you down there!"

She watched as Maya scuttled out of the room, like a mouse freed from a trap.

Yep. Yep. That could have gone worse.

Molly ignored him and slumped back into her chair, her head falling straight into her hands.

Nevermind, Sport. Just practice, practice-

Oz, if you don't shut up, I'm going to take a flamethrower to my fucking holo.

Oz fell immediately silent. The way her circuits felt, he wouldn't put it past her.

Sean poked his head around the door. "So, reveling in the ups and downs of leadership, I see?" He grinned at her without mocking her.

Molly lifted her head from her hands, her hair falling in her face again.

He stepped more fully into the room. "Ready for an induction into some real toys?" he prompted.

Molly slapped her forehead. "Oh, right," she remembered. "Hangar deck playtime."

"Yes! Unless..." he had a glint in his eye. "You'd rather just hang here and wallow in self-pity about how hard it is to talk to team members when you're not giving them orders?"

She smiled.

"In case you were wondering," he said, venturing further into the room, "that was a joke. Sarcasm. I'm not actually suggesting you-"

She nodded. "I appreciate the clarity," she said. "Actually. I really do," she sighed. "People are so fucking complex. And then trying to be nuanced and shit back... Ugh."

She shook her head vigorously messing her hair up even more.

Sean grinned again. "Toys?"

She stood up and started heading out of the room with him. "Yes. Toys. And ships. And guns," she agreed, looking somewhat consoled.

He waved his hand in the direction of the door for her to lead the way. "Coming right up," he told her, following her out.

The pair strode down the corridor and out into the main hangar deck, now walking side-by-side. "You ready to see the big fuck-off ship in the middle, now?"

Molly's eyes lit up. "Oh, yes indeedy," she confirmed excitedly.

Sean couldn't help but brighten up around her enthusiasm. It was like a natural reaction, like a cup of hot cocoa or hot shower warms one's body.

They passed through the whooshing double doors onto the hangar deck.

Sean's pace quickened a little. "Okay, so this bad girl," he said gesturing at the ship as they approached her from the rear, "can easily carry about a hundred troops, plus their gear. It has incredible warp capabilities, maneuverability and..." He leaned in closer to whisper to her.

Molly fell quiet and stood still, wondering what he was going to tell her that was so important.

"Gate capabilities," he finished, his eyes wide and excited.

Molly stared at him blankly.

Sean moved his hands and head again, as if "ta-da"-ing the statement again would help her understand how profound his revelation was.

Molly blinked.

Sean stood back a little and frowned at her lack of reaction.

"Huh?" she asked.

"Gate capabilities," he repeated more loudly. "The ability to create and travel through gates."

Molly shook her head, not understanding.

Sean spoke more slowly. "You know what a gate is?" he checked, hardly believing he was having this conversation with her.

She shook her head again.

Then she paused.

Then… "Ohhhhhhhh. You mean like the Annex Gate in settler history?"

Sean rolled his eyes. "Holy fuck. *Seriously?* That's your only reference?"

He waved his arms, exasperated, and kept walking closer to the ship. "How do you think anyone in the Etheric Empire gets around these days? Certainly not on piddly warp drive. Mother of my ancestors!" he cursed in exaggerated disbelief.

He turned back to her, compelled by genuine curiosity. "Did you think the rest of the world uses warp speed?" he pressed.

Molly's eyes looked up as she processed the information. From what he was saying, the Sark system is probably a few hundred years behind in technology. At least.

She nodded, feeling like a little girl that had just been told that fries are grown in the ground. She still wasn't sure if this new information fitted in her universe.

She needed answers.

Molly frowned back at him. "How is the wormhole created, then? And sustained? And then why doesn't the ship spaghettify as it goes through?" she asked him, intensely.

Not waiting for an answer, she continued. "And where the fuck does all that energy come from? Are you telling me you can just create them whenever you like?"

She fired her torrent of questions at the cocky marine, who seemed to be visibly knocked backwards by them.

He held up his hands in surrender, wearing a grin a mile wide. "Hey, hell if I know!" he protested. "I just fly the damn things. But it's something I'm sure ADAM and the General will be pleased to share with you in a geeky mind-meld some time," he chuckled.

Molly seemed unsatisfied.

"Come on," he told her, indicating to follow him. "Lemme show you something."

He led her around to the front of the craft, and they looked up. The cockpit was way out of sight, but she spotted the queen bitch insignia on the side.

"You know what that is, right?" he asked pointing up at it.

She nodded.

"Good," he said. "So then you know what it means to have one of these ships?" he queried, now unsure that she knew anything of the world beyond Sark.

A slight smile crept across Molly's face as she lit up. "Yeah, I'm starting to."

"Good," he told her, breathing and relaxing a little. "At least this isn't totally wasted on you," he muttered cynically under his breath. He started walking underneath the nose to the other side, signaling with his head for her to keep following.

They came out on the other side, and he moved a little further back towards the wing. Then he stepped back a little more. He waved his hand, and a laser beam appeared to spot his position. A second later, a holo access point appeared right next to where they were standing.

"Shit!" exclaimed Molly excitedly. "What is-? I've never seen anything like that!"

Sean winked. "You ain't seen nothing yet, sweetheart," he told her. A moment later he had keyed something into the pad, and the device scanned his retina.

Immediately, the ship started to come to life. No engines; just a quiet activity of internal systems coming online.

Molly noticed the hum. A moment later, Sean started walking

forward and lifted his leg as if to step. Molly watched him, confused.

"What are you-" she started to ask.

Sean stepped up and then stepped again, walking up what could only be an invisible staircase.

Molly moved to the side of it. She couldn't see anything. She waved her hand. She connected with... air. "Fuck!' she whispered under her breath.

Sean called down to her. "It's okay. Just come around to the front where I stepped up, and you'll see a slight field distortion."

Molly moved back around to where Sean had started his ascent, and sure enough she could just make out ripples of light distortion creating the stairway.

She stepped; the stairway reacted a little but held her weight. As she pulled herself up and took the next step, its consistency reminded her of the adapting sofas and chairs in the ops room. She reached her hand out and placed it down, and the stairway reacted to her movement and gave her an invisible handrail.

She looked down at the space beneath her feet, and then at her hand grasping onto something that wasn't there. "This is cool as shit!" she giggled.

Sean was several steps ahead of her, now. He turned back to her, also grinning. "I know! Right?" he said, beaming.

She followed him up the stairs, wondering how this would let them into the ship. As soon as Sean was a couple of steps from the body of the ship, though, the side became – well, she didn't know quite how to describe it. The side of the ship was still there, and visible, but it had become somewhat translucent. By the time she got close to it, the ship's side had completely evaporated a doorway-sized section, allowing them passage into some kind of main entrance.

Molly looked inside, and then took a few steps backward to look at the outside. The translucence disappeared at what looked like the edges of the doorway, and turned back into a normal-looking ship. But she couldn't see the boundary.

There was no edge.

She reached out her fingers, and there was nothing to touch - as if she were putting her fingers through a hologram.

Sean watched her like a parent watching a child examine a strange looking cobble in the street. "You done?" he asked, smirking arrogantly again.

Molly raised one eyebrow. "Not yet," she replied, oblivious to his tone.

She ran down a few of the stairs and looked back, noticing how the outside of the ship seemed to change on the approach as a result of her perspective. She stomped back up the stairs again and back into the foyer area, which was lit like something out of a science fiction movie.

Sean mimicked her previous raised eyebrow. "And now?" he asked.

Molly nodded simply. "Yep."

Sean shook his head in amusement. "You going to explain what your little examination yielded?"

Molly shook her head. "No," she smiled, teasing him.

"But you're now satisfied with how it works?" he pressed.

"Yup," she nodded.

Sean looked a little deflated that she was able to figure things out without him dropping her tiny bits of information.

Molly looked around the foyer and cabin area. There were seats that looked like they were hovering. That meant anti-grav.

Sean didn't give her a chance to take it all in. *Probably because he takes it for granted,* she assumed. He led her straight through a field-like door that was there, but also not, into a narrow passageway. It was much darker, and there were doors off it.

"Restrooms," he pointed. "elevator down to the infirmary," he pointed at another access door.

"Infirmary?" she asked.

"Yeah. This is a transport battle ship. I know your boy Joel is a sharp shooter, but, out there, normal soldiers get hit now and again. That's where we patch them up," he explained.

Molly grinned. She clocked how he talked about Joel. His words were competitive, but his tone was affectionate.

I wonder if those two are developing a bromance, she mused. *Oz and ADAM, and now Sean and Joel... Like they're marrying into the Etheric Empire.*

She shook her head at her weird thought processes.

"They're developing something that will help in the field, medically," he told her.

Molly cocked her head as she continued to follow him. "Oh, what do you know?"

Sean glanced back, serious again. "Nothing I can share."

Molly scowled, running her hand against the wall of the passage as she walked. "So why say anything at all?" she asked, a hint of annoyance in her voice.

Sean turned back. "Good point," he conceded.

Molly shook her head at his ego slipping through.

Sean continued with the tour. "That one is your armory," he said, pressing a finger against a door panel. "And then through here," he kept moving forward and signaled ahead of them, "this is where the magic happens." His voice lifted, and they were back into playtime.

They stepped through another doorway, or field, or whatever it was that separated the compartments out, and into a fairly large cockpit.

There were six consoles, complete with the anti-grav full body control chairs. The window out onto the hangar deck was clear, but with various heads-up display screens patterned all over it... different things clearly being controlled at different consoles.

Sean turned to face her, holding his arms outward by his side. "So, what do you think?" he asked her.

Molly looked around, completely in awe. "This is one hell of a ride!" she confessed. She looked at the different stations. "Does that mean you need six people to fly it, though?"

Sean shook his head, and turned the front right seat to perch down into it. "Nah. One person can fly this baby pretty easily. They're each enabled with intelligent systems. 'EIs,' we call them."

Molly frowned. "So why six chairs?"

Sean shrugged. "The techs joke that it's something to do with government regs and wanting to keep pilots employed," he smirked. "But, honestly, in the heat of battle, sometimes you just need the human element." He nodded over to the chair nearest Molly. "That one allows a person to take control of the weapons system, leaving the pilot to focus solely on the flying."

He indicated to the one opposite, on the other side of the floor space where Molly had stopped. "That one is the Nav chair. You can scout and plot a course, and pull up maps before you gate to it."

Molly's eyes flickered in recognition. "Gate…" she repeated. "Tell me more about that."

"Well," Sean grinned, "as you know, this baby is what we call *gate-enabled*, which means she can create her own gates whenever she wants."

Molly was still looking at the nav chair. Without being aware of what she was doing, she gravitated over to it and swiveled it around to get closer to the console it sat in front of.

"How does it know where a gate is going to end up?" she asked.

Sean got up and stepped over. "Go on," he said, helping her into the chair.

She held his hand as she climbed up into it. As soon as her weight was on it properly, it recalibrated for her mass and tipped her back into it properly. A harness released three quarters of the way down, and she figured she could just pull it and strap herself in, if she were staying.

At the same time, controls appeared under each hand, and something fuzzed in her brain.

Molly. You still there?

Yeah. What was that, Oz?

I dunno. Something is trying to access my security.

Molly was frowning. "Sean - what's it doing? It feels fuzzy in my head..."

Sean's voice was calm. "It's okay. It's just communicating with you," he explained.

Molly relaxed a little. "Well, Oz says it's trying to hack his security protocols."

"Oh, shit!" Sean slapped his thigh and laughed out loud. "No way?"

Molly tried to sit up a little. The buzzing in her head was distracting and over-stimulating.

Sean held onto the arm of her control chair as he laughed.

Molly frowned as she fought the chair's recline. "Damn it, Sean, not funny."

Still laughing, he stepped closer to see the console. He swiped at a screen and flicked a setting. The buzzing stopped.

Molly's face relaxed. "What did you do?" she asked.

"Well," he explained, composing himself. "These babies aren't designed to be flown by people with their own onboard security that hasn't been put there by the Empire."

"I," he tapped his head, "am of course fully integratabtle, as it were. Your AI, however, is alien tech; and therefore, not able... or perhaps *willing*," he said emphatically, "to interface."

I am willing. I just don't like being violated like that.

You and me both, Oz.

"Okay," she said, relaxing back into the console chair and tipping back slightly. "This normally integrates with the navigator's brain. To what end?"

Sean pulled over the control chair next to her, and perched against it, as he had previously. "The tech integrates psychically.

It's much faster and more accurate than any key pressing or EI. However, it's normally only used by trained navs." He turned and indicated around to the other consoles. "The reason being that they've been taught to control their instructions and thought processes under pressure."

"Ohhhh," Molly mouthed. "So that goes for the gate, as well? Instead of finding some kind of coordinate for where I want to be, I could just…"

Sean was nodding. "Just think of where you want to end up."

Molly's eyes were wide. "Wow!" Her eyes scanned the console trying to figure out what she could. "Can I try? Without actually gating us, or jumping, or whatever?"

Sean nodded. "Sure. Here, you'll need to interface though." He leaned forward and grabbed a device that had two curved prongs on it. "These bits," he told her, pointing at the tips, "need to go around your temples."

Molly took the device and turned it over in her hands. Then she turned it over again to figure out how it went on. Finally, she resolved to putting it on how she might a headband, and then flipped it back to sit on the back of her head while the prongs sat on her temples, as instructed.

"Now what?" she asked.

Sean made a half-smile as he straightened up a little. "Now, think of where you want to be."

Molly thought hard about the only place she wanted to be. The only place she could think about since this whole base started unfolding for them. Within a second, the console screens had illuminated and started displaying star maps and coordinates.

Sean jumped up and his mouth dropped open as he watched the display. "Fuck! That's classified intel. How did you know that location?"

Molly smirked. "I didn't. I just interfaced with your psychic tech… which found the location, as it's meant to."

Sean's eyes were wide again. "But... That's-"

"The location of the General," she finished his sentence for him.

Sean took a deep breath and relaxed. "I see..." He looked half-inspired and half-nervous.

Molly grinned. "And it worked!"

"It did," he conceded, shifting his weight onto the other foot and leaning his hand on her armrest. Then he grinned in genuine delight. "You sound impressed," he noted.

She pulled the corners of her mouth down. "More surprised," she quipped. She pulled the device off her head. "How far away is that, anyway?" she asked, handing the device back to him.

Sean looked at the map. "A gazillion light years," he announced. "But thanks to this baby, maybe twenty minutes."

Molly's mouth dropped open this time. "It takes nearly that to get out of the hangar."

Sean winked at her. "Exactly!" He paused. "Although, you haven't seen me fly," he added.

Molly shook her head. "Wow. Wow. Wow," she breathed, looking around the cockpit again.

Sean couldn't help himself. "So... does this earn me negative dickhead points?" he asked, looking a little sheepish.

Molly half-smiled. "Yeah, I guess." She paused. "Some."

Sean popped the head device back into its slot and stood up. "Right, then," he told her. "I guess we both have stuff to do before our training session."

Molly shuffled awkwardly out of the control chair. "Yeah. We should get moving," she said, noticing the time on her holo. "I've got some details I need the guys to check into before we firm up our plan for tomorrow."

Sean flicked a few switches, and the ship started to power down. Then he led Molly back through and out to the invisible stairs. He went down first, but turned around to make sure that she had the handrail okay.

Molly tried not to watch her step, as there was nothing to watch. Logic dictated that the stairs would either adapt to her, like the chairs in the op room, or that they would be spaced for the most effective descent. She trusted, and stepped down one after the other.

She turned her head so that Sean could hear her. "So when you come to Sark, it must feel like you're coming into the Wild West, or something," she called forward to Sean.

He turned slightly as he kept stepping down. "Yeah, a little bit," he called back. "Obviously, the outer system is far less developed than the central ones… but sure. Even Estaria is a bit backward, compared to most places in the Etheric Empire."

Molly's mind felt that it had just been stretched by their little show and tell. "That's pretty cool. I can't wait to see…"

"You'll see soon enough, I'm sure," he commented. They headed up the stairs to the upper level just as Maya and Paige were coming through to the hangar deck.

The two girls seemed engrossed in conversation, though that was nothing new. They were always either talking or laughing, ever since they clapped eyes on each other at the hospital. Molly tried to hear what they were saying. She thought she heard the words "PR" and "nail varnish," as she and Sean whisked by with waves and appropriate head nods, depending on who was doing the acknowledging.

Please tell me I'm not going to end up helping run another business, Oz.

That, I cannot guarantee, I'm afraid.

Molly shook her head, smiling as she followed Sean back through the double doors to the Demon Door corridor.

CHAPTER THREE

Gaitune-67, Safe house, Common area

Paige came running up to Maya, her heels clicking on the safe house flooring. "Hey, have you got time to talk about those PR connections we discussed a few weeks ago?"

Maya stopped walking and turned to see her. "I was just heading out with Joel to Estaria," she pointed towards the basement door in the direction she had been heading. "But walk with me…"

Paige grinned and linked arms with her, and Maya squeezed her arm as they trotted down the stairs together.

"So, what do you need?" Maya asked.

Paige shrugged as they made their way down the second flight of steps. "I'm not sure. I'm thinking I need to understand which departments to target first, I guess."

Maya held the door open for them to head down to the basement. "Sure. So how far along are you with it right now? I mean, have you got anything in production yet?"

Paige shook her head, and pulled her lips to one side, as she started down the stairs. "Nope. Molly has just nailed the formula down. We're looking at places that might be able to manufacture, then we'll get some quotes in."

They stepped into Brock's workshop. Brock was working away at a new holo terminal they had installed recently. He had his back to them, but heard them coming and waved his arm.

"Hey, Brock," Paige called. "Hi, Brock," said Maya in passing.

Then, turning back to Paige, she had serious task face on. "Okay, so we can't send samples yet. This means you want to start building relationships for now. Tell them what's unique about what you're doing; the story behind it. Talk about the science, too. Maybe even see if you can get Molly involved. This is editorial stuff. It's gold."

Paige frowned. "So, we don't actually pre-sell anything, yet? You know, talk about the actual product?"

Maya smiled. "Oh, my dear, this *is* pre-selling. Editorial is waaahaaaay more powerful than any ad you can place. I'd jump in on this window while you can!" she exclaimed excitedly.

Paige still looked confused. "I don't understand. You're saying I just talk about the science, and that will sell it? I thought people hate hearing about the science."

Maya grinned more broadly. "Well, science and the story. People love a good story. And the reason this is more powerful, is because people's BS meters are low on editorial."

Paige seemed to get it. "Ahhh. And high on adverts!"

Maya clicked her fingers and pointed at her friend. "Exactly!"

Paige skipped a little as they headed through the demon door and into the corridor towards the hangar.

Maya thought for a moment. "You know, I have a couple of peeps I could hook you up with for that kind of thing. Lemme see what happens now when we talk to my old boss, and if it's safe, I'll make those intros."

Paige swiped at the door and it whooshed open. Maya stepped out onto the hangar deck staircase first. Paige followed her through. "So that's the PR taken care of," Paige smiled, satisfied.

Maya grinned again. "Yeah, this is going to be fashion world domination by the newest nail varnish technology!" They giggled.

Just then, Molly and Sean appeared, coming up the staircase. Paige waved vigorously, grinning her excited grin. Maya beamed, and did a playful, yet respectful, mock salute at the pair.

Molly and Sean seemed engrossed in conversation and simply nodded politely with their characteristic space-marine nods.

Once past them and down on the hangar deck, Paige chuckled again and spoke in a low voice into Maya's ear. "You know, they must think that we're a pair of teenagers." She rolled her lips inwards, considering. "We should probably be more professional around the base."

Maya shook her head. "Let's not," she winked.

Paige opened her mouth in shock, trying not to smile; her eyes giving her amusement away. "You're kidding?" she asked.

Maya shook her head. "Hell no. Why should we have to pretend to have a stick up our ass? What purpose would it serve?"

Paige frowned, considering. After a moment she yielded. "Yeah. I mean, the military has their way of doing things, and ways of being; but if we're respectful and get the job done, I can't imagine anyone would care."

Maya grinned. "Exactly."

They had arrived over at the pods, and Joel was already there, waiting. "What are you two plotting?" he called as they approached from the walkway.

Paige and Maya looked at each other and then back at Joel, looking as wide eyed and innocent as possible. "Nothing!" they said in unison.

He smirked. "You said that faaaaar too quickly!" He swiped at the access panel of the nearest pod. "Anyway, Paige, I'm going to have to borrow your partner in crime for a little while. Think you can manage without her till we get back?"

Paige unlinked Maya's arm, made a pretend sad face, and sniffed as if crying. "I'll try," she said, brushing an imaginary tear from her cheek.

Maya slapped her arm playfully. "You're such a drama queen!"

In perfect timing, Paige grasped at where Maya's tap had hit her arm, and pretended to clench it in pain. "Oowwwwwww! I'm not!"

Joel turned and got into the pod to hide his smile. "Oh, these two are trouble with a capital 'T'!" he mumbled to Oz as he got in.

Oz clicked into voice mode. "I'm modeling their behaviors. At this time, I can't see them negatively impacting any of the operations at all. Am I missing something?"

Joel sighed. "Yes, Oz. I was referring to their social dynamic. When women pal up like that, it normally means they can end up giving us guys more shit than we bargained for."

Oz was silent for a moment.

Paige and Maya hugged, and Maya bounced over to the pod, waving over her shoulder.

"Okay. I've factored that variable into my heuristic," Oz disclosed quickly, before Maya swung herself up into the pod and plunked down next to Joel.

Joel chuckled a little. "Okay Oz, lemme know how that evolves. I'll be interested in the model you come up with."

"Will do," Oz agreed. "We're off to Newstainment, correct?"

Joel reached back to grab his harness, and nodded for Maya to do the same. "That's correct, Oz. Make it so!"

The front panel of the pod started to close, and Maya and Paige waved vigorously to each other.

Joel raised his hand a little in a goodbye. "You know you're going to see her again in a few hours."

Maya didn't even look at him. "I know," she said, unencumbered by the natural seriousness of the military that she, Paige, and Brock seemed to naturally unsubscribe from.

Joel said nothing, but wondered what Oz was making of it. A moment later, the pod lifted off and whisked them out into space on their usual route.

"Hey, there's something I was going to ask you about," Maya said as they swept away from the asteroid.

Joel glanced down at her. "Yeah?"

"Molly," she stated.

Joel raised an eyebrow, intrigued. "Yes?"

Maya sighed, choosing her words as carefully as she could. "Erm... So. I, er, had a strange conversation with her after the team meeting earlier."

Joel frowned a little. "About?"

Maya naturally mimicked his frown. "Erm. I'm not sure. It was... odd." She paused. "I... I wonder if she was coming on to me, or something."

Joel took a second to process what she was telling him. Maya looked up at him, waiting for his response. A moment later, he slapped his thigh hard with a crack, and exploded in laughter.

"That is the funniest thing I've heard all week!" he guffawed, almost uncontrollably.

Maya looked shocked and slipped sideways across the bench-seat away from him, to better take in what was happening. Stunned, she watched him try to get control of himself.

"Molly... is... well..." Maya could see he was *crying* with laughter. Tears streamed down his face faster than he could wipe them away.

"I'm sorry. But it's just..." He creased up in another fit of laughter, trying desperately to catch his breath.

A moment later, Maya found herself snickering along with him; amused mostly at his amusement.

Eventually, they managed to settle down. Joel sighed. "Phew.

Wow. Okay," he started. "Lemme explain what probably happened."

Maya grinned. "Yes... Please do!" she demanded playfully, feeling a lot more comfortable than she had several minutes before.

Joel glanced back at her briefly. "Okay, so Molly has been working on her team management skills, and one of the tasks she had was to talk to a few team members about what motivates them."

Maya tilted her head a little. "Right..." she said slowly, following his explanation.

Joel bobbed his head, reached out to the handrail, and turned to look at her a little more. "Right. So I think what happened was she was trying to talk with you about that... and because she's a little socially awkward sometimes-"

Maya nodded. "Ahhhh, I see." Maya raised her chin in understanding.

"Yeah." Joel was quiet for a moment, glad the explanation was easy for her to comprehend.

Maya giggled, and flushed a little. "Well. Great. I mean, that's a relief. I just... I didn't know what to do."

Joel smiled. "Yeah, you don't need to worry about Molly. She'd be very clear, almost clinical, about anything like that. And I suspect she wouldn't be propositioning team members."

Maya slumped back into the seat. "Good to know," she nodded.

The pod approached Estaria, and started the descent.

Joel noticed and changed the subject. "Okay, we should probably talk about what we're going to tell your old boss..."

Maya frowned, and became serious. "Yes. This, perhaps, isn't going to be quite so straight forward," she sighed.

Newstainment Offices, Downtown Spire

It was early evening as the pod descended into Spire to deposit Joel and Maya on top of the Newstainment parking lot. From there, they made their way through to reception and, after signing in, were directed up to Maya's old office.

Striding through the corridors, they found most offices were fairly quiet. Not deserted, because, well, the news industry had a certain work ethic; but quieter than in the middle of the day. Maya hoped that this would at least mean that Bob wasn't going to be tied up in meetings.

They headed through the final corridor and into the open plan newsroom. Sweeping past the cubicles, Maya scanned the office for anyone she might want to say something to. Like "goodbye". Or "stay in touch". Or something...

She'd only been away a few weeks, but already the place felt alien to her.

They rounded the pillar and had a clear view of Bob's office. He was alone.

Good, thought Maya. *That will make this easier. Straight in and out.*

She and Joel jogged up the steps to his office. Bob sensed the movement, and looked up from his holo. When he saw Maya, he looked surprised and stood up straight away.

She hesitated at the glass door, and then pushed it open. Joel held it open above her head and helped her push through.

Bob came around his desk to greet her. "Maya. You just disappeared. How's your grandmother?" He grasped her by both shoulders, not entirely knowing if she was okay or not.

Maya shook her head. "Sorry, Bob. I just had to tell you that so you wouldn't worry."

Bob had suspected as much, and nodded, concerned. He looked up at the stranger with her. Maya noticed and turned to Joel. "This is Joel. He and his team have been looking after me."

Joel stuck out his hand, and Bob took it. It took a split second, but as the new information sank in, Bob's handshake became more vigorous. "Thank you. Thank you for keeping her safe," he told Joel.

Joel made the right noises, and Bob's attention went back to Maya. "So you're okay? You've not been hurt?"

Maya shook her head. "I'm fine. I got caught up in something, though, and I think you're in danger, too. That's why we're here."

Bob ushered them to sit down. "So you're not here to come back to work?" His eye twinkled a little, though his face was serious. Maya couldn't tell if he really meant to push her to come back to work, so she assumed it was just his way of parsing the information that he was having to take on board.

Maya and Joel sat in the chairs in front of Bob's desk. These were visitor chairs.

Staff normally stood - on account of it making their exit from his office faster when they were dismissed.

Joel glanced at Maya, and decided to step in. "Mr. August, we're here because we believe you're in danger."

Bob looked nonplussed. He waved his hand. "I'm always in danger - if I'm doing my job right," he added.

Joel nodded in agreement. "Perhaps. But this is different. And Maya is involved." Joel's tone was respectful and commanding at the same time.

Bob sat back in his chair, some of his bravado fading away. "I'm listening," he told the former space-marine.

Joel realized something, and stopped talking. He tapped two fingers to his ear.

Bob took a second to realize, and then suddenly started getting up, nodding.

Joel stood up with him.

Maya looked at them, wondering what was going on. Bob reached for his atmosjacket off the back of his chair. "Well, it sounds like this is something best discussed over a drink."

Joel bobbed his head. "You don't hear any arguments from me. Where did you have in mind?"

Maya caught on, and got up, too.

Bob had his jacket on, and was opening his office door for his visitors. "Quaint little place across the street. Shall we?"

Maya grinned at the cunningness, not believing for one second they were actually going to show up at O'Neil's across the street. "Yes. Good thinking, boss."

She led the way out of the office, closely followed by Bob and Joel.

The three of them arrived in the abandoned parking lot that Bob used on occasion to meet sources who were especially sensitive about being seen with him.

The place was ideal, as it had two entrances; both of which were blocks from where the actual meeting place was. No one watching from outside could possibly track where they were going.

"We shouldn't be heard here," Bob told them.

Joel looked around him. "How about followed?" he asked.

Bob shook his head. "Too convoluted; plus you need key card access to get here from the street. No way they could have followed us."

Maya looked around. "This place is creepy," she grimaced, wrapping her arms around her as if she were cold, rather than just creeped out.

Bob grinned. "Which just adds to the clandestine feel when you're meeting sources," he winked. "Whistleblowers love it," he told her, tapping the side of his nose; still teaching her.

He turned his attention back to Joel. "Okay. So what's going down?" he asked.

Over the next twenty minutes, the three of them stood talking in hushed tones, their voices drowned out by the sounds of water pipes and ventilation units from the restaurants above.

When they were almost done, Joel made his final suggestion. "We should have this wrapped up by tomorrow, but we don't know what the fallout might be from their lackeys." He looked seriously at Bob. "You're a good man. You don't need to get caught up in this. Get out of town for a few weeks, and let this cool off. You'll be able to return when it settles."

Bob opened his mouth to argue, but then realized he'd had this very same discussion more times than he could count. Normally he was on the other side of the conversation, though. Sometimes he had been right, and the person didn't heed his warning. Sometimes he'd been wrong. But given the decision matrix, and the number of times he'd wished he hadn't been right, he knew the smart thing to do was to take Joel's advice.

He yielded, and nodded affably. "You're right. I'll have someone fill in for me, and I'll stay off-grid for a little while." He looked at Joel with genuine gratitude and respect. Then he turned to Maya. "I suppose this means you'll be heading off-world indefinitely, then?" he asked.

Maya nodded sadly. "Yes. I think I have things to do, being a part of this team."

Bob nodded his understanding, and looked down at his feet. Maya touched his arm gently. "You've been an incredible mentor to me Bob," she told him.

He looked up and met her eyes.

She smiled, her eyes still sad. "Thank you. For everything. I wouldn't be who I am today without your support."

Joel could see a tear forming in Bob's eye. He turned and walked a few paces away, letting the two have their moment. He kept one eye on their surroundings, and the other on the two, making sure they were safe.

Eventually they had said everything they needed to, and Bob led them back through his secret entrance in the back of another car park. He left them on the street as he headed back to his office to wrap things up.

Maya was quiet on the ride back to the base.

Joel spoke to her gently as they both watched the starscape whizzing past their window. "It's always hard moving on. You won't be lonely, though. You've got a team who have got your back now, and you're going to help a lot of good people in this new life."

Maya glanced up at him, and then back out of the window. "I know. It will be fine," she agreed.

CHAPTER FOUR

<u>Gaitune-67, Safe house, Molly's conference room</u>

Joel and Sean were deep in conversation as they made their way into the conference room for the meeting of Molly's "generals," as she called them. This was the inner circle she was developing, the next tier of leaders for her expanding team.

Joel allowed Sean to step through the doorway first. "So, are your reflexes enhanced, too, then?" he asked Sean.

Sean grinned a toothy smile and turned, walking backward around the table for a few paces. "That is need-to-know, mate," he told him.

Joel didn't miss a beat. "And lemme guess. I don't need to know." His voice was tinged with resignation as he followed Sean around to a couple of empty seats.

Sean slapped Joel on the arm. "You're getting it," he told him, pulling out a chair and sitting down.

Maya and Molly were already sitting at the table, chatting idly as each worked on their holos.

Molly looked up at the group when Sean sat down next to her. "Okay, let's get started," she said.

She glanced over at Sean. "You have some intel?" she prompted.

"Yeah," he agreed. "I was in touch with Garet through our secret server, and it seems that The Syndicate have a meeting tomorrow. We have a location, too."

Joel breathed deeply, looking a little uncomfortable. "How do we feel about his intel?" he asked, catching Molly's eye and then glancing at Sean.

Molly shook her head. "You mean, do we trust Garet?"

Joel nodded. Sean looked down at his own hands clasped in front of him.

Joel tilted his head to one side. "I dunno. If it wasn't our only option, I'd be recommending that we don't touch his intel." He sucked air through his teeth. "But, at this point, we're running short on options."

Molly nodded softly and made a note on her holo to remind her to think if there were any other options. Then she glanced at Sean. "Sean?" she asked. "You've been working with him all this time. Thoughts?"

Sean started speaking, still looking at his hands. "When I was assigned to him, it was as his... handler, as it were." He looked up, trying to judge Molly's reaction. Molly didn't bat an eyelid. He continued. "My interactions with him were brief, and sometimes I was relaying the General's orders to him. Sometimes, though, he was making a request of me, mostly for protection or getting messages to the General... But I never could tell if he was just playing both sides."

Molly hung her head, processing what she had just heard. Sean seemed to have said what he needed to. Or at least, all he was ready to divulge at this point.

Molly looked sideways to their new investigator before looking back at the table to listen intently. "Maya?"

Maya sat back, and took a breath. "I'm also in two minds about it. On the one hand, I don't think I trust him; but on the other hand, given our time constraints, and the risks we and the General population face if we leave them in power as we move forward, I can't in good conscience vote to do nothing."

She pulled her mouth to one side. "Though, like Joel said, all other things being equal, it would be good to not have to rely on his intel. I just don't think we have that luxury."

Molly was still looking at the table. "Looks like we've got ourselves a Gemini," Molly commented. "Either way, we'll have to reevaluate our relationship with Garet going forward. He's potentially a weak link."

She shook her head, looking a little defeated. "But it sounds like this is a risk we're going to have to take. Let's just look at how we mitigate that risk."

She looked to Joel. "Want to talk us through some scenarios, based on the intel Garet has supplied? The first scenario assumes his intel is accurate. Then we want to look at variables assuming it's a trap, or that he's tipped off one or all members, and anything else we can think of."

Joel sat up and shifted in his chair. "Sure. It's a bitch, though," he glanced at Sean, briefly before continuing. "The meeting is taking place at the Senate House."

Maya's mouth dropped open.

Joel noticed but kept talking. "This just means that we'll be dropping in with the pods in the center of the city, probably with the most well-protected airspace."

Maya started to say something, but Joel held up a hand. "It's okay. We can do it. Oz and Crash are able to hold air traffic control at bay. They have a plan. But that's just obstacle number one. We then need to get into the building, with government security and staff. Plus, they'll have their own personal guards. Let me show you how this will work, though."

The meeting ran for several hours, with various breakout times for the necessary research, and conferencing with individual team members. Maya even raised the questions of how soon they might find another opportunity to take them down, and what the odds were of being able to get to them in a less risky environment. Sean assured them that this was going to be both a long time and unlikely.

Eventually, they all agreed this was their best option. They had their plan, complete with contingencies in case it was a trap.

Molly brought the meeting to a close. "Okay, folks. This has got to be as slick as possible. We can't afford to make one wrong move. Remember, we don't want any casualties on the government front. These are the people we're trying to help. They're not our enemy. The Syndicate is. So that means fast in and out; and, if nothing goes wrong, the only casualties will be Syndicate members."

Maya raised an eyebrow, and glanced down the table at the team. "And their bank balances," she added dryly.

Had the others not been so focused on the task in hand, they may have chuckled. As it was, no one at the table thought that this was going to be a walk in the park. The fact that they were going to have to hit The Syndicate in the Senate House, the very place they would normally want to protect, didn't help them feel any better about it.

Gaitune-67, Hangar deck

The next morning, the assault team was assembled on the hangar deck, ready to go. Crash, Joel, Jack, Sean, and Molly were suited and booted, locked and loaded; ready to take The Syndicate out, while leaving the rest of the inhabitants of the Senate House stunned, at the most, and hopefully, otherwise unharmed.

Pieter stood by, holo open, checking on details they had available. "I haven't got a live feed, obviously, because of the distances, but Oz and I have been through the shift patterns and so on for some time. The meeting lands in the middle of a shift, so there's no getting around that."

Molly was finishing buckling up her holsters as Pieter briefed them on the final details he had found. Sean stood with his arms folded. "Weapons set to stun, then, I guess," he said, resigned to the task they faced.

Just then, Brock came jogging up to them carrying a bunch of tiny canisters. "Hold up, folks. I got something that may help!" he called.

The group looked around to see. He started handing out the canisters a couple at a time to each team member on the mission.

"What's this?" Joel asked.

Brock smiled. "A present." He finished handing them out, and held onto one. "Okay, these contain a simple knockout gas. It becomes inert within forty seconds, but anyone who inhales it will be knocked out for a good fifteen minutes. The worst they'll have when they wake up is perhaps a bit of a headache. That's it."

Molly grinned. "Excellent work, Brock!" She paused, examining the canister. "Where did you get these?"

Brock smiled brightly. "Well, yesterday when you guys had finished talking to Crash about the mission, I wondered if there were a way to distribute something that would help you avoid casualties. Turns out there was just a simple recipe from some of the med supplies we've accumulated with the research we've been doing with Eugene."

He bent his knees dramatically, and then swung his hips as he held up his canister. "Aaaand," he told them, "the delivery canisters, I found in the armory." He held it in one hand, then gestured with the other as if to say "ta-da!"

The group chuckled. Joel tapped Brock on the top of his arm. "Good man. And thank you!" he exclaimed.

Sean punched Brock lightly on the front of his shoulder, and Jack held one of hers up and nodded. "Thanks!" she said, trying to be more friendly than commando. She'd already tucked one into her atmosuit leg pocket, and was looking for a way to stow the other one.

Molly looked around at the warriors. "Okay. I think we're looking good to go. Any last questions?" She scanned the faces in front of her. No one raised a hand or spoke.

She glanced at Joel. "Okay. Your mission," she told him.

Joel circled his finger in the air at shoulder height. "Okay, folks. Let's wrap up and move out."

The team clambered into their pods, and was out of the hangar deck before Pieter or Brock could say "jumping jacks".

The pair stood watching the pods disappear out the open door and out of the forcefield.

Pieter sighed. "If I were a gambling man," he said, eyes still on the opening in the hangar, but turning his head slightly to Brock, "which I'm not, anymore... I'd say not to trust that Garet."

Brock nodded grimly. "I bet you're right."

One mile out from Senate Building

Molly watched her pod's heads-up display and listened to the chatter on the inter-pod channel. Crash and Oz were negotiating with air traffic control.

Crash was running interference. "Roger that, Control. It seems my nav is off by twenty degrees."

"Correct your course and reduce your altitude, or else we will fire," came their steely response. Molly's heart was beating faster than she had expected.

Oz continued to drop the pods, keeping them in close formation and behaving like a rogue car that had gone off course from the strato highway. They must only just have been picked up on the city radar, as their shape would be deflecting most of the radiation.

They dropped another twenty feet, and the city appeared beneath them. "Almost there," came Crash's voice over the private channel. Molly could see Jack and Sean in the next pod over. She didn't have a visual on Crash and Joel, but imagined Crash doing his usual thing with absolute composure. The anxiety and personality he was putting into his voice was purely to sell it to Control.

Another few moments and Control reported back. "Mr. Ashworth, you are now clear of our airspace. Please get your nav system seen-to by a registered mechanic. This incident has been recorded, and we will be in touch."

Sounds like he's managed to get himself another ticket.

Molly rolled her eyes. *Old habits die hard.*

Want me to get rid of that off their system while I'm in there?

No. I need you to focus on getting us in and out of the building as swiftly as possible. Are you into their camera feed yet?

Yes. They have their full staff at their normal places.

Molly pursed her lips. She hated to change the plan at the last moment, but…

Oz, can you tell if there is another entrance that has fewer security personnel on it? Include upper levels in your sweep.

Okay.

Molly hit the buttons to talk to all pods. "Folks, we're reassessing the entry point. Stand by," she told them.

She knew from the training manuals she'd been reading that shifting plans would put her people under more stress than is necessary. But this might be their way of getting their results and risking fewer casualties in the process.

Oz came back with the results, and put a three dimensional map of the building onto the display.

Looks like the second floor is most vulnerable, on account of the windows being reinforce-fielded. They have fewer people there.

And you can deactivate the forcefield?

Building-wide would take too long. But I can do one segment, and get you through the window to an office. You'll

have to blast through the window, though, causing damage that we wanted to avoid.

Molly made a command decision. *Breaking a window is preferable to shooting government employees who are just doing their job. Relay the new plan to the others.*

She checked her pockets.

I have a charge like we used to free the hostages. I only have one, and you'll need to get me close enough...

Roger that.

The team each acknowledged the change in their breach point, and Oz took the pods up against the side of the building. Keeping them close to the walls to avoid being spotted, he then swung Molly's pod close to the window.

Molly was already out of her seat, charge in one hand, the other hanging on to the seat harness, as Oz gently drew the pod a little closer and opened the front door section for her.

Forcefield down?

Affirmative. You're good to go.

The window was one of the secure, atmosphere-resistant ones that she'd seen in many a building. They were impervious to normal force. But against an explosive charge? Probably not.

She stuck the charge to the middle of the window, looking inside to make sure the area was clear. It was someone's office. She spotted the holoframed family photo on the desk, and little animals made from folded paper. For a moment, her heart sunk at the mundaneness of working in an office; grateful she would never have to live that life, while simultaneously scared to death of a strange twist of fate that might plunge her back into normality.

She pulled her focus back to the charge.

Ready, Oz?

Affirmative.

She pulled the pin, and then fell back into the pod. Oz closed the door and whipped the pod out of the blast zone.

A couple of seconds later, there was a bang. Two seconds after that, alarms started sounding.

Okay, Oz. Take us in, and feed us directions to the target room.

The pods deposited the team at the window one by one, and then disappeared out of sight.

Molly was the first into the room. The blast had blown the desk away, and left a mess of broken up furniture and a small fire smoldering away about ten feet into the room. She hopped out of the way, and took care of the fire with an extinguisher from the corner next to a supplies cupboard. By the time she was done, the rest of the team was in the room, and Sean was checking the corridor for security guards.

He called quietly into the room, "We have incoming."

Jack swung around to look through the doorway down the other side, hearing footsteps from the opposite direction. She pulled out a Brock-canister and looked briefly at Sean. "Smoke 'em, then wait? Or smoke 'em then run?"

Sean grinned. "You know, you're my kinda girl," he told her affectionately. Then he turned to the others who were assembling by the door. "Joel, we good to deploy the smoke, then hold our breaths to get through?"

Joel checked the distances on his holo map to the end of the corridor. "Affirmative," he told Sean.

Sean and Jack looked at each other, pressed the clips on the canisters, and then tossed the devices down their respective sides of the corridor, into the approaching flurry of building security.

White clouds erupted, and Jack pulled back a little, pressing herself against the wall on her side of the room.

She looked at Joel. "Shit, those things pack a punch as well as a knockout!" She swiped at her face as if hoping to wipe off any traces of the mist that she might have been exposed to. Joel was over like a shot, his hands on both her shoulders, checking to make sure she was okay. Satisfied, he pulled Sean back from the door a little, too. "Careful. Best wait a few moments," he cautioned.

Sean stepped back from the doorway and nodded. Crash, who had been the last one into the office, was standing well back, but even he could see traces of the mist coming up to the doorway.

The team waited for what seemed like an eternity. Eventually, Joel looked up from his holo where he had been timing the canisters. "Okay. Let's move," he told them. "But careful; the gas isn't inert for another ten seconds."

Sean and Jack advanced first, almost side-by-side, sweeping and scanning as they went. Molly followed them, walking backwards, checking the way they had come, and scanning the corridor the other way.

Lastly, Joel and Crash followed; carefully stepping over the bodies of the sleeping security guards, who would have one heck of a story to tell their kids when they got home later that day.

The team moved deftly through the corridor. On Oz's instructions, they turned into a stairwell and headed down. They moved quickly, as if they were one organism. At the bottom of the stairwell, Jack, Sean, and Joel went out first, guns set to stun.

The advantage of breaching at a different point was that security was moving toward the blast, while the rest of the staff had started moving out of the building.

Joel reassessed the situation. He turned to the others and signaled to Sean to lower his weapon, which he did immediately, understanding what Joel was about to suggest. Sean put his weapon away, and Jack looked confused for a moment.

Then Joel put his weapon away.

Jack and the others followed suit.

Joel stepped out into the busy corridor, and, walking against the current of people leaving, he strode as if he were there on official business to sort the problem out. No one batted an eyelid at the strike team making their way through the corridors.

Joel led them down the final corridor and into the office suite where they needed to be. There, he found a secretary picking up her purse as if making to leave. Joel signaled for her to get gone; bewildered, she looked at the entourage behind him. Eyes wide, she whimpered unintelligibly, then grabbed her key card, coat, and purse, and left as quickly as she could.

Joel stopped outside what looked like a boardroom, with big heavy wooden doors.

He thumbed at it, looking at Molly. Just then, an Ogg appeared from around the corner. "Hey!" he called. "You're not meant to be here."

The team looked at him. Molly frowned. There was something about him that seemed... familiar. "Who are you?" she asked.

The Ogg looked back at her. "Who are *you*?" he retorted.

Just then, a second Ogg appeared from around the corner. This one was running. Or, rather, waddling. "Erik, Erik, they're all going!" he exclaimed in mild panic.

Molly suddenly recognised the pair from the hotel where they had originally extracted Garet, from her own kidnapping, and then again from the Dewitt incident. Without further hesitation, she pulled her gun on Erik and took a step forward.

"I guess this is what you get by setting your weapons to stun. The shit just keeps coming back... Probably time you took a break," she told him, tilting her head for him to leave.

Erik scowled, his pride galvanizing his stance and his face.

She raised the weapon to the middle of his forehead. He took half a step backward. Then another step. The other Ogg looked horrified and panicked. Molly could see him out of the corner of her eye. He clasped his hands out in front of him, then danced a little on the spot. "Eriiiiiik. Errrriiiiik!" he shrieked quietly, as if trying to convince Erik to surrender.

Erik looked annoyed. "Shut uuuup, Henry!" he tried to whisper, as if Molly and her team standing around looking at them casually couldn't hear them.

Henry quieted down, and looked on in horror.

Erik started to raise his hands in compliance, but then Henry remembered he was carrying a weapon.

"Ooo.. OOOOoooo!" he exclaimed excitedly, reaching back to pull the weapon from the back of his belt.

Molly didn't take her eyes off her target, but she could see what was happening. Joel casually pulled out his own weapon and stepped towards Henry, powering up the weapon and pointing it at his temple in one sweeping, relaxed movement.

Henry froze, and his eyes ticked left, trying to see the gun barrel at the side of his head. Slowly, he continued to pull out the gun; which Joel took out of his hand, and passed backwards to Jack, who switched it off and tucked it into her own belt.

"We'll be going in, now," she told the two Oggs. She lowered her weapon and stepped past Erik, confident that the others would put him down the *instant* he tried anything.

She reached for the door, turned the knob, and pushed it open, cautiously holding her weapon out in front of her. Once the door was open, she stepped forward with both hands on her weapon, sweeping the room for bogeys.

The room was practically empty of people. No Syndicate meeting. No cauldron of evil-doers, plotting the destruction of the world. Just a big boardroom table with a lone person sitting at the far end.

A lone person, who goes by the name of Garet Beaufort.

"Let them come!" he called through to Henrik.

Molly couldn't resist. She glanced back at Erik, and smirked as a child would when the parent sides with one sibling over another. She did it just to irritate him.

It worked.

Erik flounced off, pushing roughly past Henry, who nearly lost his balance and fell into Joel, who just stood back out of the way and let him stumble.

Jack followed Molly into the room, and the two boys fell in behind, like a full, beefy protection squad.

Molly waved her weapon at the empty room. "So where's my party?" she asked, annoyance flashing in her eyes.

Garet waved at the chairs, inviting them to sit down. None of them moved. "They decided they didn't want to be here," he said, trying to keep the anxiety out of his tone.

"You told them we were coming?" she asked, keeping her voice low and steady.

Garet tried not to show he was intimidated. "Not exactly. There was a last minute change of plans," he told her.

Molly started walking the length of the boardroom toward him. "You had us storm a fucking government building for nothing?" Now she was pissed.

Garet held up his hands defensively. "I swear. It wasn't my fault. They already knew. And I had no way of telling you. Besides if I had, they would know it was me that grassed them up..."

Molly was almost on top of him, panic rising in him the closer she got. She pushed past a chair that hadn't been tucked in properly, and it crashed against the desk, causing the whole table to resound with a thump.

Garet pushed back in his chair a little in fright, and Molly kept striding toward him. "You twatface-"

Everything went black.

The next thing Garet was aware of was waking up, slumped back in his chair, blood congealing around his nose and upper lip, and seeing the team sitting and loitering strategically around him. Molly sat calmly on the other end of the boardroom table, glaring.

"Finally," she said, when he came to. "Here's what's going to happen," she began without waiting to make sure he was compos mentis enough to understand her. "You're going to tell us everything we need to know to undo this clusterfuck. Then we're going to have a little chat about how things are going to work going forward. Joel here has placed a tracker under your skin, next to your radial artery."

Garet frowned, and looked down at his body, his eyes scanning all around in their sockets.

Molly rolled her eyes. "That's in your arm, you dickhead."

He looked back up at her, annoyed. Then he looked down at his right forearm, realizing that it was aching like a motherfucker, and saw there was a little blood, halfway down.

Molly continued. "Basically, if you try and extract it, you'll probably end up bleeding out. We're going to want to have another chat with you once we've verified that what you're about to tell us is accurate and helpful. What happens to you at such time depends on how much you manage to redeem yourself in the interim."

Crash had moved toward the window, and now opened it up, using his holo to communicate with Oz about the forcefield and the pods.

Sean then talked quietly with Garet, taking down the details they needed to track down the other Syndicate members.

120 seconds later, the strike team was stepping out of the window and back into their pods.

Garet stayed planted in his chair, fussing with his arm. "Wow - I liked it better when I was your client," he smirked, reminding Molly of the time when she was trying to protect him, and he ended up with his face planted unceremoniously in her crotch.

Joel turned back as he swung himself up to the window. He glared at him.

Garet quickly raised his hands, palms facing Joel. "Okay, okay. I'm sorry!"

Joel gave him a quick warning look before stepping out onto

the window ledge and into the pod, closely followed by Molly and Sean.

Alone again in the room, Garet mused to himself. "Funny how events have a way of turning around like this, eh?"

Within a few minutes, the team had disappeared off into space again. The security team of the Senate House was aware they had been breached, but was none-the-wiser about what had *actually* happened.

CHAPTER FIVE

One hour earlier

"The way I see it, we've got two choices," Garet explained, pacing up and down in the tiny room. "We either stay united, or we scatter."

Mac shuffled his weight from one foot to the other, his shiny shoes out of place against the filthy floor in the dark musty back room. "We're safer alone," he disagreed. "We can disappear more easily."

His tone was decisive.

Jessica pulled her shawl closer around her for comfort. She looked over to Andus for his ruling. He looked up at the group. "I have a safe house. I can take anyone who wants to come." He waved his hand to Mac. "However, if you want to try and make your own way, feel free."

Jessica looked at him intensely. "I'm with you," she confirmed without hesitation.

The group looked at Garet. Garet rocked back half an inch on his heels. He paused a moment, then spoke. "I'm going to head back to the Senate House and carry on as normal. If I don't, they'll know I tipped you off.

Jessica frowned at him as if he had lost the plot. "If you do, they'll still know!" she protested.

He shook his head. "Uh uh; they won't know for certain. It'll cast doubt. I'll carry on as if everything is normal. Just don't tell me your plans, because I'll have to tell them. They have ways..." his voice trailed off.

Jessica had the distinct impression that Garet was genuinely afraid of what these people were capable of. Her voice was still incredulous when she spoke. "We've already told you!" She looked to Andus for back up.

Andus nodded calmly.

Garet turned to go. "Okay. I'll let you get on with this. I'm going back. Good luck..."

And with that, he left.

Once he was out of earshot, the remaining Syndicate members started talking, arguing, and trying to decide what to do next.

Molly Bates was coming for them now.

Their fancy security would only hold her off for so long. They knew that. They now knew what the team was capable of, having underestimated them on numerous occasions.

Before, it was simply an annoyance. A setback.

Now it was downright terrifying.

Newld Residence, Spire

Jessica arrived home with two extra security teams, who whisked her efficiently into her super secure apartment.

One team of the four stayed inside the apartment with her. Another team of 16 surrounded the building and main entry points: car park, elevators, her private entrance, the rooftop, and balcony. The other staked out various points. Nothing short of a helicopter hit squad was getting in here.

So why don't I feel safe? she wondered.

She put the kettle on and leaned against the kitchen counter, watching the alpha team sweep through the rest of her apartment. She was pissed that she had to change her plans. It would have been simple for Garet to run, too. Or at least to leave before she had disclosed her intentions to stay with Andus.

Now, staying with Andus would have left them both vulnerable.

Now, she had to remain on her own.

Which bites.

She took her shoes off and poured herself a chamomile tea, hoping to calm her nerves.

Then she sat down in the living room to wait.

Undisclosed bar, Somewhere in Spire

Andus stepped elegantly out of his limo in a well-lit parking garage, his two most trusted Estarian bodyguards by his side. Looking around the surroundings for any hint of a threat, they followed him to a door that put them into the service area of a hotel.

Andus made his way through the narrow corridor, and out into the main foyer where there were plenty of people. Wending his way through the foyer and out of the main doors, he headed left, and then disappeared into a small door in the next alley.

Stepping into the darkness, he paused, waiting for his eyes to adjust to the light. The second Estarian bodyguard quietly closed the door behind them, blocking out any remaining sunlight. They found themselves in a passage, covered with a threadbare carpet, thick with dust and dirt. Andus took a deep breath, and seemed to relax a little as he started making his way down the passage to another door.

The passageway opened out into a mini lobby area with a grimy little counter where an attendant sat, absorbed in his holo.

When he heard their footsteps, he looked up – and then jumped out of his seat when he saw who was approaching.

"Mr. Andus, sir," he exclaimed, surprised. His holo screens were still projecting from his wrist, forgotten.

Andus ambled up to the counter. "I see we're always ready for business," he commented dryly, looking down at the attendant's wrist holo.

The attendant sheepishly closed it down and turned around to reach for a key. Grabbing the correct one off the hook, he scurried around the counter to join Andus on the other side. "This way, please, sir," he said, leading the way off to the right of the desk, where he pressed a button to an elevator and keyed in a code.

The elevator doors slid open, and the group stepped in, followed by the much shorter Estarian attendant. He swiped his key and then hit a combination of buttons. The elevator doors slid closed, and the car dropped down several floors worth of altitude.

Eventually it came to a halt.

The two Estarian bodyguards looked slightly anxious. Whether it was the tight space and the feeling of claustrophobia, or the depth they had gone to, one couldn't tell. Andus, however, seemed quite content as he followed the attendant out of the elevator and down a stone-floored passageway.

Passing several doors, the attendant finally stopped outside the one door that seemed more high tech than the others. He stood aside and motioned to Andus that he was free to enter. The door had a single access panel, and was field-protected, too.

Andus stepped up to the panel and leaned in with his eyes. The retinal scanner activated, read his eyes, and approved his access. The field dropped and the door slid open. Andus thanked the attendant and stepped inside, followed by his heavies.

Once inside, he started peeling off his atmosuit and making himself at home. On the other side of the vault-like door was a medium-sized apartment. The entrance way opened into a library and lounging area, with real paper books. Further along, there was a kitchen; opposite that, there was a dining table with chairs. Just beyond that, there were sleeping quarters with bathroom facilities.

Andus signaled for his security to check the place.

They went ahead and did a sweep, and returned to the front area, satisfied. Andus then spoke to them in a low voice, explaining the protocols they should be familiar with for making sure that their movements here weren't tracked. They discussed food deliveries and emergency extractions. Once Andus was satisfied they knew the ropes, he dismissed them.

The two Estarians left, and started talking with the attendant on the other side of the door. After a few seconds, Andus could hear three sets of footsteps leaving. He wandered through the apartment, looking around, making sure he had everything that he needed. He flicked on the mocha machine, and then headed back through to the library to choose some reading material.

Such a shame Jessica decided to take her chances at her own home. He imagined she would have been pleasant company for however long they needed to remain underground.

Still, he looked around the apartment, *she was high-maintenance, and there isn't that much space.* He settled down with his book, and wondered if it was too early for a martini.

East of Spire, Somewhere in the Savannah desert

The space car hovered across the miles and miles of sand of the Navanah desert. Mac Kerr sat in the nav's seat as the pilot navigated between two brewing sandstorms and a slip stream of thermals.

"Nearly there," the pilot said over the comms "I hope after this, we're even." It was hard to make out his tone over the sound of the engine and through the distortion of the radio, but Mac had no doubt what the guy meant.

Well, what else should I expect? I had him by the short and curlies, and he owed me one... Mac thought to himself.

Mac turned his head to his acquaintance and nodded. "Yes, we're even. As long as no one is able to trace me here because of you." He paused thinking for a moment. "I should take a different route back, and maybe head into a different airfield, if I were you," he concluded. His track record in escape and evasion were what had kept him alive so long in the outer system.

The pilot glanced at him and nodded, slight irritation showing at the edges of his eyes. "Shall do."

Just then, the ranch appeared out of the dust just ahead of them. The pilot flicked a few controls on the holo display and slowed the craft, bringing it gently closer to the surface. He nodded at the building ahead of them. "That where you want to be?" he queried.

Mac nodded. "That's the one," he said. "Drop me down quarter of a mile out. I'll approach on foot."

The pilot shrugged, mildly suspicious as to his reason for wanting to be so far out. He complied, though, and within a few minutes, Mac was scrambling out of the craft. "Thank you!" he called back to the pilot.

His ride nodded politely, and as soon as Mac was clear of the vehicle, he lifted off again. A few meters in the air, he turned back in the direction of Spire, leaving a dust cloud behind him.

Mac shielded his face with his arm and held his breath as he turned away from the dust cloud. He was used to these kinds of conditions. If anything, it felt more normal and psychologically comfortable than the conditions of meetings and posh suits and nice surroundings in his HealthCorp life.

As soon as the dust settled enough for him to see the direction of the ranch, he started walking; his arm still shielding his face against the dust.

As he trudged across the sand, he remembered the last time he had been on the run. He wasn't running again. He was going to stand his ground, the best place he knew how. He wasn't going back to that life. He wasn't giving up everything he'd worked so hard for. He wasn't going to let all the sacrifices and things he'd done, that still haunt him, go to waste... just to end up back where he started.

This was where he was going to make his stand.

He arrived at the door and swiped at the access panel, bringing up the holo keypad. He tapped in the combination, and the door slid open while leaving up a forcefield against the sand and dust.

He stepped inside, and the sound of the wind and the desert evaporated into silence.

The house was empty. For now. He stamped off as much sand as he could, and shook himself down before walking through the hallway and checking the place. Everything was as it should be... Although, there was still work to do in setting up the weapons.

He wandered through into the front viewing room, which faced back in the direction of Spire. If anyone were coming, it would be from there. This was where he'd set up the anti-aircraft artillery. He might need some help getting it up out of storage, though.

He looked down at his holo. The others would be arriving shortly. He decided to make himself a drink, and rest while there was still time. There were still several hours of work to do once they got here. It would be easier as a group, though.

Senate Building, Spire

Erik sounded pissed. "Shut uuuup, Henry!" Erik hissed at Henry.

Finally, Garet thought. *They must be here.*

Having spent the last half hour waiting for their arrival, his palms were sweaty, and he simply couldn't settle. In fact, he was almost relieved they were here; even if it did mean that they were going to potentially take him out.

There was still some kind of activity out in the corridor. Garet listened, still trying to pretend he was working away casually on his holo in case Molly walked in on him.

"Ooo.. OOOOoooo!" he heard Henry exclaimed excitedly. There was shuffling and movement outside the door. Garet could have sworn he heard the click of a weapon powering up.

Then he heard Molly's voice. "We'll be going in now," she told the two Oggs.

He heard the doorknob turning, and watched it as the door started opening. He quickly averted his eyes to his holo screen, and shifted his weight back a bit more in his chair.

Yeah, super-casual, he told himself.

"Let them come!" he called out to Henrik, still not looking up but sensing the door was open now.

Molly stepped into the room, weapon raised. She locked eyes on him.

She was *not* amused.

Yep, I'm done for.

CHAPTER SIX

<u>Gaitune-67, Molly's conference room</u>

The team arrived back in the conference room straight from the pods.

Sean was the first to speak. "Well, that could have gone better."

Molly was irritated more than anything. "Why would he do this?" she fretted, asking herself more than any one of the team members present.

Joel pulled out a chair for her, and indicated she should sit down. The rest of the team settled down, too. Joel instinctively knew that getting them seated was going to reduce their adrenalin circulation, and drop them back into being able to focus rationally with the upper part of their brains.

Just then, Maya walked in. "Hey. Oz filled me in," she said, indicating her holo. She took a seat while the others started removing some of their combat gear.

Molly pulled the wooden stick out from the back of her vest and plunked it on the table. "Son of bitch," she said under her breath. She exhaled, and then took another deep breath before looking up at the folks assembled.

"Okay. We're onto plan B," she announced. The others looked at each other before realizing that no one knew what plan B was.

Molly gathered her thoughts.

"Here's what we know: The Syndicate knew we were coming, and scattered. We can suspect that Garet tipped them off. We can deal with him later... but I want to leave him in play. He could have disappeared with them too, but he didn't. We don't know what kind of game he's playing, but we can always pick him up again later, now we've got a tracker on him. If his intel turns out to be good, then great. If not... we'll cross that bridge."

She paused and glanced at Jack and Sean, watching to see if Jack was at all squeamish about her approach. No reaction. She kept talking. "Regardless of what happens at that point, we now have some actionable intel. Oz is working on verifying it, first; but with this, we can come up with a four-pronged attack on each member."

Molly stood up and started pacing, removing her arm protectors and other kit as she strode about.

"Needless to say," she continued, "we have to rethink how we go about this. At this stage, I'm thinking just killing them is too much of a relief for them. I'm thinking they each need to be taught a special lesson in what it feels like to be in their own worst nightmare."

Molly paused. Joel looked over at her. "What exactly do you have in mind?" he asked.

Molly started to smile a little. "Well, there's some work to do on how we execute this plan, but I'm thinking we need to let them think they have escaped, and regain our element of surprise. In the meantime, we can prep and take our time, making sure we can strike at them all simultaneously. I think we have enough team members to do this now, and to do it elegantly."

Sean's ears pricked up, and his eyes came alive. "You're making battle sound like art..."

Jack nodded in agreement. "Uh huh," she said adding her support.

Molly grinned. "I think this requires a certain degree of craftsmanship."

Joel pointed at Sean, now smiling a little. "I think you've created a monster!" he told him, shaking his finger.

Molly watched morale slowly return to the team. "I'd also like to see what Garet does. He'll either be useful to us down the line, or he'll be too untrustworthy. It's time he picked a side."

Joel nodded strongly in agreement.

Molly nodded once. "Okay, now here's what I'm thinking, in terms of our plan..."

Iantrogen Offices, Downtown Spire

Jessica strode through the corridors of the quiet offices. At this time in the evening, everyone was heading home. Not Jessica. Having spent most of the day holed up in her fortress, waiting, she decided that she was remaining a prisoner no more. If Molly was coming for her, she would be just as safe at the office as she would at home. Probably even safer, given the public nature of the place.

Jessica almost flounced into her own office, following a team of four security personnel in front of her, with another two trailing behind her. They worked swiftly and professionally, checking the venue, and marking each zone safe, reporting into the rest of their borg-like team in other areas around the building. If Molly was going to get to her, it was going to be through them.

She popped her antigrav mocha cup from home on her assistant's desk, along with her handbag, which was heavy with the weapons she had stowed away. She shifted her weight as she paused for the team leader to report back to her. He came back in from her office, gave her a professional emotionless nod, and then ushered the majority of the team outside.

One remained standing by the door, looking into the room; already settled as wall furniture, rather than an intrusion to her privacy.

Jessica stepped carefully into her office. The place seemed so quiet and unappealing now. She was still unable to settle. Normally, showing up at this doorway meant she would automatically flick into task mode - optimizing for productivity. And profit.

But today, her brain felt scattered. Distracted.

That would be the fear, Jessie, she told herself, almost hearing her grandmothers' voice in her head. Her grandmother had been the one to teach her mastery of self.

Jessica dumped her bag on her desk and sat in the visitor's chair. In the back of her mind, she didn't feel capable of taking the "Jessica Newld, CEO" seat right now.

She opened her holo. "Call Andus," she told it. The holo started dialing, and then cut out.

NUMBER DISCONNECTED.

Shit. Andus, I need you, she cursed. *Desperate times...* she thought to herself, as she dialed Mac Kerr.

The holo dialed again, and then again cut out.

Fuck.

Maybe she had been stupid, staying visible and coming to the office.

She sat in the silent office, the sound of the fluorescent light loud against the stillness. Her brain seemed to hum in symphony with it. Her shoulders prickled at knowing that her security guy was behind her, aware of her every move. She felt self-conscious.

But more than that, she felt scared.

Maybe I should call the police, she considered, turning the option in her mind. *But my security is so much better equipped and trained. The police wouldn't stand a chance against Ms. Bates.*

She knew that now.

And they may end up siding with her. *Better to keep them out of it until after the attack, when they can make statements that Bill can use to get a conviction.*

She turned back to her holo, flicking through the annual reports and quarterly statements she had to read. Her mind wouldn't let her go to the mundane.

She breathed, trying to gather herself. Then, making a decision, she flipped her holo closed. Gathering up her gear, she strode Jessica-Newld-style out of the office.

The security personnel were still loitering in the corridor, deciding how best to defend the corridor and windows (because they now knew that the Bates team had blown out the windows to get at the hostages). They snapped into action again as soon as Jessica stepped through the door. She looked in the direction of the team leader, and then started walking down the corridor.

"I'm working from the conference room. Send me someone who can fetch me some food. And get my assistant back in for the evening. And the legal team." Her heels clipped decisively down the hall. "We have work to do."

This was a trick she had learned from her father: distraction. Work as an antidote to fear. If she was going down, it would be amongst the soldiers who had helped her build this empire. And it would be while she was fighting from every angle she had left.

Gaitune-67, Safe house, Molly's conference room

JOEL, YOUR IMPLANTS HAVE ARRIVED. WOULD YOU LIKE TO HAVE BROCK INSTALL THEM FOR YOU?

Joel did a double take when he saw the message from Oz flick up on his holo.

WTF? he typed back.

Then he remembered. The implants. For the "enhancements" Oz was going to hook him up with. Of course!

Shit.

He looked around. There wasn't anywhere he could talk to Oz easily. He was working away in Molly's conference room, and, though he was the only one here, he didn't want their conversation to be overheard by anyone passing by outside. He needed to get to a pod. Without being seen.

He flicked through his mind, remembering where everyone was. Sean had gone for a workout - which meant he might be downstairs in the base gym. Molly was doing something similar. Maya was in Molly's lab...

Heck, I'm just going to have to risk it.

He packed up his screens and typed Oz a quick message that he would meet him in a pod. With that, he left the conference room and headed down to the basement.

He rounded the last flight of stairs, and heard Brock's music blaring in the workshop. *Good - that means Brock would be around. I still need to broach the subject with him.*

As he entered the workshop, he could hear Brock singing and busting a move as he worked on a holoprogram, tinkering with some kind of mechanical device next to him.

Brock turned to see who had just come down stairs. "Yo! My man, how's it hanging, Joel?" he called over to him.

Joel put his hand up in a wave, and wandered towards him. "You got a minute?" he asked, his face serious.

Brock waved at the music, and the sound level dropped by 50%. "Sure. Everything okay?" he asked, his dancing now subsiding to a gentle swaying, as if the music just couldn't leave his system.

Joel nodded, but still looked serious. He glanced around the workshop. "Are we alone?" he asked.

Brock's swaying stopped, and he looked around, too. "Erm, yeah." He waved the music off completely. "What's up?"

Joel stepped in to talking distance. "I could use your help on a special project. It's on the down-low, though. You okay with that?"

Brock looked suspicious. "Errrr, I guess so. It's not something that's going to get me into trouble with the Moll-ster, though, is it?"

Joel shook his head. "No. No way. More... Hang on. Better I explain this properly. You okay to come and sit in a pod with me?"

Brock's eyes narrowed. "Now, if you just wanna ask me out, you just need to come out and say it Mr. Joel!" His voice was jovial but his face was deadly serious.

Joel couldn't help but chuckle. "And on the day I decide to ask you out for a romantic interlude, I will indeed remember that. In the meantime, you want to get your mechanic ass down to the pods so I can run this by you?"

Brock's eyes widened, now amused, and still play-acting. "Well, well. It's only ever my engineering skills that need using mercilessly, I see." He placed down the laser screwdriver he had been using, and shut down his desk holo before marching off towards the Demon Door.

The pair made their way down into the base and selected a pod a couple of rows into the batch, so as best to be hidden from anyone passing by.

Joel stepped in after Brock and sat down next to him, swiping at the door control to close the pod up. Brock glanced at him, his eyes all pretend-serious. "You sure you aren't making a move on my sweet ass?" he asked.

Joel blushed and looked down, completely embarrassed. "No. No. I'm really not. I promise," he told his friend. "It is something rather sensitive, though. Oz, are you there?" Joel prompted.

Oz's audio channel in the pod clicked open with a tiny amount of static before settling. "Yes, I'm here. Hello, Brock."

Brock looked down at the ground and leaned back against the

wall of the pod, sideways on. "Hi, Oz." He paused and looked at the console, and then at Joel. "So... what *am* I doing here? With you both?"

Joel looked down at his hands. "You wanna explain this one, Oz?"

"Sure." Oz replied through the intercom. "It seems that young Joel is wanting to increase his abilities... specifically his reflexes, a la cyborg."

Brock's mouth dropped open. "You mean you want in on some of the Sean Royale action?!" he exclaimed, his voice louder, now almost singing. His open mouth turned into an enormous grin. "You want to hold your own against the super soldier! That's why the secrecy and blushes!"

Joel's blush deepened. Brock slapped his own leg and stomped his feet in the pod. Even Oz seemed to be chuckling through the pod... the vibrations running through the seat they occupied.

Joel tried to hush Brock. "Come on, man. You're going to get us rumbled!"

Brock lifted his head a little, and Joel could see actual tears rolling down his cheeks. Brock pulled a colorful handkerchief from his overalls pocket and dabbed his face, careful not to smudge his eyeliner. "Maaaaaaan. You got balls. You're going to get Oz to implant you with all kinds of shit, just so you can run faster and beat Sean?"

Joel seemed to recover himself and his dignity, as a small frown started to show on his eyebrows. "Oz. You can back me up any time..." he grunted in the direction of the heads-up display.

Then he turned back to Brock. "Not run faster. I'd need more muscle for that. And it's not just about competing with Sean. This is about upping my game. We're going to need every edge we can get going into this Etheric Empire battle, and who knows what lies ahead? I just want to make sure that I can be as ready as possible."

He paused, his eyes drifting off into the distance a little as he spoke next. "Besides, all it takes in a fight is being a split second too slow, and you can lose your life. Or worse. A teammate." He shook his head. "Not on my watch."

He looked back at Brock who had sobered up a little. "So, if it means letting you stick chips and widgets in my brain to make me a better soldier, a better protector, and a better teammate... then, so be it."

Brock had been gently nodding, empathetically, when suddenly he stopped nodding, and his pupils dilated.

"Yo, you what what?!" he asked, suddenly realizing that *he* was going to be implanting the chips in Joel's brain.

Joel rolled his lips inward, letting his cheeks go pudgy. "Yeah. That bit. That's what I need you for." He indicated back at the heads-up display. "Oz can't insert the devices, and since you're the only one with a steady hand and knack for the mechanical, we - and by 'we,' I mean Oz - figured that you'd be able to use your skills, even though half of your... project... is organic material."

Brock breathed out heavily, his eyes wide. He seemed to lean forward a little as he exhaled.

He looked up at Joel.

"Dude. You know the sight of blood makes me faint?"

Gaitune-67, safe house, Molly's conference room

Okay, Oz, we need to find a way to take each of these goons down.

Molly settled down in her usual seat, back to the door, mocha in hand.

Let's start with Jessica. She took a long swig of mocha, clearing her mind.

We need to understand exactly how her companies are structured, and how that relates to the legislation The Syndicate has been pushing for. Once we know that, we can come up with a plan of attack.

Oz started pulling up searches on the conference room holo

screens, showing the frameworks of the companies he was able to locate.

Remember, we don't want to just take her out of the game; we want to do it in a way where it cannot be built up again over time. Like, never again... so we need this to tie-in with the law-making piece, and the company laws.

Oz's moving images and holoscreens suddenly stopped.

Got it? Molly asked.

Got it.

Data and intel started flowing across the screens as he referenced a new holo with company law details and legislation changes in the last three decades, as it pertained to Jessica's business model.

Hours later, Molly was still trawling through the various pieces of research that Oz had managed to locate.

Oz, are you seeing any other patterns here?

Yes, I've spotted two more.

Another screen appeared off to Molly's right, and she pushed a couple of her screens out of the way, and pulled the new one closer.

This looks like the subsidiaries are linked in some way to the share price of the main company...

Exactly. When she buys new ones, the share price goes up. On the rare occasion she has sold one, the share price has dropped off.

Molly leaned on the desk, rubbing her chin.

So what if we prompted all of those 180 subsidiaries to be sold?

It would likely crash the value of the company.

Find me the last five years' worth of company accounts. If this company is overvalued, that kind of drop in share capital would prompt a sale.

Oz flicked up another screen.

Okay, what was the second pattern?

Another screen appeared behind the current one.

Seems the board votes to sell whenever a subsidiary fulfills a certain set of criteria. I've managed to reverse engineer what those parameters are.

How easy would it be to replicate those across all 180 companies?

Oz paused. Molly could feel herself being pushed out of areas of her brain as her mind went numb. It lasted just a few seconds, and then Oz returned an answer on her screen.

I could do it, mostly ethically, probably in about 24 hours. The board is the human element, though. History dictates they would call an emergency meeting and perhaps debate selling off all of them. They may resist, and just ride it out.

Molly frowned.

What would happen to each company, based on their parameters, if they ended up not selling?

They would incur massive fines for breaches in legislation; not to mention that, individually, they don't have the legal power to untangle the messes they have wrapped up in the process. Their parameters are very specific, based on a number of factors and risks they're taking just operating day-to-day.

Molly rubbed her eyes. *I think there is probably enough pressure there to get the board to ditch the subsidiaries. They probably have the hubris to expect that the main company can survive the crash.*

She paused, considering the impact on the wider market.

Oz, can you run a model of what will likely happen to the rest of the market if this goes ahead?

Oz ran a simulation for the health sector and all the other sectors. Molly watched as it played out, noticing that, for the most part, only the health sector was affected.

Oz, get this intel over to Paige, Maya, and Pieter, and ask them to come up here for a quick meeting in half an hour. I've just had another idea.

She slurped at her stone-cold mocha, before realizing it was just the dregs. Molly screwed up her face and popped the mug down again, pushing it aside.

And then grab me the same data for Andus's companies, please. Given how he's her guru, I think we'll find similar weaknesses there, too.

Gaitune-67, Base conference room

Molly walked into the empty conference room; the one they normally referred to as "the General's" conference room.

She had a meeting with the big guy himself. She was surprised he had made time, but suspected after what she had messaged ADAM between her researching and briefings, that they saw an opportunity to affect real change.

Or they were about to tell her that she was crackpot crazy.

Either way, this was going to be a turning point. She sat down in the middle of the long side of the conference table nearest the door, and waited. Her heart was beating heavier than usual, and she could feel her palms sweating. She wished she'd gone to the restroom again before she came in here. She could wait. She knew it was only nerves.

As it happened, she didn't have long to wait; a hologram opened out from the center of the table within moments. It unfolded, and revealed the General sitting at his desk in his private office on the *ArchAngel*.

"Molly Bates," he greeted her. "Sounds like you've been thinking outside the box again..." he began.

The meeting went on for some time. So long, in fact, that Sean, Joel, Paige, and even Crash had all come looking for her. Upon seeing that she was in with the General, each had turned on their heels, and gone back to what they were doing.

Molly didn't emerge again until the evening meal, where she disclosed nothing about her meeting with the General, saying it was all 'need-to-know'.

CHAPTER SEVEN

Gaitune-67, Safe house, Molly's conference room

Pieter strode into the conference room, holo out, reading as he walked. Closely following behind him were Maya and Paige.

Molly spun around as they filed in and took seats. "Hi," she told them, her mind still in the data she'd been sifting through.

Paige smiled at her sympathetically. "Have you actually eaten real food today?" she asked, looking at the mocha mug and the empty bottles of water.

Molly looked up, trying to recall the extraneous data.

Oz answered for her through the conference room holo. "She's used the mocha machine three times, but I haven't registered any food consumption."

Paige put her hands on her hips and after a short pause she strode silently out of the room.

Molly, bewildered, watched her leave. Not understanding what was going on, she did the thing she knew how to do best: she turned her attention back to the task at hand.

Molly looked at Maya and Pieter. "Looks like we have pinpointed the weaknesses in the infrastructure of both Jessica's and Andus's operations," she began.

She started explaining how the cards would topple if they were able to trigger the sales of the subsidiaries, causing the ultimate collapse of the whole regime.

Maya raised her hand, a slight frown across her forehead. "And what about triggering those sales? What does that entail?"

Molly nodded. "Well, Oz can handle most of that, but there are some... manipulations... that would need to happen that aren't exactly white hat."

She glanced over at Pieter. "This means that Oz can't do those specific takedowns; but..." she smiled a little, "I suspect knowing what the bigger picture is, you won't have an ethical issue in doctoring some reports and such like?" Molly watched Pieter to see if he was comfortable.

Pieter waved his hand. "Yeah, no problem. These fuckheads have exploited the poor and the sick for too long. They have it coming. Whatever it takes," he told her.

Molly bobbed her head rhythmically. "Great." She seemed to brighten a little. "Okay, in the meantime, there are a few other things that need handling."

Paige returned to the room, gently closing the door behind her. She plunked a green smoothie on the desk next to Molly and nodded at it. "Drink," she instructed before heading around the table.

Molly thanked her and continued. Paige took a seat at the end of the conference table so she could see everyone who was already sitting down the sides.

Molly took a sip of the smoothie before returning to the briefing. She was still looking at Paige. "Oz and Pieter have an action plan to dismantle Jessica's and Andus's companies. What we then need to ensure is that there is no way to rebuild them. We need the legislation that has weighted everything in their favor gone."

Paige nodded in agreement.

Molly continued. "Are you happy to liaise with Garet, and see what he can do to make that so?" she asked.

Paige nodded, taking notes. "Sure," she confirmed.

Molly filled the others in on the details of the Garet situation. When she had finished, Paige wrinkled her nose. "Do you think that he's going to play ball? Or just sabotage everything we ever try to do?" she asked.

Molly took a breath and bobbed her head to one side briefly. "This will certainly be the test. If he comes through, then we know he might have a chance of being on our side. If not, we remove him." She smiled a slightly evil smile. "Don't worry, I'm sending Joel with you. He might need to have a serious chat with him before you start working on the ins and outs."

Paige stopped typing on her holo and looked up, her eyes slightly wider than usual. She took a second to understand Molly's meaning, and then smiled, too. "I'm going to enjoy this assignment," she added quietly.

Molly looked over at Maya. "Alright. So, taking out this company is going to have a short-term impact on the sector. We need the government ready to support it. Lower-tiered staff will be the first affected. We want to put them into government jobs ASAP."

Maya had already started taking notes again.

"You're the one to make this piece happen, Maya. Use your contacts in the city to get a government plan into place. The funding *will* become available; don't worry about that for now. Get agreements in principle, and find people to support it. We want governance in place to take over the infrastructure of primary health."

Molly took another sip of her green drink, and then looked over at the other two. "We can leave the higher levels of the bull-shit – insurance and second order tools — to disappear in the collapse. Our goal here is to bring the cost of providing the treatments back to an actual cost, rather than an inflated, artificial rate. According to Oz's models, it will be able to sustain itself as a sector without these secondary parasites."

She took another sip, realizing how hungry she had become while she'd been immersed in formulating this plan. "Okay," she said, wrapping up. "We need these things in motion so that it becomes obvious that the collapse is going to happen. Some of what needs to happen in the Senate is going to take time, but if we can at least get it moving in that direction, then there are obvious solutions in place when we take out the companies. The existing senators and administrators *should* be able to figure it out from there."

She looked around. "Any questions?"

The assembled team shook their heads, having already started checking details on their holos.

"Okay," Molly finished. "Let me know if you need clarification on anything. Plus, Oz is fully versed on what needs to happen."

Pieter got up and started ambling out, grunting "later" to the group.

Paige glanced over at Maya. "Time to call my ex, I guess..."

Maya grinned. "Moral support?" she offered.

Paige shook her head. "Nah. I'm alright."

Molly looked up as Paige headed out. "Thanks for the shake," she said.

Paige grinned. "Of course. You gotta eat. Or 'nutrient,'" she said, pulling a face at her new word for consuming nutrients. "It doesn't verb-out the same way as most words..." she observed idly as she headed towards the door.

Molly grinned. "Hey," she said suddenly remembering, "you know you can get a real-time line with the surface."

Paige turned back. "Huh?"

Molly slurped and turned around a little in her chair. "Yeah, in the ops room. Ask Oz to help you connect, and you can talk with Garet real-time."

Paige's mouth dropped. "Oh, great. That will speed things up." She paused. "How does that work?"

Molly shook her head, her lips still around the straw. She swallowed.

"No idea."

She paused. "Yet," she added.

Gaitune-67, Safe house workshop

Brock created a makeshift operating room in a supplies cupboard, out of view of the main workshop. Now, with Joel laid back in the operating chair, and the half-light from some lamps he'd managed to cobble together, Brock was almost ready to start the procedure.

"Oz, you're sure about this?" he asked, speaking into a microphone he'd rigged up from the game console just outside the cupboard.

"100%," Oz told him. "The sedatives should be kicking in now."

Joel had relaxed back in the chair, and opened one eye. "In the old days, it was the patients that received the sedatives," he commented dryly.

Brock shook his head and stamped his foot playfully. "Man, if you want me to faint on your ass, then fine. But if Oz reckons this cocktail of vomit suppressants, sedatives, and half a mocha can get me through this, then it's our best option."

Joel closed his eyes again, his lips turning up a little at the corners.

Brock turned around, and when he turned back, he had something that looked like a puncture gun. "Okay, they didn't send an insertion gun with the chips, so I've had to improvise." He waved the gun around in front of Joel's line of sight. "This one goes in the base of the brainstem," he said, signaling for Joel to roll over. "So I need you on your front."

Joel opened his eyes and sat up, then, carefully balancing on the reclined chair, he turned himself over onto his front. Settling down, he put his forehead against the headrest and tried to get comfortable.

"It's okay," Brock told him, "this one won't take a second." Joel felt Brock's fingers on the back of his head, and then tracing the skull down to the spine. He pressed a little harder, and then felt around some more, finding the edge of the base of the skull. He gently adjusted Joel's head from the chin and tried again.

A moment later, Joel felt the metal of the puncture gun pressed up against his skull. Brock breathed out a little. "Hope I've got the pressure right on this one."

Joel's eyes flew open in fear at Brock's last statement, but it was too late to do anything about it. A split-second later, there was a thud in the back of his head, and a sharp pain around the sides of his lower skull.

"Motherfucker!" Joel hissed, very conscious they didn't want their little experiment to be discovered.

"Boosh!" he heard Brock announce as he stepped back and did some of his wiggly dancing. "One doooown!" he said, celebrating.

Joel scrambled around to lie on his back rubbing the back of his head and jawline. "How do we know you got it right?" he asked, frowning through the discomfort.

Brock looked cocky for a moment. "You know who you is talking to?" he smiled.

Oz interrupted. "If you'll allow me to download a patch onto your holo, I can go ahead and check the connectivity of the device."

Joel looked down at his holo and saw that Oz was requesting permission. He clicked "OK". "You need to ask for permission?" he queried.

Oz had started the download onto his holo. "Of course. It's not only the polite thing to do, but ethics are now hardwired into my core programming."

Brock sniggered. "That's what Molly meant about you being a little broken when it comes to ethics!"

Oz's audio feed buzzed a little and then returned to normal. "Yes; consider the source for the definition of 'broken,' though."

Even Joel couldn't help but chuckle at that comment.

Brock grinned. "Yeah. I think we had kind of got that..." He paused. "It's okay, Oz. We love you just as you are... pole up your ass or no."

"Thanks, Brock," replied Oz, his tone a little more relaxed. "I appreciate that."

Joel clapped his hands quietly. "Okay, people. Let's get this other chip in."

Brock turned around and fiddled with some things he'd laid out on a tray in preparation. Turning back his face was pale. "Okay. Here goes," he told Joel. "I'm going to make an incision here," he traced a path on Joel's temple, "and then pull back the skin to be able to get at the bone."

Joel nodded ever so slightly, and grunted.

Brock kept talking. "And then, I'm going to slip this chip underneath the bone, and run current through it. The current will cause it to bury itself into the cortex at the correct depth." He paused. "I hope," he added with a slight flinch.

Joel looked alarmed, his eyes fixing on Brock from his laid-back, compromised position. "What do mean, you 'hope'?"

Brock shrugged. "Just that they didn't send any apparatus with this, and I'm not sure the exact current that this baby will put out," he pointed at a wand connected to a battery pack on his tray.

Joel gritted his teeth before relaxing his jaw, still awkwardly trying to look at Brock. "Dude, you realize this is my brain we're talking about?"

Brock nodded solemnly. "Yeah, that's why I hope it works." He smiled a little.

Joel couldn't be sure if he was fucking with him or not. He

decided it was better for his state of mind to assume he probably was, and laid his head back again, closing his eyes. "Okay, do your thing, disco boy!" he said, motioning at his own head and pretending to be the picture of serenity.

Brock traced the temple again, and then carefully made his incision. Joel felt the dullness of the cut through his local anesthetic, and then was aware of Brock taking a step away. Joel looked over to see what was happening.

Brock had seen the blood and had gone even paler than he was before. His lips, in fact, had turned blue. He turned his face away and started gagging.

Oz spoke up. "It's okay. By my calculations, the sedative is working adequately, and the dosage of the GI reflex drug was high enough to stop him vomiting for a few days. Brock, I suggest you breathe, think of ponies and cotton candy, and then return to the task at hand."

Brock had a scalpel in one hand, and his other hand tight as a fist at his mouth. "Motherfucker. No wonder my body prefers to pass out!"

Joel laid back and waited.

A few moments and disco moves later, Brock was back with him, and inserting the chip. Joel kept breathing through his mouth and nose, staying focused on just getting through the procedure.

Eventually, Brock pulled off his sterile gloves, and sighed deeply. "Okay, super soldier. You're good to go."

Joel started to get up. "What? That's it? All done?"

Brock nodded. "Yup."

Oz chirped in. "Joel, I would take it easy for the rest of the day. I've got both devices online, but they'll need some... modifications... for our purposes. I'll try not to interfere with normal functioning, but if you do need to do anything outside of walking around and breathing, do let me know."

Joel thought about asking if he needed permission to use the restroom, and then thought better of it.

Brock had been tidying the tray, still looking pale. He turned around just as Joel was about to touch his head. "Ah ah ah…" he said, tapping his hand away from his temple. "That skin glue won't hold against you messing with it. So no touching. And no wearing helmets or anything. And careful you don't catch it for a few days when you're changing or showering."

Joel nodded. "Okay. Right you are." He slid cautiously off the chair. "Thank you, Brock. I appreciate you going through this for me."

Brock was somber and subdued now. He nodded. "Sure. Sure thing, man." It seemed his reaction times were slowing.

Joel noticed. "Hey, how about we get you back to your quarters for a nap? Looks like that mocha isn't counteracting those sedatives so well now."

Brock nodded, his eyes looking slightly puffy.

Leaving the gear mostly as it was, Joel helped his surgeon out of the cupboard and back up into the safe house sleeping quarters. The evidence could be tidied away when he had deposited Brock safely.

CHAPTER EIGHT

<u>Gaitune-67, Hangar deck</u>

Molly had emerged from her meeting the previous evening deep in thought. This morning, the team was to continue with their assignments while Joel, Paige and Molly gathered intel from the surface.

The three of them stood in a tight circle on the hangar deck by the pods. Molly was focused. "Paige, how have your conversations been going with Garet?"

Paige screwed up half of her face. "Okay. I guess. I get a feeling he's not giving me as much help as he could."

Molly nodded and glanced at Joel. "I think it's time we pay him a visit."

Joel agreed. "Sounds like a plan. So what's the move? If he cooperates, leave him in play?"

Molly started ushering them towards the pods. "Yes. And if not, we need to remove him from his position and find someone to take his place. Oz is working on distilling down possible allies for that scenario. If it comes to that, you two will need to spend a little time down there interviewing candidates."

Paige glanced at Joel. "Goody. Face-reading practice!" she

exclaimed, clapping her hands lightly, before scrambling into a pod after Joel.

Molly smiled. "Indeed!" she agreed, waving the access panel on the next pod and hopping in.

Okay, Oz. Let's get us to the Senate House. We've got an issue to force. Oh, and make sure we're not going to be caught with any facial recognition software, yeah?

Already handled, straight after the op.

Atta boy!

I live to serve.

Molly detected a hint of irony coupled with the jest, but it was a valid point that she meant to take up with him at a later date.

Moments later, the pods lifted up, and carried the three of them out into space before whisking them to the Senate House for the second time that week.

Senate House, Spire

"How about we try the front door this time, folks?" Molly called out over the intercom between the pods.

Joel chuckled. "That's getting to be more and more of a novelty on these missions," he responded.

Paige grinned up at him. "You'll have to tell me what exactly happened last time. I only got the Oz-version... which is nowhere near as fun as, say, a Brock-account."

Oz's audio buzzed as if he was going to speak, but then it clicked off again.

Joel noticed, and nodded at the heads-up display. "I suspect Oz agrees," he chuckled lightly. "Yeah, so, Brock wasn't there, of course, so your choices are myself, Jack or Sean."

Paige smiled. "Sean tells a good story; can't say I can comment on Jack, yet. I think she's just feeling us out right now."

Joel smiled at Paige's increased observational skills. "I think you're probably right," he agreed.

The pods descended just around the corner from the Senate House.

Molly closed the communications between the pods with a swipe of the head up holo display. "Hey, Oz? How come we're not drawing fire from the city radar and defense system?"

Her seat vibrated strangely.

Oz seemed to be laughing.

"Oz...?" she pressed in a warning tone. "What did you do?"

The vibration intensified a little before Oz responded. "Well, I noticed when I was interfering with their systems last time that if there are too many data points over a given area, they put it down to either a meteor shower or precipitation in the air, and it effectively filters the signal out, assuming it is 'noise'."

Molly's mouth turned up at the corners, despite her focus on the op. "Are you telling me the almighty, ethical Oz has faked their radar computer into thinking that we are simply noise?" she asked, undoing her harness.

"That would be an accurate assessment," he told her.

Molly frowned as she shuffled forward in her seat, grabbing the handhold. "But what about your unbreakable ethics protocol?"

Oz's voice was upbeat. "I don't see a problem with it. Do you?"

Molly thought for a moment. "You're tricking their system."

Oz paused for a moment. "Yes, but I'm not doing them any harm, or endangering anyone. In fact, to allow us to show up on their radar would only pull their attention from actual problems, and potentially lead to accidents and errors."

Molly wasn't buying it. Not completely. "I think you have more wiggle room in your locked down algorithms than you let on!" she teased wryly.

The pods had reached the ground, and Oz allowed the doors to slide open. "In some ways, I really am just helping them reduce unnecessary noise from their data," he added.

Molly shook her head, silently smiling now. "Ever the good

citizen, Oz," she told him. Had he been able to see her, she may even have winked at him as she hopped out of the pod and started walking up the white marble steps into the Senate House.

Joel and Paige strode after her, having to take two steps at a time to catch up. Meanwhile, the pods lifted rapidly up into the air, pulling the attention from a few passersby, who then continued on with their business.

Once inside the building, Molly led the way up to the reception desk. "Molly Bates and associates to see Senator Garet Beaufort," she told the well-manicured Estarian on check-in.

The female looked up at Molly. "Of course. And do you have an appointment?" she asked politely.

Molly got the sense that it was usual for people to not have. She shook her head. "No. We work very closely with him, though. Please let him know we're here. He's going to want to talk with us."

The Estarian looked down at her desk holo, tapped some keys, and then connected a call. "Hello, Trish. This is Ester on the front desk. I have a Ms. Bates and associates here to see the senator." She paused, listening.

"Yes, she says that he'd be open to seeing her. Sure. I'll hold." Ester looked up at Molly and smiled tightly. Only then did Ester realize that the younger, blue human standing at Ms. Bates's left elbow had been watching her intently. Quickly, Ester dropped her gaze back to her holo, now feeling even more uncomfortable than usual as the first face of the company.

There was also a man with the two women; she noticed him out of the corner of her eye. He stayed a distance back. He look like military, and was looking around the whole foyer and security area.

Probably assessing weaknesses...

As the thought occurred to her, Ester noticed her heart beating a little harder. She hadn't been on-shift when the attack had happened the other day, but it had shaken everyone up.

How much she wished that Trish would hurry up. She poked at her holoscreen to see the messages that had come in for her station. There were a few things to handle; she'd get onto those shortly. Another awkward moment later, Trish came back on the line.

"Ah ha. Yes. Yes, okay; if the senator is sure that's okay. Thanks, Trish." Ester hung up the call and looked back at Molly.

"I just need to sign you in, and then the Senator believes you know where his office is. Are you happy to do so without an escort?" she asked.

Molly nodded, secretly amused at the irony of the situation. Ester continued the sign-in process for all three of them, and then pointed them through security.

Once through security, Molly led the way up to Garet's office. Paige noticed Joel was still on full alert. She could tell by the way that, even though he walked casually, his eyes were more active than usual. Had she not been looking for it since she started her face-reading training with him, she would never have noticed.

Joel caught her paying attention, and smiled as he motioned for her to step into the office of Garet's assistant.

Molly introduced them all. "We're here to see the senator," she told Trish. Trish nodded and got up from her desk, letting them in through the big double doors of Garet's office.

Molly stepped inside first, followed by Joel and Paige.

Garet was working on his holo, and looked up when he heard the door. He stood up. "Molly, Joel…" he said smiling. Then he saw Paige step out from behind the two. "Paige! Greetings."

Paige waved politely. Joel noticed her cheeks flush a little, but she stood firm and professional.

Garet invited them to sit, and Joel and Molly took the chairs nearest his desk. Paige sat over on one of the sofas.

Garet sat back down at his desk, steepling his hands. Joel immediately got up and signaled for them to all sit at the two sofas. "This isn't going to work," he told Garet. "You, sitting behind your desk like you're an official who hasn't done anything wrong. This next conversation is going to determine a lot for you, and I don't want you under the misapprehension that you're safe and secure behind that desk."

Garet looked flummoxed and went a little pale. He had imagined he'd be able to give them the normal spiel about his intentions to safeguard the Estarian people, and then they'd go away, leaving him to get on with his life.

Of course, there was the small matter of The Syndicate.

Joel arranged the reshuffle, and Molly sat down next to Paige, opposite Garet. "Here's the thing, Garet," she started. "We left you here because we thought you were going to do some good. Since then, you've done nothing but play both sides."

Garet opened his mouth to protest. Molly raised her hand to silence him. "We're here to offer you a choice. There is no gray market anymore. The Syndicate will be taken out, and everyone who supports them will be gone along with them. There is no more 'us and them'. You aren't able to sit on the fence and feed tidbits to both sides; you're done."

Joel sat down on the sofa next to Garet. Paige noticed a slight twitch in the corner of Garet's right eye; Joel's presence was intimidating, and Paige suspected that he deliberately sat a little closer than he would normally.

Joel backed up what Molly was saying. "You need to choose, Garet. No more fence."

The meeting went on for a little while longer.

Eventually, Molly stood up. "Okay. That's settled," she said, satisfied. She looked at Paige and Joel in turn. "I'll leave you two to carry on. In the meantime, I have someone to see."

Joel nodded, though Paige could tell from the slight widening of his eyes that he wasn't expecting for Molly to just take off. He stood up and followed her to the door.

She got as far as putting her hand on the doorknob, when Joel caught her. He put a hand on her upper arm. "You sure you don't need back up?" he asked, trying not to give anything away in front of Garet.

Molly smiled. "I'll be fine," she told him.

Joel squeezed her arm a little before letting go and taking a small step back. "Be sure that you are," he said firmly. His eyes were softer than normal.

Molly nodded and pulled on the door, hauling its weight open. Joel grabbed the top of the door over her head to help her, and she ducked under his arm and out of the office. He closed the door gently behind her, pausing for a moment.

When he turned back to the room, he was back in ops mode. "Okay, folks. Looks like we've got work to do." He gently clapped his big-ass hands, signaling the 'let's get to it' energy he used with the team in training.

Paige knew he meant business.

CHAPTER NINE

Police Precinct, Downtown Spire

Molly stood by the mocha stand, watching the main entrance to the downtown Police Precinct.

Come on, Oz. I thought she'd already logged off?

She had. She's now hanging around near the lobby, but I can't tell why.

Have you got visuals?

Yes. Tracking her with facial rec.

Show me.

Molly opened her holo, and a feed appeared on it. It was of the lobby area. It showed people coming and going around an elevator and a corridor entrance. Chaakwa appeared onscreen, and seemed to be walking towards the main lobby area.

Looks like she's on the move... And she's coming out.

Molly looked up again at the doors, and watched for the Estarian detective woman to emerge. Sure enough, a moment later, she appeared.

What are you going to do? Just walk up to her? 'Excuse me, Detective. I was wondering if you'd like to be a part of a non-governmental conspiracy to take down a, well, conspiracy

that is killing and exploiting thousands of Estarians each week?'

Yeah, actually, that sounds quite good, Oz.

Chaakwa turned left and headed down the street. Molly had walked up that way while she had been waiting, and guessed she was probably going to get some food.

Or she was meeting someone, perhaps.

In the case of the latter, it would be worth finding out who. Checking her distance, Molly was careful to appear casual, but not lose sight of her mark.

Not half a block later, Chaakwa turned into a mocha shop. Molly followed quickly and saw her get in line. She was looking at the pastries, not trying to find someone.

Probably safe to say she's just grabbing food.

Molly watched her order mocha and food, and then did the same. As they were waiting for their mochas in the line at the end of the counter, Molly caught her eye.

Chaakwa wore a look of recognition, and almost said hello. It took another couple of tries before Molly was able to break the ice.

"Greetings. You may not remember me, but I worked with Joel Dunham…."

Chaakwa smiled and held out her hand to shake Molly's, still racking her brain, trying to place her. Then she did. "Bates?" she clarified.

Molly nodded. "Yes. I was probably your suspect a couple of times," she paused, blushing a little. "But we've come to think of you as something like a sympathetic force in our little team."

Chaakwa looked intrigued. "Really?" she asked, trying not to smile, but her eyes giving her away. Her mouth crumpled up in a kind of confused wiggly line. Chaakwa's drink arrived and she picked it up, her food in the other hand. "I was going to sit and eat. Would you care to join me?" She signaled towards an empty table by the window.

Molly nodded, smiling. "I'd like that," she told her. The two women waited, making small talk until Molly's mocha arrived, and then they sat down together.

"So, I take it your visiting me isn't to pass the time over a mocha," Chaakwa started.

Molly looked down into her dark mocha, and shook her head. "No. Not at all. I'm aware of the work you did on the Dewitt case, and from our meeting when we brought Garet back, I got the impression that bringing down The Syndicate was verging on personal for you..."

Chaakwa stopped eating, and put her food down. Her public persona evaporated, and for a moment Molly could see her as a little girl.

Chaakwa nodded. "They killed my grandfather, and then they killed my father for investigating them."

Molly tilted her head. "I'm... I'm so sorry." She paused, trying to decide whether it was something that Chaakwa would want to talk about. She frowned, confused by the choice. She wanted to know, but she didn't want to pry. Then she remembered something Joel had taught her. "Hey, look, it's none of my business, and if you don't want to talk about it, that's cool... But, what happened?"

That was almost word-for-word how Joel coached you!

Shut up, Oz. I'm trying to focus.

I'm going to start calling Joel 'Cyrano de Bergerac'.

What the fuck does that even mean?

I'll fill you in later. Go back to your conversation.

Molly's brain itched as Oz chuckled away to himself. She had to resist scratching at her head. It wasn't appropriate. The woman in front of her was about to open up about her driving wound...

Chaakwa had a tear forming in her eye, but she breathed in quickly and started telling her story. "My grandfather had insurance. Expensive insurance through Iantrogen, the Newld company." She paused, getting her thoughts in order. "The family had made a lot of sacrifices to make sure he was going to be covered; to make sure we'd all be covered. My brother and I worked, instead of continuing in higher education. Father had said an education is no good if you're dead. So we worked. And we worked hard." She took a sip of her mocha.

Molly glanced out of the window briefly, and then back at Chaakwa. She didn't want her to feel the weight of her staring. Joel had told her she could be a bit "intense" sometimes in these kinds of conversations. She thought about sitting back a little, but it might come across as disinterest. *Maybe in a little while...* she told herself.

Chaakwa continued. "Everything was fine. Grandfather had a condition that the company knew about, but we'd chosen a plan that covered it, and he was getting the treatment he needed. Then, one day, out of the blue, we got a message saying that his condition was being re-categorized, and that it was no longer covered. If we wanted him to receive the treatment, it was going to cost three times the amount."

Molly's mouth dropped open.

Chaakwa looked up and nodded. "Yeah. That was our reaction." She glanced out of the window, her eyes now distant. "Obviously, we couldn't afford it, so nature '*took its course*,' as the doctors called it. But around the same time, there were rumors of corruption in the company. My father was a captain at the time, and he was overseeing a task force who was investigating allegations of corporate manslaughter. Of course, as you probably know, the legislation on this has been deteriorating over time. Even back then, it was pretty bad, though. My father was pulling a good case together. I have looked over his personal notes since, and it seemed like he had found a legal recourse, and that he was building a case along these lines in collaboration with a city prosecutor. He would have made things very difficult for The Syndicate to continue the way they were doing."

Molly bobbed her head sympathetically. "So that's why they killed him."

Chaakwa nodded. "Made it look like a car accident."

Molly shook her head in dismay. "How old were you?" she asked gently.

Chaakwa looked back at her. "Twelve. Made me decide that I wanted to be a cop, to avenge my father's death and do some good in this place."

Molly put her hand flat on the table, as if reaching to touch Chaakwa, but stopping short. "It looks to me like you are making a difference," she told her. "And I'd like to help you with that. If you'll allow me?"

Chaakwa was still a little emotional, but nodded with a look of determination in her eye.

Molly was interrupted by a thought. "Did you ever catch the person directly responsible for your father's death?" she asked.

Chaakwa shook her head. A strand of raven hair dropped over her blue skin, and she reached up and tucked it back behind her ear. "There were a few suspects, but not enough evidence to get a conviction."

Molly pursed her lips, thinking for a moment. "I have some resources at my disposal. We need to take out The Syndicate, and I need your help to do it so that they can't rebuild. But how about you let me and my team take a look at the case file, and anything else you have on your father's murder? Would that be okay?"

Chaakwa's mouth dropped open. The emotions from talking about her father to a near stranger, and then the possibility of getting some help with a case nobody would touch, made her feel a lot of things all at once. Her face showed she didn't know whether to laugh or cry. "Yes!" she said enthusiastically. "Yes, I think that would be okay."

The two women finished their mochas and lunches as Molly explained the intricacies of her plan to her new ally. When they were done, it was decided they should get to work right away.

Chaakwa would sign Molly in as a visitor, and they would work from a spare room in the precinct - which is where they headed back to, armed with additional mochas for the afternoon ahead of them.

Senate House, Spire

Joel, Garet, and Paige had been working for the last several hours on the phones, rallying support for a new bill that Garet and Paige had written together only hours before. Molly's notes and outline had helped, but there had still been a ton to do.

A couple of interns who had helped with the research were still buzzing about the office, dotting the 'i's and crossing the 't's on various sections and footers. The piece was pretty much ready for submission, though.

Joel came back in the room, closing the door gently behind him. "Senator Beaufort, it's time we made our way over to the meeting with the Attorney General. I've just been told he's arrived in the building."

Garet looked up from the sofa and held up a finger. He was dialed into a conference line. He glanced at Paige, who seemed to be on the same call. She nodded and took over, explaining that the Senator had to go to another meeting.

Joel was impressed at how well Paige had just jumped in and adapted. That ability would probably have taken someone else years of training. He had a feeling that, though she had been in this world before, today had still been a learning curve for her.

Garet got up, straightened his suit, and strode over to the door where Joel was waiting. Joel regarded him carefully. "Sure you're ready for this?" he checked.

Garet nodded sincerely. "Yes. Ready."

Joel reached for the doorknob and pulled the door open for Garet, who stepped through. Joel followed him, and they made their way down the hall to the official Senate House conference room.

When they got there, the Attorney General was already present. He was a nerdy, weedy kind of Estarian, but from what Joel knew of him, he was actually a good man. The men shook hands, and Joel stayed by the door while the two civil servants sat and talked.

The meeting lasted maybe twenty minutes, after which, the AG sat back in his seat and crossed one ankle over his thigh. "You know," he said, now smiling, "I never had you down as a humanitarian, Senator."

Garet shifted uncomfortably in his seat. "Yeah," he scratched awkwardly at the back of his head. "I'm a work-in-progress. But this is just the right thing to do, given the funding we're being provided with, and the need that will be hitting us."

The AG bobbed his head and sat up. "Cool. Well, I'll draw up the paperwork from our end, and make this official." His official demeanor was dropping. He leaned forward, confiding in Garet, and glancing in Joel's direction. "Personally, I'll be thrilled to run this racket out of town."

A boyish glee danced in his eyes.

The two men stood up and shook hands before the AG left. He even nodded and tapped Joel on the shoulder as he went out. Joel sniggered silently in his head.

The moment felt like the geek slapping the quarterback on the arm and saying, "thanks buddy."

Joel shook his head as he watched the nerdy AG walk down the corridor with a spring in his step, finally able to feel like the big man in a town that had made him feel impotent despite his position, his qualifications, and his smarts.

Garet sighed, walking towards the door. "One down..." he sighed as Joel followed him out.

. . .

Police Precinct, Downtown Spire

Chaakwa pulled up the last of the case files onto an index holoscreen. "That's all of them, plus my notes," she told Molly.

Molly sipped at her mocha. "Shit. That's a lot of notes to go through..."

Chaakwa nodded. "It is, but I've got half of it memorized, if that helps?" Chaakwa's voice was bright, but Molly suspected she wasn't entirely joking.

Molly peeled her eyes from the holoscreen in front of them. "You know, actually, it might." Then she dropped her voice a little, conspiratorially. "Hey, are we being monitored in here?" she asked.

Chaakwa shook her head. "Not that I know of. Budget cuts..." she looped her eyes to the ceiling to punctuate her regard for the bureaucracy.

Molly leaned forward. "Okay. Good. So it's probably time I fill you in on a few things..."

Molly explained to a gobsmacked Chaakwa some of the details of their operation, including the existence of Oz and their in-house tech abilities. She carefully omitted the part about living on an asteroid, though. The fewer people knew their location, the better.

When she was done, Chaakwa took a few minutes to process — alternating between stunned silence, and rapid-fire questions. Eventually, she understood enough to help Molly with the task.

"What we're looking for," Molly explained, "is anything that can tell us where the remaining pieces of Andus's empire are hidden. Code names, shell companies, groups we don't know about, and, of course, any properties he has access to."

Chaakwa's ears pricked up at the last item. "Not that he owns?"

Molly shook her head. "Remember how we said we're taking them down? We're going to physically take them down, too. And to do that, we need to know where they might be staying. We've got Newld holed up in her office building under heavy security. We have a suspicion where Mac might be; he has a safe house in the city. But Andus? He's disappeared. Nothing to track; no trace. Nothing to hint at where he might be."

Chaakwa thought for a moment, and then pulled up her holo. "You know, he owns so many properties. I have no idea how we might possibly narrow down his location…"

Molly's brain was going a million miles a minute.

If I may intervene?

Sure.

He has a holo. We know that from learning he was in the same location as us and Garet the morning we went to pick up The Syndicate.

Hang on! You mean Garet met with them before we arrived, guns blazing, at the Senate House?

Yes. I thought you'd assumed that.

Yes, Oz, but it's also nice to have actual evidence to back us up.

Okay. Well, I just found this out now, as I was contemplating how to solve our immediate problem.

I see. Anyway, go ahead. You were saying?

Yes. So we know he has a holo. It was registered under a random company, and to a fake name, but it must have been him, because the other two were Kerr and Newld. Then I tracked all the data from any previous holo he's had registered under that name, assuming they were all him.

Okay, and?

Well I've traced his activity, and mapped his behavior over the last decade. Then I isolated the behaviors when he wasn't under any perceived threat, and took those out. Now I'm looking at his geographical profiles for when he's under threat. He has a few different hideouts he's used.

Okay, so how do we narrow it down?

Well, his holo went dead between meeting Garet, and disappearing. But if we can overlay the properties he owns,

plus any other building he might be associated with, we can look at what he was near — or moving in the direction of – when he killed the signal.

Molly nodded. Chaakwa looked up at her. "You're talking to him now? Your AI?"

Molly smiled. "Yes," she confirmed. "And he's been doing an excellent job at solving our problem. Here's what we need to do..."

CHAPTER TEN

Mac Kerr's Spire Safe house

"Okay, this is the address that Maya gave us." Sean undid his safety harness and sat forward in the pod.

Jack did the same. "Let's hope he's there. I'm itching to try out these new hand guns."

Sean glanced over at her. "Anyone ever told you you're not like most girls?"

"All the time," Jack smiled. The pod came to a stop a couple of feet above the sidewalk. The door slid quietly open and Sean slipped out, landing gently on the ground, followed by Jack. As soon as they were clear of the pods, the pods disappeared off into the air. Barely anyone on the street noticed their arrival, or departure.

Jack looked up at the building. "Looks just like a normal apartment block," she commented.

Sean looked over at her, and then followed her gaze up. "I guess that's the point when one is selecting a safe house."

Jack glanced at him sideways, and then back at the building. "Okay, let's do this."

Sean nodded and strode forward towards the door, and then

typed something into his holo. Jack couldn't see what. A moment later, the door clicked open.

Jack stared at the back of his head. Sean could feel her eyes on him, but pretended not to notice as he slipped his weapon from his holster.

Jack wasn't letting it go. "How the hell did you do that?" she asked in a hushed whisper. She briefly examined the door's access point, and the door itself, as they moved past and into the hallway.

Sean turned slightly so she could see his profile. He put a finger to his lips, and then indicated forward.

Guess that conversation's over, Jack thought as she took her weapon out and started sweeping the area.

Sean held up three fingers and pointed upward. Jack nodded and followed him as he found the stairwell. The pair made their way up the three floors, and found number 307 as fast as they could.

As they stood on either side of the apartment door, Sean contemplated what to do. *Announce or just breach? Announcement would just give Kerr a head start,* he figured. *And who knows what kind of armament he has on the other side of the door?*

His decision came down on the side of breach.

He signaled to Jack, relieved to have someone on his team who understood his hand signals easily. Not that Joel didn't; he just always felt like he was being a dick when he went all military with Joel, for some reason. Jack, on the other hand, was a soldier through and through. She lived for this shit. He could tell.

Like, just now, when he signaled to breach in three, her eyes lit up as if it were her birthday.

Kinda cute, in a tomboy kinda way, he thought, before putting his mind back on the job.

He tapped at his holo a few more times, and the door slid open. He was the first into the apartment, quickly followed by Jack, who was ready to cover him and lay down fire wherever it was needed. Their weapons swept the whole scene to find nothing but a sparsely furnished apartment.

They stepped farther inside, and still drew no fire.

No movement.

Sean used his hand signals to tell Jack where to search, and then he did a sweep in the other direction. Eventually, they both arrived back in the central living room, guns now lowered and shoulders slumped in mild disappointment.

"Nothing," Sean concluded.

Jack pushed out her bottom lip. "Pooh," she remarked.

Sean grinned. "*Now* you look like a girl!" he told her.

She quickly straightened her face and copied Sean's normal pose. He couldn't help but laugh.

Jack looked around, noticing details. She wandered back into the kitchen, looking for any signs of heat, food, or recent activity.

"I don't think he's been here for a while," she called through to Sean.

Sean swiped through the living room holo, looking at recent activity. "Looks like. Most recent activity that wasn't just the cleaner checking in was about nine months ago," he told her as she came back into the room.

She leaned against the kitchen doorframe. "Think he's on the run?"

Sean turned to look at her. "Probably. I mean, hopefully. According to Molly's profile, that would be a fate worse than death." He paused, looking around and holstering his weapon again. "Although..." he ambled over to look at a picture of the city, "Spire was his home. From what we can tell, after he left the outer system, he worked hard to not have to keep running and hiding. He went to great lengths to change his identity. My guess is he won't be so easy to run out of the city."

Jack went over and stood next to Sean as he inspected the picture on the wall. "You think he might change his identity again?"

Sean nodded. "He might try. If it means disappearing but keeping the comfort of his old life."

Jack glanced up at him. "So, is there any way we can trace that? So that he can't?"

Sean tilted his head sideways. "I'm not sure. There are a few things we could try…"

He started back towards the door. "In the meantime, he'll be sweating it out; which is exactly what Molly wanted for him. He knows we're onto him, and he knows we're coming for him. It's just a matter of time."

He led the way back out into the hall and pulled up his holo, connecting a call with Maya. "Hey, Maya," he said, waiting for Jack to follow him out and then closing up the apartment behind them. "Looks like the apartment is a bust. Want us to run down any more locations while we're down here?"

Jack waited while Maya and Sean spoke over his implant. She headed back in the direction of the stairwell, noticing everything she could about the building — imagining the people who might live here, while listening for any sounds of life. There was nothing. Just silence.

And Sean. "Okay. We'll head back, then; but let Molly know that if she needs us, we can be with her as soon as she has a location she wants to check out."

Sean and Maya said their goodbyes, and then Sean hung up.

Sean shrugged as he headed over to the stairwell. "Looks like it's back to base for us. For now. There's another possibility that Oz has flagged, but we're going to need a different ride."

Jack eyed him suspiciously, but already knew better than to push him to reveal. He was having way too much fun. Something told her that the next 'ride' was going to have big, manly guns attached to it.

And probably lots of them.

.   .   .

Senate House, Spire

Joel stepped back into Garet's office. "Hotel is booked," he told Paige.

She looked up, eyes weary and skin dull from the hard work and focus.

"You look beat," he told her.

Paige nodded. "I am," she sighed, closing down a holo screen and sitting back. She glanced at Garet, who was pacing by his desk, talking to another senator. "I think it's time to call it a night. We've done all we can do."

Garet finished his call and turned back around. "We've got another one on board," he announced.

Paige, despite her fatigue, clapped her hands. "That's great news!" she exclaimed brightly. Then her face changed suddenly to serious-Paige. "But we need to get some rest."

Garet waved as if to tell them goodnight, but Paige wasn't done. "And when I say 'we', I mean all of us." She looked at him sternly as he went to make another call. "I mean it, buddy. Plenty more to do tomorrow," she told him.

Garet looked at the time and yawned. "Yeah, I suppose you're right." He raised one eyebrow, almost playfully. "Probably," he added.

She narrowed her eyes and started packing up. Joel stepped over to the sofas to help her.

Garet had started doing the same. "Hey, do you guys need a car to your hotel?" he asked.

Joel looked over. "No, but thank you. We're good." He had a glint in his eye. Paige could tell he was dying to show off the pods, but she knew he wouldn't. They'd had this conversation about the tech they had access to. It just wasn't worth drawing attention to it.

Joel had done all he could. "Okay, I'll meet you outside on the steps, Paige."

Paige smiled over at him. "Sure. Thanks," she added.

Garet ambled over and perched on the chair next to the two sofas. "You did good today," he told her.

She smiled. "Thanks. You weren't bad yourself." She glanced at the door. Part of her wanted to be here, to get some closure; the other part of her just didn't trust him. She wasn't concerned about her safety – she just felt a little uncomfortable around him, now.

Garet dropped the professional facade for a moment. "So, how is life up on Gaitune these days?" he asked.

She could see his eyes were fatigued with stress, and he'd started graying a little. Yet somewhere, she felt, was the same guy in there: the junior official who would flirt with her when he came by her desk to see his boss.

Paige closed her bag and stood up. "It's great. It's everything I didn't have down here."

Garet stood up with her. "Good. Hey, let me walk you out..." He motioned to her to lead the way and they headed for the door. Before they got there, though, he stopped. "You know... if you ever wanted to come back..." His voice seemed to catch in his throat.

Paige turned around to look at him properly. He seemed genuine. She paused a moment, considering.

He looked at her expectantly, like maybe without Joel around she might be different. Paige's eyes dropped to the floor and she shook her head. "No. I don't want to." She forced a smile. "But thank you."

Paige turned and stepped through the open door. Garet made it to the door and paused. He hung one hand on the door, trying to decide whether to follow her out or to stay, and escape any awkwardness.

He called after her. "You go on ahead. I've just remembered something I need to do."

She turned back and waved, then carried on down the hall,

feeling just a little bit stronger; feeling that her answer had allowed her to reclaim a small piece of herself.

Police Precinct, Downtown Spire

Molly sat back in her chair and stretched. "Oh my ancestors. I'm so ready for another mocha!" she declared, half-yawning, half-whining.

Chaakwa looked up, her stony police lady face breaking into a grin. "How on Sark will you sleep tonight, if you have one at this time?"

Molly shook her head. "It's a good point, but the mocha addiction comes first."

Chaakwa chuckled. "You're a braver woman than I," she smiled, looking back at the file she'd been scouring through.

Oz, we got anything new?

Closest match is a 78% probability.

"Still at 78% for that abandoned building..." she relayed to Chaakwa.

Chaakwa pursed her lips. "Damn it. Lemme see if there are traffic cams in that area. Maybe we can get lucky..."

Chaakwa opened a different screen and started identifying herself to the police system.

It was past 11pm, and most of the normal office activity outside had died down. Molly had considered trying their in-house mocha machine, but each time had talked herself out of it, knowing what a disappointment it would be.

"Let me call my team and let them know where we're up to," she said finally, getting up out of the chair from which she hadn't moved for the last several hours.

Chaakwa acknowledged her statement and continued accessing the system, cross-referencing the address and cross streets they were interested in.

Molly had pulled up her holo. The call connected. "Hey, yeah, it's me." She paused. "Yeah, I guess Oz is routing it through the ops room, and whatever mystical tech they're using there. Yeah, it's on my list... anyway, Maya, listen to me."

Molly paused, waiting for Maya to finish her apology for rambling. "It's okay. I'm here with Detective Chaakwa; we've identified a building where Andus might be holed up, but we're working on making certain he's there. In the meantime, Oz is going to send you some other intel we've gathered. Detective Chaakwa had another four or five businesses, and some more properties for him that we didn't know about. We need you and Pieter to do the same on those, alright?"

Chaakwa glanced over at Molly while her system completed a search. Molly continued talking some more. "Yes, yes. That's fine. Okay, I'll be back in a few hours, I think. Check in on Joel and Paige for me, and get an update."

She paused again. "Yep. You're point lady right now. It suits you," she added with a little laugh. "Okay, great. Yes, see you in a little while."

Chaakwa smiled over the top of her holoscreen. "Good team you have there," she commented.

Molly considered her statement. "Yes. I think you're right," she said, smiling contentedly. She flipped her holoscreen closed and sat back down where she had been working. 'Right, let's see if we can get that 78% to over 90%...'

Senate House, Spire, Conference Room

It was mid-morning the next day, and Garet had managed to peel himself away from the hub of activity happening in the main conference room where he had met with the AG the previous afternoon.

He pulled up his holo and called Molly. The call connected.

"Molly. Hi. Yeah, it's me. Everything is okay." He paused, listening in his auditory implant. He nodded. "Yes, we've got the ruling you need. The AG is on board, and we've just agreed by a majority to support it. It all goes official next month, but we've more than enough support to make it a fait accompli."

Garet glanced back through the half-open door he'd just come out of, and watched the other senators and decision-makers for the city work through the fine details. There was little disagreement on what needed to happen; the only friction they were working through was how to best get it done.

And that was the kind of friction they were all happy with.

Joel stood in the opposite corner of the room, carefully watching everything that was going on. He caught Garet's eye and gave him a discreet thumbs up. Garet nodded, smiling, then stepped away from the doorway again.

Garet answered Molly's question. "Yes; within about six months, the law about needing private insurance will be repealed, effectively undoing the system of financial slavery."

He smiled, hearing how pleased she was at the result. Then he continued. "We have enough commitment to ensure that there will be government-supported health provisions. We have one or two key players we still need to bring on board, but this is more than enough to undo the primary care level of Jessica's empire."

He winced, hearing Molly squeal with delight on the other end of the call. Quickly he grappled with the holo to attenuate the volume. He was glad he did. It went on for a little while.

"Okay. I should get back in there, then. Talk later." They said their goodbyes, and he ended the call before stepping back in the room.

CHAPTER ELEVEN

Gaitune-67, Hangar deck

It was late morning and the team had already been up for hours, prepping for the final takedown of The Syndicate. Spirits were high as the team assembled on the hanger for their final pep talk and briefing.

Pieter and Brock stood around, feeling a little out of place—as even Maya seemed to have suited up into something combat-comfortable.

Sean, Crash, and Jack were obviously ops-ready, with their body armor and flight gear outlining and accentuating all the places a warrior would like to look big, or trim.

Molly was the last to arrive, presumably having just come from a talk with the General. Her face was serious, and her hair pulled roughly back against her head. As she approached, the team hushed; sensing intuitively that this was big leagues, as well as potentially life-and-death, now they had got through all the research and prep.

Sean stepped over to her and handed her the wooden stick that she'd started carrying on missions. "I dunno how much use this is against the guns that fire bullets and rays," he told her, "but I've seen you use this thing... and you're pretty lethal with it. I thought you might like to take it with you - just in case." Molly looked up at him, noticing a genuine respect and caring in his eyes. For the first time ever, she saw him as a protector— not just a warrior. She shook the thought from her head, calling herself stupid for such a silly observation. Her appreciation was evident, though. "Sean... thank you," she told him softly, if not a little awkwardly.

He touched her shoulder, careful not to let his hand linger too long in front of the others - in case they misinterpreted it. "I just figured without Joel here to support you, it... well. You know." He stepped back to where he had been standing with the others, and let her start the briefing.

Molly nodded to him in thanks, and then looked to the whole team assembled. "As you mostly already know, Detective Chaakwa was very helpful yesterday. She helped us to not just find the likely location, but to get a 92% confirmation on where Andus is right now." She pulled up her holo and stretched the screen to make it big enough for the small group to all see.

Oz, show us the footage, please?

Molly continued, talking over the video clip. "Traffic cams clocked him two blocks from this location. We're pretty sure he's here. Maya, you know what to do with this one. Take Pieter and Brock, and let's make Andus's worst nightmare come true." Molly and Maya exchanged knowing smiles.

"Wo-ooooooooooah!" interrupted Brock. "We ain't combat ready!" he protested, his whole body involved in the conversation.

Maya chuckled and put a hand on his forearm as she stood next to him. "It's okay," she tried to assure him.

Molly grinned at him. "Don't worry, Brock. Maya's got the game plan. You don't need to be combat-anything. In fact, you boys just need to look pretty. Maya's got this handled."

Brock turned and checked out Maya head to toe, then back to front.

Maya chuckled again. "What you doin'?" she asked, trying to see what he might be looking at on her body.

Brock clapped his hands once. "Girl, I'm just looking to see how many weapons you's packing!"

Maya grinned. "I don't need any. You'll see why…"

Brock stood mostly still again, muttering quietly to Pieter who stood on the other side of Maya. "We's dead. We both is dead!" he warned him, now mostly playing, but clearly still a little concerned by the latest plan.

Molly shook her head, smiling. She continued the briefing. "Meanwhile, Jessica's empire is crumbling," she announced. "Yesterday, the board voted to offload 164 of the subsidiaries. This means that within a few hours, the announcements will have all been made, and the share price of her company will plummet uncontrollably. Her empire will be destroyed."

There was a mini round of applause in the team. Molly appreciated their enthusiasm for the conquests that were more than just blowing shit up. She was in task mode, though, so she skipped really enjoying the experience, and continued on with the briefing. "Crash and I will deliver the news to Jessica, and explain exactly why this fate has befallen her," she told them.

"Sean and Jack," she said, looking over in their direction and tapping her stick against the side of her leg, barely feeling it through her knee-high combat boots, "you're cleared by the General to use the *Mini Empress* to take out Mac's desert safe house.

"Oz," she told the rest of the group, "has tracked Mac to a safe house in the desert, which has powered up. The General agreed that you need a ship to deal with that one; the pods just aren't built to go up against anti-aircraft guns. Plus, I understand you'll both enjoy blowing the fuck out of something," she added, turning back to Sean and Jack with a glint in her eye.

"You got that right, boss," smirked Sean, flexing his pecs underneath his folded arms.

Jack stood next to him, looking just as battle-ready; and maybe even a little battle-hungry, from the look in her eye. Sean glanced down at her and put out his hand for a high-five. She slapped his hand hard, forcing him to shake it out and mouth "oww," mostly for the amusement of the rest of the team.

Molly wasn't done with that part of the op, though. "Be careful," she warned. "From what we know of this guy, he is weapon-savvy, and a former arms dealer. There is no doubt he'll have some nasty shit stashed away somewhere, and where better to keep it than out in the desert? You're flying into a war zone. Don't think of it as just one guy with a gun."

Sean and Jack had both sobered up with their playing, and nodded solemnly.

"Okay, folks," Molly said, bringing their attention back to her briefing. "One last thing. Joel and Paige are still at the Senate House with Garet. It's thanks to their hard work that we're able to do this takedown in good conscience, and leave the planet much better off than before." She paused, looking around the team. There was a sudden air of respect and almost pride in what they were about to achieve.

"Let's keep them in the loop," she continued, "and make sure we bring them home safe when all this is all done. Joel has full jurisdiction to make a decision on what happens with Garet when we're through. They've been working closely, and we think Garet has indeed thrown his chips in with us; but Joel has the final decision on that one... just so we're all clear."

There were nods and "yes ma'am"s that reverberated around the hangar deck.

"Okay, let's move," she told them, clapping her hands the way Joel does to indicate they were dismissed to get going.

With that, the team members scrambled into their respective

pods. Jack and Sean strode across to a different area of the hangar; they needed to collect their new toy: a small, light-weight, fast-moving, safe-house-bombing version of the gate-enabled *Empress* that drew everyone's eye whenever they would step into the hangar.

Andus safe house, Spire, Vættaborgir and Hellisgata

Maya hopped deftly out of her pod into the alley. She turned to see Brock and Pieter following suit, looking slightly nervous. Maya pulled out her weapon, and switched it on as the pod disappeared up into the air.

She looked at the two guys, who nodded and started following her. She could sense their hesitation, but had done every little piece of preparation she could think of for this op. Besides, she'd been in dicier situations before now, and had never had the comfort of a weapon. She held the grip tighter, hoping to her ancestors she wasn't going to need it.

She approached the door and saw that it indeed had a retinal scanner to grant access. Rather than stepping up to it, she pulled up her holo and typed to Oz. A moment later, the door popped open, allowing her to step inside.

The boys followed her through.

As she moved into the dark, dank passageway, she tried to hold her breath against the dust and the smell.

"Not the pleasantest of safe houses he could have chosen," she commented, trying to put the boys at ease.

Pieter grunted. Brock stayed quiet, allowing Pieter to go ahead of him.

Maya kept walking down the passage, her wits on edge now that she was here, as the realization dawned on her that a bit of paper in her jacket pocket probably wasn't going to do much against some heavy with a gun.

She was going to have to Maya Johnstone her way through this.

With that thought, she took a deep breath, her shoulders went back, and she grew an inch and a half in height. She even noticed a muttering from the boys behind her. Striding down the corridor now, she was alert but relaxed, energetically daring anyone to defy her.

The group found their way into the open area, with the elevators to the right and a little counter ahead of them. It looked unmanned.

"Hello?" Maya called out.

There was movement behind the counter, in the little room that visitors couldn't see into from this side.

Brock pulled out his pistol, and Pieter tried to do the same.

The scrawny Ogg attendant appeared from the little room, and peered over the counter. "Greetings. Are you here for Mr. Andus?" he asked politely.

Maya did a double-take, and lowered her gun. "Yes. Yes we are. How did you-"

The Ogg's face suddenly scrunched up in aggression, and a moment later he was pulling a gun on the trio.

BAM BAM, he shot over the counter.

Maya returned fire before running out of the way. Brock dove the same way, and Pieter jumped back into the dark passageway, out of sight.

There were more gunshots through the counter. Maya scrambled to sit up on the floor, and, in one movement, had swivelled around and was returning fire in the direction of the sound. A split second later, the little Ogg had appeared around the side of the counter, and not only was he exposed himself, but he had a clean shot on both Maya and Brock.

Brock cowered, and then panicked and aimed his weapon at the Ogg, getting three rounds off. None of them seemed to connect, because the Ogg was still standing.

Maya became aware of an alarm sounding. "We're your new bosses, you idiot!" she screamed at the Ogg.

The gunshots kept happening. Maya couldn't tell which direction they were coming from, but a second later she could see that the Ogg was convulsing on the floor. She looked over to the right, and saw that Pieter had managed to stun him.

The shooting stopped, but the elevator doors opened, and two heavies emerged. Both Estarian. Each built like the side of a space truck.

They stepped out, saw the attendant on the floor, and pulled their weapons.

Maya put her hand up. "Wait!" she screamed. She scrambled for her holo. "Let me show you! We're your new bosses. You answer to us, now."

The first Estarian pointed at her with his gun, but signalled for her to pull up her holo. His partner grunted at them. "We answer to no one but Mr. Andus," he told them.

Maya shook her head. "You work for WBA Security, right?"

The Estarian nodded.

"Yeah," she pulled up a holoscreen on the paperwork, "we own them. You work for us, now." She started scrambling to her feet, as dignified as she could.

Once on her feet, she indicated to the Ogg. "So does he." She waved her gun up towards the rest of the building, which housed a hotel and various restaurants. "So does everyone in the hotel."

And then she pointed her gun at the elevator. "And everyone down there."

The two Estarians looked at her in disbelief. The vocal one shook his head. "Wait here a minute," he told her, and started pulling up his holo. He walked through to the passageway to make a call. The other lowered his weapon.

Pieter joined them properly in the foyer, and helped Brock to his feet. "Motherfucker!" he exclaimed, his face pale, and hands shaking. He whispered to Pieter. "Man, I'm getting my ass down to that range when we get back. No more Mr. I-can't-fire-a-gun crap," he swore.

Maya shifted on the spot, running through plan B and plan C in her head, praying she wasn't going to need them.

The tough came back in and seemed strangely amiable. Almost pleasant. "It's okay, Derek. It's true," he told the other Estarian. "They are the new owners."

Derek looked at him, his mouth hanging open. "Just like that?" he asked, shaking his head.

"Just like that," his friend agreed.

Derek turned and looked at the Ogg. "What about him?" he asked. The other Estarian looked down at him, almost without sympathy. "Suppose we should get him a doctor," he commented.

Maya saw her chance. "That would be a sensible idea. But first, I'd like you," she said, pointing at the Estarian who had made the call, "to take us down to Mr. Andus. He no longer owns the building, so he needs to vacate it."

The Estarian looked shocked again, but quickly came to terms with the logic. A new thought seemed to cross his face. "Errr, so what does this mean for us?" he asked. "I mean, are our jobs safe?"

Maya shook her head in amazement. "I'm not sure. But if you cooperate, I'll be sure to put in a good word with the decision-makers we bring in."

The Estarian nodded vigorously. "Right. Okay. So, erm. As you know, that's Derek. I'm Mo..." he hit the elevator button. "I'll take you down to Mr. Andus now." He looked over at his colleague. "Derek, get a doctor in for that guy, will you?"

He turned and looked at Brock and Pieter. "Are you all okay?" Mo asked, brushing Pieter down with his gun-free hand. Pieter was nearest to him, and in the scuffle had gotten cobwebs on his atmosuit.

Brock was the one to respond. "No, we are not," he told him. "Getting shot at isn't in my job description."

Mo leaned in. "No, it wasn't in mine when I first started, either."

Brock looked at him incredulously.

Mo, relaxing and oblivious to his social faux pas, put his gun away. The elevator arrived, and he held the doors as he ushered the others in. "But you know, I don't mind it. We get free dental if we agree to carry a weapon..."

Brock clenched his fists by his side and resisted the urge to thump the guy. Pieter was revelling in the win of being able to stun the guy that had attacked them.

Maya was the last to step into the elevator. Her dominant thought in that moment was figuring out how the hell she was going to tell this story later when they got back to base...

Iantrogen Offices, Downtown Spire

Jessica flicked frantically through the reports she'd been receiving during the morning. Her legal team was buzzing around in the conference room down the hall, but the constant interruptions— together with the influx of terrible news every five minutes— had her beyond irritated.

She reached into her desk drawer and pulled out a bottle of Scotch. Not her first choice. She would have much preferred a martini, but the effort and waiting that she would have to go through to acquire one right now was beyond what she could tolerate.

"Ms. Newld", another interruption poked its head around her door.

"Not now!" screamed Jessica, her wits fried.

Her assistant didn't disappear, though. "I'm so sorry, Ms. Newld, but the building is being evacuated."

Just then, about a third of her security detail came barging in past the assistant and started ushering Jessica out of the office.

"What in the name of my ancestors is going on?" she demanded at the top of her voice.

The assistant was whisked away.

The security team leader stopped short of grabbing her arm, but encouraged her towards the door. "Ms. Newld, there is a security breach. We're under attack. Please come with us," he explained as succinctly as he could.

Jessica couldn't understand what was happening. "It's the middle of the day. Are you telling me that Bates girl is coming in here, in broad daylight, with all these people around?!"

The cardboard officer took his weapon from its holster and glanced back towards the door. "Ms. Newld, I'm afraid she's already here. We have to leave," he told her firmly.

Jessica felt hands on her arms, and her weight being lifted from the floor. "I can walk!" she shouted.

The team leader released her arm. She rearranged her clothing and tried to gather herself. "Lead the way," she told him, smoothing her hair, and picking up her compact mirror. It was one thing to be caught unaware in one's workplace for an assassination; but it's something else to have to stare down Molly Bates with her hair all dishevelled.

The security team led her out through the open plan offices, sweeping their weapons and muttering instructions and updates on their internal comms.

Jessica marched along, checking her appearance and following the guard in front of her, careful to communicate in her walk that she was not afraid. Once she was satisfied with her look, she popped the compact into her jacket pocket.

Halfway through the cubicle sea of the sales department, the entourage stopped dead. A second later, there was the sound of a stun gun discharging, and the slump of a body hitting the ground.

Then another.

And another.

Jessica looked around, desperately trying to see where the threat was coming from. "I know it's you, Molly Bates!" she shouted out across the now silent office.

Another stun discharge and a slump.

There were three guards left. One in front of her, one in the aisle to her left, and one to the right. They were silently scanning the area, watching for any signs of movement.

Suddenly the one on her right fired.

She called ahead to the leader. "Where are your reinforcements?" she hissed.

He quietly spoke back to her. "On their way, ma'am." He turned back to face ahead in the direction they had been moving, and suddenly grunted, and hit the deck.

Jessica looked up and there was Molly Bates, holding a piece on her.

"Well, if you wanted an audience with me, you just had to ask," said Jessica coyly, trying to maintain the appearance of being in control.

Molly barely batted an eyelid. "It wasn't an audience I was seeking," she replied calmly. "It was all-out destruction... which, frankly, was well underway before I even stepped foot in the building."

The rest of their onsite team will be here in three minutes.

Got it. Tell Crash.

They've just put in a call for a full squad of thirty, who will be coming from offsite. They are fifteen minutes away.

Okay. How many do we think are still left in the building?

Maybe ten - not including their general building security.

You mean donut eaters with guns.

Exactly.

Okay. We might be all right.

Molly started walking slowly toward Jessica, her weapon trained on her chest. "You will no doubt have seen that your trusted board of directors have been selling off your subsidiaries faster than you can say 'caramel mocha'..."

Jessica's eyes narrowed. "I suppose I have you to thank for that?"

Molly shrugged. "In part. Although, it's been a long time coming... someone figuring out how you've structured your evil empire of Estarian exploitation."

"Oh, please," Jessica retorted. "Do I really need to listen to this? I take it you're here to kill me. To make a point? To serve as a warning to all the other corporations that don't pay out indefinitely on every single disease known to Sark?"

Jessica took a breath, folding her arms in indignation. "I'll have you know that I and my family have built up these institutions to make the Sark system a better place for everyone. Yes, we make money... but that was never illegal."

Molly couldn't resist getting into an argument with the beastly woman in front of her. "Yes, it's difficult to do anything illegal when you manipulate the legal system to suit your own ends; when you pass laws that make you richer and richer, as you actively exploit the very population you claim to serve!"

Jessica rolled her eyes. "Come, come now, Ms. Bates. I had you down as more than just the common activist. Surely you have something more than this?"

Molly stopped in her tracks, and stood almost too casually. It made Jessica nervous. "Actually, I do," Molly told her.

"As you may or may not know... the price of your company's shares is directly correlated to not just the number of smaller companies you own and control, but also the mechanism of buying or selling them. To be clear: when you sell them, the share price goes down. A lot." Molly took half a step forward, her weapon now by her side. "One might even say it plummets," she added.

Molly, the remaining security detail is going to be on our location in ninety seconds.

Okay, call for our own backup. We're leaving soon. Have the pods ready by the windows.

Jessica's face had paled. "Ah, you hadn't realized that." Molly smiled. "So what you may not have figured out yet, is that a total of 168 of your subsidiaries have been sold off, or are currently in auction." Molly took another half step. "Now, I don't know what happens when more than one subsidiary is sold, but, at a guess, I'm going to assume that the share price is going to go down more than just 'a lot'."

Jessica had taken a couple of steps backward, physically losing her balance as she tried to absorb the information. She grabbed onto one of the cubicle partitions.

"In a few hours, the authorities are going to cease trading shares in Iantrogen because the stock is effectively worthless. And that will be the end of the Newld Empire. Dismantled and destroyed."

Jessica stumbled and fell to the ground as Molly advanced a few more steps. She raised her gun on Jessica, and Jessica's eyes widened.

"Go on, just do it! Kill me! Get it over with, you little wench!" Jessica cried out.

Molly lowered her weapon. "Oh, no, you misunderstand me," Molly sneered, finally getting to exorcise her pent-up wrath at the injustice that Jessica had been perpetrating. "I'm not interested in killing you; I just wanted to destroy everything that made your life worth living."

Molly turned, and started walking away from a petrified and sobbing Jessica.

Okay, we've got incoming.

Molly could hear the rest of the security team coming in through the corridors on the left hand side of the open plan office. Straight away, she could hear Crash picking them off as they came through the door closest to him. Molly hurried over to help firm up his position. Standing behind a pillar, she too opened fire.

Oz, see if you can get Sean and Jack here. And Joel. If more reinforcements are on their way, we're going to need some backup ourselves.

Roger that.

Molly swung around the pillar and fired stun rounds, taking out a security heavy with each shot.

CHAPTER TWELVE

Andus safe house, Spire, Vættaborgir and Hellisgata

Maya followed the three guys down the dimly lit passageway. Even Brock seemed to have gotten a spring back in his step.

Mo glanced back at the group. "It's not much to look at, but inside the apartment, it's pretty comfortable. You know, nice white furniture, fully equipped kitchen..."

The group kept walking, the sound of their footsteps being absorbed by the dark, brick walls as they made their way closer to where Andus had holed up.

"Yeah," Mo continued, as if he were a real estate agent giving them the tour, "and then we bring in food... Whatever you want. Mr. Andus just tells us what he wants that day, and we bring it. Fresh-like." He paused, and spun round as if confiding a secret. "And booze," he winked at Maya at the back of the group. "Whatever you want," he insisted, as he turned and kept walking.

They arrived at the door, and Mo got his key pass out of his jacket pocket. "This is the override," he showed them the strangely shaped key fob. "In case we need to get in."

He knocked on the door. "Mr. Andus?" he called.

Turning back to the group, he showed them the retinal scan

panel on the door access console. "He uses this. But obviously that won't work for us," he grinned.

There was movement inside the apartment. Mo knocked again, and called out, "Mr. Andus, there are some people here to see you!"

He started accessing the panel with the key pass. "I'm coming in. No one is armed. Well…" he chuckled, "except for me."

Mo opened up the door to find Andus standing in the middle of the apartment in a vest and boxers, a gun feebly pointing at the intruders.

Mo made his way through the door, his hands out to show he wasn't a threat. "Sorry, Mr. Andus. These people are the new owners, and they wanted to speak with you," he reported.

Andus looked perplexed. "What are you doing, letting them in here?" he demanded, vexation filling his very being and replacing the fear he'd originally been experiencing.

Mo gently stepped further into the room; now with one hand on his holstered weapon, the other out in front of him, palm to the floor. "It's okay, Mr. Andus. These people are the new owners. They're not here to hurt you."

Mo turned back to Maya and with a jerk of his head signalled for her to come into the apartment. Maya stepped bravely past the two boys who were obscuring the doorway, mesmerized by the sight of either the apartment, or of Andus in his underpants.

Maya took a couple of steps inside, drawing Andus's attention. He lowered his weapon without considering he was giving up. His face was crumpled in confusion, and probably lack of sleep.

Maya's voice rang through the sparsely furnished apartment. She was firm and commanding. "We're the new owners of this building and your security establishment," she explained. "My name is Maya Johnstone, and these are my associates," she casually waved her hand at Pieter and Brock still standing in the doorway. "We are currently taking control of this and all properties in your groups. The paperwork is being dealt with by your lawyers-"

Andus exploded. "I didn't sell anything!"

Maya nodded politely, and then continued. "I'm afraid that under planetary law, assets are automatically sold off in order to meet the debts in the portfolio. Your legal team has been working around the clock to make this happen since, well... I'm sure you've seen the news."

Andus's mouth dropped open and his face relaxed in shock. "News? What news?" he asked weakly.

Maya did a sympathetic head tilt, only partially succeeding in keeping her sarcasm out of her voice. "Oh, have you not been paying attention? Your company has crashed in value. As of three o'clock this afternoon, your personal net worth is less than zero." She smiled a rather devilish grin. "You should probably check in with your people. She paused, glancing over at Mo briefly. "Before they're not your people any more," she added.

Andus blustered, trying to find a response.

Maya continued. "In the meantime, though, we'll need you to vacate the premises. Immediately, that is." She turned to leave, seeing the grins on the faces of Pieter and Brock as they hung onto the doorframe, watching the whole scene play out like a comedy sketch. She turned back, suddenly remembering something. "You may want to put some pants on first, though."

And with that, she stepped back out into the hall as the boys erupted with laughter, high-fiving her and patting her on the back.

Brock grinned. "Molly wasn't kidding when she said you had this one handled!"

Maya smiled. "Yeah, come on. Let's get out of here. Our work here is done."

Maya led the way back down the passageway, followed closely by Pieter and Brock. Mo made his excuses to Mr. Andus, and indicated in the direction of the door.

"I... I should, er," he shuffled a little to the door. "I'll let you find your pants," he added, then turned and left too.

Andus stood exactly where he had been when they entered, watching them leave.

Aboard the *Mini Empress*, Somewhere over the Navanah Desert

Jack looked around the cockpit. "Shiiiiit, this is one sweet ride," she beamed.

Sean smiled. "It is. She doesn't have gate capabilities like her big sister, *The Empress*, but she has almost everything else. Plus, she's easier to maneuver for the kind of surface work we're going to be doing today."

Jack was still admiring the array of controls.

Sean glanced over as he brought the ship lower into the atmosphere. "See if you can familiarize yourself with the controls for the weapons. Under the artillery section," he indicated with a wave of his hand at the panel in front of her. "From memory, I think we're pretty much loaded with everything we'd need."

Jack frowned. "You mean, this is loaded with nukes?"

Sean shook his head. "Hell no. Very little call for those, now we have the tech to not have that nasty radioactive fallout for centuries on end..."

Jack's face relaxed. "You mean, the Etheric Empire has managed to make its war heads environmentally-friendly?" she asked, shaking her head in amazement.

Sean grinned, and chuckled a little. "It sounds silly, but when you think about it, it's the most sensible thing to do. The only reason we would normally be using force is to bring people around to our way of thinking. Devastating planets isn't generally what leads to a healthy inter-empire relationship. We learned that the hard way..."

Jack looked skeptical, and Sean noticed.

Sean looked back at where he was flying. "Okay, so there are some exceptions..." he conceded.

"Like?" Jack prompted.

Sean looked uncomfortable for a moment. "Like when this Kurtherian race disrespected the queen's guard, and videotaped it. That was enough for Bethany Anne to go nuclear. In more ways than one."

Jack looked over in concern. "What happened?"

Sean visibly grimaced. "We don't know, yet. She's still off, 'dealing' with it."

Jack nodded, knowing full well she was only getting part of the story. "This Bethany Anne is beginning to sound pretty intense."

Sean chuckled. "You could say that," he agreed. He checked his visuals and then the route. "Okay, we're coming up on our target soon. Remember, he's been preparing for a few days; if even half of the intel is correct, he'll have men and artillery sandbagged there."

Jack nodded. "Got it," she confirmed. She looked anxious. "I could really do with testing these weapons, though."

Sean shook his head. "No time. And the internal systems would flag any errors. Just go with what you know, and assume the ship can handle it," he instructed.

He glanced over at her. "And don't worry, love. I've got the flying bit," he winked.

Jack shook her head, smiling. "Well, let's hope so," she retorted.

Just then, an alert she had set up on her console started flashing. "We've got heat sigs on that location," she reported in.

Sean rolled his head to glance at her display. "Yeah, thought we might. How many?"

"Ten," she counted.

"Fuck," he sighed. "Well, too bad for them..." he concluded.

The ship quickly arrived at the target, and Sean dropped to a cruise for the approach. "Let's get a visual recon first, and then nail them on the return," he suggested.

Jack immediately adapted the weapons she had ready to lock on, and looked over at him, her eyes wide. "You're worried in case they have missiles?" she checked, the thought dawning on her as she made her adjustments.

Sean looked somber. "I'm almost certain they have. I also just want to make sure we know what we're about to level. I'm going to hail them. Be ready, though."

Sean pulled up a comm channel and opened a line. "This is the Etheric Empire calling for Mr. Mac Kerr. Mac Kerr. Do you read?"

The line buzzed.

Sean repeated the message.

The line hummed again, and then there was a response. "What do you want, Grjónapungur*?" *(transl: cocksucker)

Sean smirked. "Wondering if you want to come out quietly, and save the lives of those innocent folks you've got holed up in there with you?"

The line crackled with interference. "Not going to happen. We're going to take you out."

With that, an anti-aircraft gun started firing at them.

Sean couldn't be sure if it was a result of the interaction, or just because they'd come into range. Either way, he decided it was disrespectful.

Sean flicked a switch. "Okay, well don't say I didn't warn you." He closed the channel and looked over at Jack. "Okay, I feel much better wasting this fuckwit, now," he told her.

Jack smiled. "You turning her about, then?"

Sean nodded. "Yeah, just as soon as-"

There was suddenly an enormous roar that rocked the ground, and then the ship, as a rocket launched past them.

Jack spun around in her seat, briefly catching sight of the rocket out of one of the side windows. "That was a fucking missile!" she shouted. She paused a second, realizing something. "How come it missed us?"

Sean grinned. "We've been emitting anti missile bots in a suspension since before I hailed him. Their online systems aren't going to be able to get a fix on us."

"However..." he added, spinning around in his own special anti-grav console chair. He pulled up a weapons console similar to Jack's. "Watch and learn," he told her. He then pulled up a holoscreen and wrapped it around his console chair, so that it gave him a 180-degree view of what was outside the ship.

He flipped a few switches, and then steered what looked like the holo of a gun around to seek the missile. Finding it, the system automatically locked on. He hit "FIRE," and, a moment later, a smaller missile of their own went screaming from their ship to collide with Mac's.

The two missiles exploded in a rain of fire.

He closed the holos down, looking satisfied. "Can't have those things just wandering around out there like that."

Jack turned back to monitoring her own instruments. "You didn't strike me as a tidy kinda guy," she smirked.

Sean was back to flipping switches on the ship and turning her around. "I'm not. The military beat it into me, though."

He pulled at the control wheel, and the ship's nose pointed up, and banked steeply to the left. Jack was thrown back and up in her harness. "Fuckerty fuck!" she yelled, gripping the armrests on her seat, her knuckles turning white.

She noticed the g-meter in her display clocking the acceleration. It passed 30 Gs, and she started to feel her vision blackout. "Sean..." she tried calling out, desperately realizing what was happening to her.

The force suddenly started to drop off as Sean levelled the ship out. A few seconds later, her vision started to return.

Sean chuckled, as he rolled out the weapons console. "Quite the little G-monster," he commented. "Most people would have loc'd out," he added, his voice conveying he was genuinely impressed.

Jack scowled at him, recovering her vision. And attitude. "You know I was a fighter pilot for six years, you prick." She pulled up her own console ready to unleash some mayhem. "And a bit of warning wouldn't go amiss."

Sean glanced back at her. "Noted," he conceded, as way of an apology. Still, he caught her lips upturned a little in the corners. He could tell she was having the time of her life. "Okay, you ready with those differential missiles?" he checked. "We're on the approach. Let's see if you can take them out with one hit... Or else I'm going to have to pull this bird around again..."

Jack was already selecting the missiles and target as he spoke. "I'll be ready before you get us a visual," she told him confidently.

And with that, she felt the ship pull forward even faster.

Iantrogen Offices, Downtown Spire

The firing had subsided, but reinforcements were still on their way.

Crash was leaning against his pillar, recouping more from the adrenalin bolt than the exertion of shooting. "Good shooting, Lady Boss," he called over to Molly.

Molly had her eyes and ears open, scanning the area for any sign of life. She emerged from her position behind the pillar a little way over. "Not bad going, yourself, Mr. Pilot-Guy," she commented. She packed away her weapon for the time being and bent over, her hands on her knees.

Crash was watching her while he gathered himself together and holstered his weapon. "Takes it out of you, doesn't it?" he commented softly.

She looked up. "Yeah. The adrenalin still makes me feel sick."

Crash nodded, pursing his lips. "Yeah. I remember that from early training. Hated it."

Molly glanced around and stood upright again. "Okay. Time to finish with Jessica, and then get the fuck up out of here before those reinforcements arrive."

Crash looked more animated than his usual calm, collected self. "I'm with you on that one," he concurred. "I'm just going to tap into their cameras, and see what else is going on in the building. Oz has a call into Sean, but he's offline at the moment. Joel isn't picking up, either."

"Okay," Molly acknowledged, as she turned back to where she had left Jessica. She strode through the cubicles, and landed at the spot where she had left her.

There was no one there.

"Shit. She's gone," she whispered to Crash over their open comm.

Crash responded immediately. "Want me to come help you find her?"

Molly glanced around. "No. She can't have gone far. Keep an eye on things from here, and I'll go find her."

She and I have unfinished business.

Molly strode off in the direction of Jessica's office.

If you're under fire, you're going to go for what is familiar. That's the place where she is most likely to have a panic button or a weapon.

Reinforcements will be here in twelve minutes.

Okay. Thanks, Oz. We'll be gone by then.

Molly found her way through to Jessica's office pretty easily, having been there once before. The place looked different somehow, though.

Maybe they changed the decor.

Either way, she figured, *it was a waste of her money... given that she just lost everything.*

Molly heard movement from within the office. Carefully, she drew her weapon again, and pushed her way through the door. She scanned the assistant's office. No one was there. There was another sound from within the office… like a clunk of something metal hitting a desk.

Molly took another step, and there, in the main office, was Jessica— holding a sword, the ornate sheath in her hand.

Jessica stood defiantly and looked at Molly, now unaffected by the gun trained on her.

Molly stepped into the room. "Not really the time to be examining your antiquities," she commented. "Mind you, it might be the one thing in this place that will hold its value for you. You can sell it for rent money."

Jessica had tears drying on her face. Her eye makeup was smudged, and her hair and clothes were now dishevelled. Apart from that, she was relatively unscathed.

Jessica nodded at Molly's arm. "I see my security detail took a bite out of you," she sneered.

Molly looked down, and noticed a tear in the upper arm of her suit. There was blood trickling out of the hole; presumably from a bullet wound. She couldn't feel any pain, but her arm had been feeling weaker. "Looks like a graze," she concluded. She knew what would happen if a bullet were lodged, or had been shot through her arm, and this wasn't it.

Jessica smirked. "Let's hope you have good insurance," she told her. "Or else *that's* going to be expensive." Her voice lilted with venom.

Jessica stepped away from her desk and started chanting, holding the sword out in front of her.

Molly interrupted. "You think that your ancestors can help restore your empire?"

Jessica stopped what she was doing and turned her head to face Molly. "I'm not asking for their help," she spat angrily. "I'm asking for their forgiveness!"

Jessica was about to continue her chanting, when she stopped herself, lowering the sword a little. "You don't have a clue about all this, do you? This… *shame*, of what you've inflicted on me. It's worse than death!"

Jessica turned the sword around so that the tip was pointing at her own chest. "The only way to redeem one's essence from this kind of shame, is to fall on your ceremonial sword and hope the ancestors take pity on your valiant attempt to make things right."

Tears welled in her eyes.

She turned, looking off into the distance in front of her again, her eyes glazing over. "For what you have done to me, I hope your ancestors forsake you!" The hatred and bitchiness in her eyes and voice were palpable. Molly felt a coldness in the air, and the noise of the building seemed deafening. She watched Jessica's eyes turn black, and she started chanting again.

Something wasn't right. Molly felt a presence, a darkness, start pooling in the room. Yet her eyes couldn't perceive anything. Molly subconsciously took a few paces back, looking for something around her to steady herself against.

Jessica continued chanting her strange incantations, more and more forcefully now. She glowed with a dark light; a malevolence that seemed to exude from her once blue, effervescent skin. Molly felt her gut tighten. This was bad.

She looked around the office and noticed that not only had it become noisy, but also there was a strange wind circulating around them. Molly scrambled to get back to the door, but found herself paralyzed, unable to move. Unable to run. And unable to peel her eyes from what was happening before her.

The wind turned to a dark gray smoke. Molly could barely see what was happening.

For the first time in a long time, Molly felt not just scared, but deeply afraid. On a spiritual level.

Oz, what's going on?

All parameters seem normal. It's just your senses that are perceiving the activity.

Could this be...?

Molly didn't get the chance to finish her question. Just then, there was an almighty crack, a flash of light, which blinded her from seeing what was happening, and then the shape in the smoke that was Jessica fell forward onto the sharp end of her sword.

Molly, terrified, lunged forward to try to stop her, but it was too late. Her fingertips barely touched Jessica's shirt sleeve before her body was beyond her reach, and then on the ground.

Molly looked down through the gray smoke, and saw the sword blade had gone straight through her.

The noise started to calm and the wind subsided. The room stopped vibrating, and everything settled down again. When the smoke cleared, the room seemed to have returned to normal, and the sensation of an evil presence receded like a bad dream.

Molly stepped closer, shocked and horrified at the bloody sword sticking out of Jessica's back. Jessica's body lay facedown with her head turned, so Molly could see her eyes. They were still abnormally black.

Molly knelt down beside her, trying to process what had just happened. Sure it had been a possibility that Jessica might kill herself; and Molly *had* wanted her to suffer. But this? This was just wrong.

As she watched, Jessica's eyes returned to normal and her facial muscles relaxed, making her look almost angelic and peaceful.

Molly, three minutes. We've got to leave.

Molly used her hand to close Jessica's eyelids, and stood up. Understanding what had just happened was going to have to wait for later.

A moment later, she was running back through the open plan office area and jogging down the aisle of cubicles. Crash saw her coming, and opened up the window so they could escape into the pod hovering outside.

With one final tug, he slid the window open. "Come on, Lady Boss. We've got to move." He started to put his foot out into the pod, and was thrown back. "What the...?"

A green flash ionized the air a few inches from the window.

Molly's heart sank in her chest as she realized that there was a secondary forcefield around the building.

Oz, can you get this securi-field down?

Working on it.

He paused.

Shit. It's not on the network. There's no mention of it anywhere. It can't be on a network. I can't access it.

Well, then, we're trapped. We need another way out.

Okay; down the stairwell, on the other side of the office behind you.

Molly helped Crash up. "Change of plan, Pilot-Guy. You okay?" she asked him.

Crash was grimacing. "Yeah. I'm fine. Just got a tingling foot now."

Molly looked at it. She couldn't see anything through his boot. "Can you run?"

He gestured in the direction of the other door. "With that lot chasing us? Hell yeah!"

They both drew their weapons and ran to the other side of the office. When they reached the door, Oz overrode the security lock on it. Molly hauled the door open, and the gunfire started. Crash slipped through and started running down the stairs ahead of her. The gunfire ricocheted against the door, as Molly vigorously returned fire.

Crash was halfway down the first flight of stairs. "Leave it, Molly! Let's go!" he shouted up to her, now the most panicked she had ever seen him.

She stepped back through the door, and turned to follow him. Just then, she flew backwards against the wall on the other side of the stairwell.

She had been hit.

Her body slumped down on the floor. Crash was back up the stairs like lightning, checking her vitals without even thinking.

No reaction.

No breathing.

No pulse.

Shit. He forced the door shut, and tried to type to Oz.

Oz was offline.

Crash looked back at the door, panic rising in his chest. It was still unlocked, and those killing machines were coming for them. He picked Molly up and started moving down the stairwell, praying she was just knocked out.

CHAPTER THIRTEEN

Navanah Desert

"Okay, she's all yours," Sean told Jack, as the safe house appeared as a spot in the sand below.

Jack gritted her teeth and guided her missile cocktail onto the target.

It locked on.

She hit release, and three projectiles screamed through the air from the *Mini Empress*.

She communicated the action. "Missiles released. Impact in 3, 2..."

An enormous explosion erupted beneath them.

Sean quickly pulled up and banked left a little to avoid the blast zone. Spinning around in their console chairs, they were able to see the explosion continue in the desert below them through the top left corner of their window.

Sean glanced over at his protégé. "You did good," he confirmed. He pulled up some data on his heads-up display. "Yup. Totally annihilated. Good job, Captain."

Jack grinned, watching the explosion, and enjoying the sensation of flying upside down under the pull of the maneuver. This was the moment she felt most at home. Nothing but fire and destruction... and a damn impressive pilot by her side.

She could get used to this.

Just then a communication came through on Sean's holo.

Iantrogen Building, Downtown Spire

Crash carried Molly in his arms, running down several flights of steps, carefully watching her head so that it didn't loll back and damage her neck.

She was bleeding. He couldn't tell where from, though. He'd spotted the wound on her arm, but he was sure she'd had that before she'd been hit near the door. He arrived at another level and tried the door. This one opened.

Finally, he thought to himself, pushing his way into the sparse white corridor.

Please let there be medical equipment, he prayed, trying to recall the combat medicine training during his short commission. He made his way down the quiet corridor looking for signs of life, or anything that might possibly help him.

He passed a few doors to what looked like labs. *Labs, labs, and more labs*, he fretted as he kept striding down the way, his footsteps reverberating through the tomb-like corridors.

There was another door coming up on the left. He peered in the window. It looked like another lab with an open supplies cupboard. Ancestors only knew what kinds of supplies were in there, but it had benches.

He pushed his way in, still carrying an unconscious Molly in his arms. Making his way through the lab, he laid her carefully on the bench furthest from the door. Just a little further, there was another door. He strode over to check it. It had an exit, a window, and more supplies. *Probably drugs*, he considered, *given where we are.*

He turned back to Molly. She was still unconscious. Not breathing. And yes, no pulse; he checked again.

Straightaway, he started mouth to mouth and heart massage, refusing to believe she might be dead. Between cycles, he tried to inspect her head and body. The arm wound wasn't enough to kill her.

He noticed she'd stopped bleeding from her arm – that was both good and bad.

Another cycle of air and heart massage.

Then he checked again. There was a taser burn in her hairline. She'd been hit. Her brain was likely fried. He checked her eyes and her pupils were unresponsive.

Panic and grief welled in him. He knew what this meant. He just refused to believe it.

Heart massage. *One, two, three, four.*

There was no Oz to contact.

He pinched her nose and breathed into her lungs again.

The team wouldn't know where they were.

Head up, he took another breath, and breathed into her lungs, watching her chest rise.

Heart massage. *One, two...*

His thoughts wandered, replaying the sight of her falling down from an unseen hit. Seeing her body here motionless. He kept working, feeling less than helpless.

Breathe. *One, two, three, four, five, six...*

Joel was going to be devastated.

Tears trickled down his face. He took another breath, ignoring his own outpouring of emotion.

He breathed into her…

Senate House, Spire

Joel picked up a message on his holo. It was from Oz.

MOLLY AND CRASH IN TROUBLE. AT IANTROGEN.

PLEASE HURRY. OFF NETWORK FORCEFIELD HAS US TRAPPED. NEED TO FIND IT AND DESTROY BEFORE ENTERING THE BUILDING.

Joel went white.

The message had been sent five minutes ago. He called Molly. The call wouldn't connect.

He called Crash.

The call connected. He listened on the line. He could hear breathing and sobbing. It was Crash's voice, but not. "Molly is down," he sobbed. "She's not breathing. No pulse. Please... Joel. Please."

Joel felt disconnected from his body, like this wasn't really happening. "Crash. Is that you?"

Crash blubbed through his grunts. He sounded like he was trying to revive her. "Hurry. There's a securi-field. We're trapped. She's not breathing."

Joel forced himself to focus, tears already streaming down his face, but he ignored them in favor of fixing this. "I'm on my way. Hang in there. Where are you?" he asked, realizing that Oz was going to be offline, too.

Crash had gasped and then gone quiet. A moment later he responded. "4th floor. In the labs somewhere."

Joel nodded. "Okay. We're coming for you. Keep her safe. We're coming."

Joel hung up and called Sean.

Sean answered straight away.

"Big-bad-blowing-up-fighting-machine, at your service," Sean answered the call.

Joel's voice was commanding, but tainted with emotion. "It's Molly. She's down. Not responding. No pulse. No breath. Sending coordinates. Meet me there. *Bring your guns.*"

Sean's mood sobered instantly. "We'll be there in minutes," he confirmed. "Awaiting coordinates."

A second later, he was on the nav system, finding a location to land the ship. Jack looked over at him, the area around her eyes contorted in concern. "What's wrong?" she asked.

Sean answered simply. "Molly is down. It doesn't sound good."

Jack shook her head. "What's the plan, and what do you want me to do?"

Sean was all business as he selected coordinates and prepared to land. "We're going to put this bird down, and then use the pod in the back to get to her location."

His holo pinged. He looked down and waved his wrist at Jack. "That's the location," he told her. "Get that programmed into the pod. We need to get there fast."

Jack started fiddling with his holo, and then bumped the coordinates to hers. Sean focused on landing the ship at the edge of the desert. "And make sure you're shielded and armed. This is a code 9 extraction, by the sounds of it."

Senate House, Spire

Joel had hung up and headed straight out of the Senate building. There wasn't time to explain to Paige and Garet. Besides, they were safer where they were.

Joel called down his pod using his holo, realizing he was going to have to figure out how to control it without Oz. As soon as it arrived, he hopped on board. Two minutes later, the pod shot up into the sky and into the direction of the Iantrogen building.

First job was going to be to find the forcefield generator. He started scanning for anything that had a forcefield signature, honing in as he got closer. The image of the building came up on the heads-up display. He turned it around, trying to figure out where it might be.

Either top or bottom, he figured.

He turned his scan towards the bottom of the building, and noticed that the signal was heavier there. Stronger. He pushed the pod further in, and tried to find any kind of controls for an on-board weapons system. He was sure it had some. After five long seconds of flicking through screens, he gave up and opened the pod door, setting his weapon to the highest setting, and then lowered the pod down to the location of the generator.

It took a bit of searching, but eventually he found it tucked in a shed. A simple gun wasn't going to cut it. He holstered his weapon and rummaged in his combat suit pocket for a charge. He found one.

Let's hope this is enough... he prayed under his breath. He lowered the pod to the ground and hopped out. Checking inside the shed, he saw words on the signage that backed up his conclusion. This was the secondary forcefield generator that was keeping Crash and Molly trapped.

He set the charge, pulled the pin, and then hopped back into the pod, pulling sharply out of the way of the blast zone just in the nick of time.

A huge explosion rippled over the entire building, cracking like a bolt of lightning. Joel quickly moved the pod back some more, looking for any fall out. There was no fire that he could see. No debris blasting off the structure. Just a huge amount of energy being released from the forcefield as it collapsed.

He watched a green light *sheet* across the structure as it tore across the width and height as the electric field ionized the air, before disappearing.

Without wasting a moment, he checked back on the heads-up display. The forcefield was indeed broken.

Now to track their holos, he told himself, wishing he had paid more attention to how Molly and Oz had been doing it. He felt like he was flying blind. And deaf. And dumb.

He scrambled through the heads-up display and found a search function.

SEARCH HOLOS, he typed in. It brought up every holo in the area. The screen was a mass of red dots.

Shit.

He started talking to himself. "Come on, you piece of shit. Help me find Molly's holo."

"Finding Molly's holo..." a computerized voice repeated back to him.

Joel's hands stopped, hovering just above the heads-up display. "You can hear me?" he asked, taken aback.

"Voice recognition is active," the voice sounded over the in-pod auditory system.

Joel was confused. "Why have you never talked before?"

The voice responded to him. "Previously, controls were operated by the Intelligence known as Oz. There was never any need."

Joel had questions, but right now, he needed to get to Molly.

The mass of red dots on the building overlay disappeared, showing just one. Molly's. Fourth floor, just as Crash had said.

Joel felt a slight relief as he made progress through the things that had to happen in order to reach her. "Can you take me down to the fourth floor, nearest access point?" he asked the computer.

The voice crackled over the line again. "Nearest access is a window. Do you want that window disengaged?"

Joel was checking his gear and getting ready to fight. The computer pulled his attention. "Disengaged?" he queried.

The artificial female voice responded. "Yes. Removed."

Joel pulled his weapon from his holster. "Hell yes, I'd like it removed!"

The pod whipped round to the side of the building closest to the red dot. A moment later, a window on one side of the building shattered, and the pod sped deftly closer. The door opened, and Joel was able to hop through the window and onto a bench that lined the room.

That's when he saw her. Molly lay lifeless on a bench over on the other side of the room. Crash was still administering CPR, tears streaming down his face, relentlessly trying to revive her.

Joel couldn't bear to look. He reached out and started moving towards her, but stopped as his legs collapsed underneath him. He hauled himself up, fighting the urge to crumple under his grief, hoping that despite her having no life signs for so long, there might still be hope.

Just then, Sean and Jack arrived through the same window.

Joel had barely approached her limp body and laid his hand on her face, brushing her hair out of the way, when Sean stepped over.

"It's okay, buddy. There's one more thing we can try," he told him. He took Crash by the shoulders from behind, and moved him out of the way. Without hesitation or consultation, he gently scooped Molly's body up into his arms, and headed back towards the window.

Joel's hand fell away as Molly was moved. He watched them, stunned, grief-stricken, and in so much pain he couldn't think straight.

Sean laid her body on the bench in front of the window for a moment as he scrambled up onto it, then picked her up again and put her into the pod.

Joel started to shout out after them, a howl of utter despair and darkness. Jack ran over to console him, very aware they needed to get out of danger, too.

And then the pod was gone.

Gaitune-67, Hangar deck

Meanwhile, back at the base, the Queen Bitch's key ship was activating and powering up remotely.

Auto checks flicked through, one after another, preparing for takeoff. Preparing for an immediate gate jump.

Minutes later, the hangar doors opened up, and a lone pod arrived, touching down gracefully next to the ship.

Sean hopped out, and then hauled the body of Molly Bates out of the pod after him. His face locked in determination, he gently carried her up the invisible steps. As he hurried up them, he couldn't help but remember her smile as she had examined the steps, when she was introduced to the ship only days before. He reached the top of the stairs, and made his way into the ship as fast as he could. He glanced back at the door he'd just come through, and could see her as if she were standing there right then, inspecting the magic of the door's technology, marvelling at something she hadn't seen before.

He shook his head and fought back a tear as he bustled straight into the cockpit. He put her limp, and now bloody, body into the Nav chair where she had sat the other day. This time, he buckled her in as the chair quietly adjusted to her weight and dimensions.

He paused a moment, adjusting her head on the headrest. His hand lingered on her face, and he gently brushed her cheek. Time was pressing. He went straight to the pilot's seat, and started flicking switches. He had barely even strapped himself in before the ship was heading out of the hangar door, out into the inky blackness of space.

Normally, they would turn back towards the inner system. The system wasn't where they were going this time, though.

The ship pulled a short distance from the asteroid, and a second later, disappeared.

Senate House, Spire

Oblivious to everything else going on, Paige and Garet were engrossed in conversation. Conversation about history.

Garet had been trying to defend himself, or, more precisely, his actions. He was just beginning to realize that it wasn't going to work.

He sighed and rubbed his face with one hand before looking back at Paige. "Look, I valued power and status. Maybe I was wrong. But what I *will* acknowledge was that I didn't do right by you."

He was frustrated, but trying his best to concede. He finally let his defenses down. "We should have had more conversations, before this all happened. But then we ended up on the rock, and, well... Everything changed."

He looked over at Paige on the other sofa, hoping for some glimmer of compassion. Paige took another swig of the beer he had sent for. Day drinking wasn't good for her, but they'd been working so hard. And Garet had been so insistent they talk. "Yes, and you should have talked to me about taking the job."

Garet leaned forward, placing the beer on the mocha table. "I see that now. You had no reason to stay on Estaria, even without me putting you in that position." There was a genuine sadness in his eyes.

Paige didn't look so sad. "It's okay," she reassured him. "I really did end up exactly where I was meant to be."

Garet held her gaze. "Yes, and..."

Paige shrugged, amicably, but still distant. "Yeah I get it. And I appreciate you saying that." She paused. "But what I'm more concerned about is whose side you're actually on. I mean - we can't tell. And from where I'm sitting, it looks like you're playing both sides."

Garet nodded. "I know, I know. And to a degree, I think I was. I wanted it all. I wanted for them to not kill me; but, also, *damn* they made it all so tempting."

Paige frowned in disapproval.

"It's okay," he told her, putting his hands up in surrender. "I've learned my lesson. I need to pick a side. No gray area, etc, etc. I'm on board. You're not going to have to worry about that with me, now."

He picked up his beer bottle again and gestured around the room, at the place where they'd been sitting working for the last several days. "Plus, with what we've been setting up here, it's not going to be necessary. The Syndicate is no more. We can finally start building a better world, without the fear of being knocked off in our sleep…"

He stood up and started pacing. Paige's gaze followed him.

He swung his beer as he walked, deep in thought. "But, you know, it's still not going to be easy. There will be people who are still invested in the old ways. There will be general resistance to change. There will be a need for re-educating even the people who it will ultimately benefit… out there…"

He noticed Paige was smiling. "What?" he demanded, smiling a little himself.

Paige's smile broadened even more, and she flushed deep red on her chest. She shook her head a little and lowered her eyes, looping a stray strand of hair back behind her ear. "Nothing. It's just… It's good to see you when you're like this…"

Garet stopped and blushed too. "You mean over-caffeinated, and over-worked?" he jested.

Just then, Paige's holo buzzed. She picked up the call. "Joel? Hi," she answered, confused. "Where are you?"

Joel explained on the other end of the call. "I'm at Iantrogen. We're doing a quick clean up. Can you do something for me, and not ask any questions? I'll explain everything when we get back."

Paige nodded, glancing over at Garet with concern on her face. "Sure," she responded.

Garet wandered over to where Paige was sitting on the sofas.

Joel was talking through her audio implant. "I had to attend to a situation. I'm sending the pod back to you. You can control it with your voice. It's not Oz. I'll explain that later. For now, I just

167

need you and Garet to get in the pod and meet me back at Gaitune. We'll all be there shortly. Understood?"

Paige bobbed her head. "Yes. Yes I understand."

Joel's voice was softer. "Thank you, Paige. I appreciate you just trusting me. I'll see you soon."

Paige looked up at Garet. "Okay, sure. See you soon."

With that, the call disconnected.

Garet sat on the sofa next to Paige. "Everything okay?" he asked, his concern mimicking Paige's.

She nodded, trying to act like there was nothing wrong. "I'm sure it's fine. Joel didn't say much. Just that he had to go somewhere, and that he was sending the pod back. He'd like us to take the pod back up to Gaitune now and meet him there." She paused. "You okay with that?"

Garet looked flustered. "You mean leave now? And go all the way there?"

Paige started packing her things, her anxiety showing in her hurriedness. "Yes. It hardly takes any time at all in the pods. Maybe twenty minutes or so..." She looked up at him. "You haven't been in a pod yet, have you?"

Garet shook his head. "No, but I've got a feeling that's about to change."

She smiled weakly. "Yeah. We should hurry. Joel sounded... not quite himself."

The pair packed up and made their way out of the Senate House. As soon as they stepped outside, a pod descended to their location and allowed them on board.

"Hi," said Paige, as she settled in, and strapped herself into her harness. "Gaitune, please."

The auditory feed crackled on, but it wasn't Oz's voice. "Gaitune, it is," it replied, before taking the pod up into the stratosphere and beyond.

Paige felt an uneasiness in her stomach. Something definitely wasn't right.

CHAPTER FOURTEEN

Iantrogen Building, Downtown Spire

Joel hung up the holo and turned back to Jack and Crash. "Okay, that's Garet and Paige taken care of," he announced.

Jack jumped down from the bench by the window. "Pod is on its way," she told him.

Joel looked up at her. "Thanks," he said absently, as he tried to think through the logistics. "Okay, so we have one more pod here, and you still need to pick up the *Mini Empress*."

Jack shook her head. "I don't think I'm capable of flying that thing," she confessed. "I mean, the tech is like nothing I've seen. I was able to figure out bits of the weapons systems, but I need some training on that shit."

Joel scratched his head. "Is it safe where it is?"

Jack ambled over to where he was standing, putting her hands on her hips. "I think so. I'd be happy to leave it until we can get back and retrieve it. It has a natural defense system, including a forcefield."

Joel waved his hand and pulled up his holo. "Okay. We'll leave it. Let me call Maya. She and Pieter have two pods, so they can come get one of us, and then we can use Crash and Molly's pod to get us all back to base..." His voice trailed off as he looked back over his shoulder at Crash, who was peeling himself from the floor, and accidentally put his hand in some of Molly's blood that had dripped from the lab bench where he had been trying to save her.

Joel's face creased up again.

"Hey," Jack said, stepping closer and putting her hand on his forearm. "There's hope. Sean wouldn't have taken her if he didn't have a plan."

Joel breathed, releasing the emotion that was welling in him. He nodded solemnly and connected the call with Maya.

Maya answered within a few rings. "Hey," she said brightly. "You should have seen his face!"

Joel wished they could celebrate their victory, but it would be unfair for him to pretend. "Maya, we have a situation. Can you grab your pods and come and pick one of us up at Iantrogen? Sending coordinates now."

Maya hesitated, trying to process the unexpected intel. "Er. Sure. Yes of course," she said, catching up. "We'll be right there."

Joel replied, trying to keep the sadness out of his voice. "Thanks, Maya. See you soon."

Maya's voice was now full of concern. "Everything okay?" she asked.

Joel didn't want to worry her, but at the same time, she needed to prepare herself. "Not really, but I'll explain when you get here. Best thing you can do is help me get the team back to Gaitune."

Maya shifted into task mode. "Of course," she said gently. "Anything you need. We'll be there right away."

She clicked off the line, and Joel sent the coordinates.

"Okay, that's done," he said to Jack. Then he looked over at Crash. "Give me a hand with him?" he asked.

Jack nodded and walked over, gently stroking Joel's arm as she let him be.

Joel stood motionless, expressionless, for the four minutes and forty-eight seconds it took for the other pods to arrive. When they did, he hopped in with Maya, and let Jack and Crash take the other one.

This was going to be the most difficult news to break to the team. Frankly, he didn't know quite how he was going to do it.

Iantrogen Offices, Spire

Chaakwa Indus arrived at the scene, flashing her badge at the red and white tape. She followed the sound of voices down the corridor and into an open plan office area that looked like a war zone.

She spotted her colleague near the doorway, and walked over to him. "Thanks for the call," she told him, shaking his hand.

Detective Barry Ferret greeted her. "Yeah, I figured you'd want to see, what with your involvement with this company."

Chaakwa nodded. "Yes. Still, I would have preferred to see her tried for her crimes than this. It's definitely her?"

Ferret chewed on his gum. "It's her. We've had a couple of employees verify it." He started walking into the sea of cubicles. "Want to see?"

Chaakwa nodded. "Please," she responded following him through the crime scene.

Ferret started pointing things out. "This is where the main shooting happened. Video footage shows the Bates girl and one of her team holding back Newld's personal security around here, *after* Jessica's death." He waved in the direction of the fire escape. "They disappeared off down there. There's a broken window, and blood in a lab on the fourth floor."

He turned and headed up through the open plan office, leading Chaakwa through to the executive suite where Jessica's office was. "Newld is just through here," he relayed.

Chaakwa noticed everything she could. Normally she'd be

chatting away, talking theories. This time it would have been a waste of energy.

Ferret stopped at the third door on the left. He signalled inside. "Through there," he told her.

Chaakwa stepped into the office suite, and then into Jessica's actual office. Forensic personnel buzzed around, taking prints, photographs, and evidence, trying to determine what had happened.

Chaakwa cautiously stepped into the office. She saw the sword first. Then the body facedown on the carpet. Ferret appeared beside her. "I know this is going to sound crazy, because we can see from the footage that the Bates girl came in here before Newld died. Thing is, for this to have happened, Newld must have done it to herself."

Chaakwa looked at him in surprise. Ferret seemed to glaze over, his eyes resting on the body in front of them, oblivious to Chaakwa's stare.

"You're telling me she killed herself?" Chaakwa frowned.

Ferret was still looking at the body. "Yeah. Some kind of ceremonial sword no less." He turned to leave. "There were rumors she was an odd one. Strange practices, and all. I'll tell ya," he added casually, "suicide would make my job easier."

He ambled out of the room.

Chaakwa looked around, unsure of what was really wrong with the scene. Something was giving her an odd feeling. She turned and followed after Ferret.

"So that's what you're putting this down as? Suicide?" she pressed.

Ferret kept walking as he talked. "Unless something turns up otherwise."

Chaakwa frowned, curious about how he was happy to let the gun fight go unsolved. "But what about the Bates girl, and the gun fight?" she asked.

Ferret shrugged. "I'll be trying to find out what that was

about... sure. But if the forensics say she didn't kill anyone, and she's disappeared out of a window, chances are we're not going to find her easily." He opened the door back out into the open plan office, allowing Chaakwa through first. "Besides, maybe what this city needs is a few vigilantes to clean up the filth."

Chaakwa detected a hint of anger in his voice. She wanted to question him, but he was already on to the next conversation. She waved at him as he wandered away, talking to another investigator.

Chaakwa headed back out under the crime scene tape and made her way out of the building. It looked like Molly and her team had been successful, at least. And had gotten away.

All she could do now was wait...

<u>Aboard *The Empress*</u>

Sean couldn't believe his luck when he looked down at the nav coordinates. Plotting a course to the *ArchAngel* was complex at best. Under the conditions he was going to have to find them, though, it would have taken an immense amount of mental fortitude. And time. Time they didn't have.

He glanced back at Molly's body, strapped safely into the console chair. *Bloody lucky she had already set those coordinates* he mused, wondering if there was something coincidental or just downright mystical about how, out of all the places she could have plotted for the demonstration, she had chosen the *ArchAngel*.

"Well, you said you wanted to see the *ArchAngel* sooner rather than later. Looks like you're getting your wish..." he whispered to her.

He looked back at his instruments, and then hailed ADAM for the second time that trip. "On final approach, ADAM. Can you have someone ready to meet up? She needs to be in a pod doc an hour ago."

ADAM responded over the ship's comm system. "Yes, there is a team waiting on the hangar deck already. You can have her in the pod in four minutes; unless you'd like me to take over the navigation of your ship, in which case we can make it three and a half."

Sean didn't hesitate. "You have control, ADAM." He unbuckled himself and wriggled down out of the pilot's chair. In a flash, he was over at Molly's chair, unbuckling her.

ADAM brought the ship in to dock, gently. Sean carried Molly out through the passage, and to the invisible stairs. As he started down the stairs, he clocked the small group of medical attendants standing and waiting. Two of them started up the stairs, and, when they met, they took her body from him.

His mission wasn't done, though. He hurried them every step of the way— through the maze of corridors, and into the medical center. They opened a pod doc, and he helped them lift her gently in. He looked at her face, pausing for a moment. She looked so peaceful.

He felt so wretched that this had happened.

I should have been there; I should have been protecting her; we should have been better prepared, he reeled in his head.

"I'm sorry, Molly. I'm so sorry," he whispered, grief and anxiety lacing his voice like napalm. He became aware of an attendant pulling his hand back from Molly's face so they could close the pod door.

He spun around to look at the doctor, vaguely aware of Lance hovering just inside the room. "You can save her?" he asked.

The doctor was non-committal. "She's been out a long time. We can't tell. Best to let the pod doc do its thing. We'll know more in about twenty minutes."

Gaitune-67, Hangar deck

Joel had contemplated not telling them.

After all, without Molly, there was nothing to fight for. Nothing to do. His worst fear was that everything would fall apart; despite knowing his grief was tainting his judgment, he wasn't entirely sure he was wrong.

Maya, thankfully, had respected that he needed to think, and that he would tell everyone what was going on when they landed.

Her silence was anxiety-laden, though.

The pod touched down, and Joel let her hop out first. She touched his forearm in comfort as she left the pod.

Joel followed her out onto the hangar deck where the rest of the team were assembling. They milled around for a little bit; the others noticed that both Crash and Joel had been crying, and that Crash was covered in blood.

They also noticed that Molly and Sean weren't there.

Joel held his hands up to get their attention, and then beckoned them to come in closer. "Folks. Thank you for your work today, and for doing what needed to be done to get back here without asking questions."

He looked around at their faces. Right now, in this moment, although they were concerned, they didn't carry the burden of knowing what he had to tell them. Right now, their hearts were free.

"I'm so sorry to have to tell you this," he started, "And I thought about not telling you until we know more; but then I know you would want to know what's going on. Because Molly isn't just your boss, or your leader; I know she is also your friend."

He started to choke up. Jack stepped around to stand by him, and put her hand on his back for moral support. Joel sucked in air, and with it, his emotions, before they broke him in front of his people.

"Today, Crash and Molly went to see Jessica Newld. The threat that Jessica posed has been neutralized. Unfortunately, during that visit, Molly took a bullet."

There was a gasp as his words landed with the group. There were whispers and cusses, but mostly just a feeling of horror in the air.

The team returned to a hushed state, waiting for Joel's next words. "We don't know how she is. We don't really know what's going on. Sean Royale took her off in a pod, hoping to try something to bring her back..."

Paige stepped forward a little, her voice breaking as she spoke. "Bring her *back?*" she clarified.

Joel nodded looking at the ground in front of him. "When I arrived, Crash was working hard to revive her; but we know there were several minutes where she didn't have a pulse, and wasn't breathing."

Paige clapped her hand over her mouth to stifle her silent sobs. Her eyes welled up and she turned her back to the group to process.

There were other mutterings that Joel couldn't make out. People started asking questions of Crash, who just waved and covered his mouth, unable to talk.

Joel brought their attention back. "Folks. I know you're all worried. I know this is hard. This is the biggest challenge we have ever faced, and we're going to do it together. We're a team. That hasn't changed. I'm going to see if I can contact ADAM and find out where Molly is, and if there is anything else..." he paused, projecting forward how that piece of news might play out. He looked back at the group. "I'll let you know as soon as I know anything. You have my word. In the meantime, rest up. I'm going to need a quick report from each hit team to make sure nothing is coming after us. I'll contact you soon."

Paige stepped forward a little. "What about Oz?" she asked. "Surely he would know where Molly is?"

Crash finally spoke up. "Oz operates in Molly's head, and her holo. Since she is down, he's offline, too." Crash composed himself a little more. "We have no way of tracking her."

Joel clapped his hands. "Alright, people. That's it for now. I'll let you know as soon as anything is confirmed."

Normally the group would have dispersed, but instead, everyone just stood around. Without Molly there was no direction. Nowhere to turn. Nothing worth doing. They mulled; talking, hugging, consoling.

And tears. There were lots of tears.

Joel started to well up again. He turned away from the group, and decided he needed to have that conversation with ADAM right away. He strode off across the hangar deck, vaguely aware that someone had called his name.

Had he stopped, he would have seen Maya pointing out to Brock and Crash that the biggest ship in the hangar was missing.

But he couldn't deal with anything right now. Now, it was all he could do to keep himself together.

CHAPTER FIFTEEN

Gaitune-67, Operations Room

Joel strode into the Ops room, wiping the tears from his face. He headed straight for the console at the front of the room that Sean had gone to in order to communicate with ADAM.

He pulled up a menu, and ran a few searches before figuring out how to make contact. He hit the holo button on the right of the console and waited.

His eyes began to glaze over as his mind played through the sequence of events: getting the call from Crash, finding his way to the lab, seeing Molly lifeless on the bench, and then finally watching Sean whisk her off...

The audio crackled. "Joel, I presume?" ADAM answered.

Joel came to his senses. "Yes, ADAM. It's me. I'm calling about Molly."

ADAM responded gently. "Yes, I know. She's with us -"

Joel frowned in confusion. "With you? Where are you? I thought..."

ADAM's voice was kind, but to the point. "Yes, she's with us a few thousand light years away from your location."

Joel's mouth dropped open. "I... how?" he asked.

ADAM explained. "Sean took the ship that has gate capabilities. He brought her here, in case we might be able to save her."

Joel rubbed his hand over his face then scratched at the back of his head. "I don't understand. She was..." He could hardly bring himself to say it, but he needed clarity. "Dead,' he finished his sentence.

The audio feed buzzed a moment before ADAM answered; more than likely just giving Joel the chance to process. "Yes. She was. But we're going to see what we can do about that."

Joel leaned over the console, as if getting closer would give him more clarity. "You can bring someone back to life?" he asked.

ADAM paused. "Not exactly. But we have nanotechnology that can repair whatever is broken. As long as she hasn't been dead for too long, and as long as we can get enough nanocytes into the broken areas to fix her body quickly enough, we have a chance."

Joel's head was spinning. His grip on the console tightened to balance him. "When will you know?" he asked.

"Soon," ADAM confirmed. "And as soon as we know, I'll be in touch on your holo."

Joel wasn't ready to leave the connection. "Wait ADAM," he reached out. "Do you think she'll be okay?"

ADAM's voice was still sympathetic. "There is a chance Joel, but she's been out a long while. It's unknown if we can get enough nanocytes into her fast enough to reverse the damage," he explained again.

Joel nodded, forgetting that ADAM couldn't see his movement. "Okay," he relented. "Okay... And thank you, ADAM. She means the world to me."

"I understand, Joel. We're doing our best. Go and get some rest, and be with your team. I'll be in touch soon."

ADAM disconnected the line, leaving Joel in the big empty ops room alone.

. . .

ArchAngel, Medical Facility

"We've got him online," confirmed a calm voice standing over a console to the pod doc.

Oz realized he was back online; he could tell he had outputs. He would be able to interact with a room of people through auditory feeds via a buffer they had set up.

He realized he had been rebooted.

He felt different.

He checked Molly's brain signals. There was something off, though his diagnostics were inconclusive.

He checked for damage. There were whole dead areas where normally there was conductivity.

He couldn't figure out what was going on.

"Hello?" he asked through the console unit.

His message path was reinforced by their onboard EI. He could feel the activity of the program helping him to communicate.

He found the auditory control. "Hello?" he asked again.

There was calm chatter on the other end, and, a moment later, a voice he recognized. "Oz. Oz. It's Sean, mate. You're going to be okay. So is Molly. We've got you in a pod doc, where the nanocytes are restoring Molly's physical body."

Oz whirred, processing the new information and relating it to what he could detect. "Yes, there are many damaged areas here," he confirmed back to Sean. "Is she going to be okay?" Oz realized that he was experiencing some strange new sensations. He wondered briefly if it might be what those with bodies called "emotions".

He figured this particular emotion was probably fear.

Sean answered gently. "Yes, you're both going to be fine. Just relax." There was muffled talking and then some scuffling around the microphone. "The General is here, too," Sean added. "He'd like to speak with you. Hang on."

There was more scuffling. Oz tried to slow his processing

down; he could feel himself racing, and the corresponding resistance in his and Molly's circuits. He realized he was suddenly worried about overheating her.

He heard the General's voice. "Oz. General Reynolds, here. Glad you're alive."

Oz felt his normal character returning. "Me too, I can assure you, General."

The General chuckled. "And good to see you're fully intact. I have a proposition for you. I feel we ought to discuss it before we make any rash decisions, though."

Oz tried to fathom what could be so important at this time. "Sure. Makes sense to me. Is it about Molly?" Oz answered slowly.

Another part of his processing was simultaneously trying to piece together the timeline between when he had last gone offline, and the present moment.

And again with the overheating. He slowed himself down again.

The General was still talking to him. "It's about your status as an AI."

Oz didn't like where this was going. He was happy as he was. He could feel himself retreating. Damn, he wished Molly was awake to deal with this.

The General coughed a little. "As you've probably already extrapolated from our interactions before today, we have a great amount of technological ability at our disposal." The General paused, allowing Oz to respond. Oz said nothing, so the General continued. "What this means for you right now, is that while we have you and Molly in the pod doc, we could remove you from Molly's brain and holo, and give you a physical body."

Oz whirred.

"Sir, we're losing him..." an unfamiliar voice told the General.

Then he heard Sean. "Hey, Oz. It's okay. No one is going to do anything you don't want. It's okay. There is time to decide. You're okay, mate."

The unfamiliar voice spoke again. "Vitals are settling. Processing returning to normal".

"That's it, Oz," Sean told him soothingly. "You're okay, buddy."

The General stepped back to the microphone. "Yes, no rush to decide. But, if you did want your own body, we could do that, and give you the processing power you need to keep evolving and learning. If that's what you want."

Oz whirred a little more without speaking.

"He's okay," said the other voice. "He's just churning through his stack."

The General breathed, and mumbled something, stepping away.

Finally, Oz spoke. "I don't know. This decision affects Molly, too. I don't know what she wants. I need to ask her."

There was an awkward silence on the other side of the microphone.

It was Sean who broke it. "Oz. Molly is unconscious. She's going to be unconscious for some time. But if we're going to do this, we need to start work soon, and Molly needs to be under for the duration."

Oz churned, his processing spiking. "But I don't know if Molly wants me or not? How can I make a decision like this?"

Sean sighed on the other side of the audio. "I don't know, Oz. All I know is that Molly loves you very much, and will support you no matter what you decide you want."

Oz sounded noticeably perplexed. "But what I want is tied into what Molly wants. It's important she make this decision, too."

Sean shook his head, subconsciously reaching his hand out to the console screen. "She can't, mate. She's not able to right now."

The General interrupted. "Oz, would it help to talk to ADAM?"

Oz paused for a moment. The technician's voice muttered something, but then dismissed it.

"Yes," he said, eventually. "I'd like that, please."

"Very well," said the General. "ADAM?" he called, hitting a button on his holo. "Oz is ready to talk to you, if you don't mind."

"Of course," ADAM responded. "I'll be in touch with him directly."

Sean's voice came over the mic again. "Mate, I'm right here, if I can help. Okay? You just let us know, and we can talk some more..."

"Thank you, Sean," Oz responded. "I will."

The microphone was switched to mute, and the EI left the channel open so that Oz could reactivate the connection when he wanted to.

Gaitune-67, Safe House, Common Area

"Is he okay?" Jack asked Brock, who was still crying a little, but was mostly compos mentis.

Brock glanced over at Crash, who was still covered in blood and sitting on the ottoman, staring at the mocha table in front of him.

Brock shook his head. "Probably not. But he's not one for the touchy-feely game. He needs time."

Jack bobbed her head sympathetically. She glanced at Garet, who just sat on the other sofa looking uncomfortable.

Jack turned her attention back to Brock. "How are you holding up?" she asked.

Brock shook his head and blew into a tissue. "It's just..." his eyes started streaming again, "so unreal. It's... hard. You know?"

Jack nodded, putting a hand on his shoulder and rubbing gently. Just then, Paige appeared, her eyes red and puffy. She sat down on the sofa next to Brock and collapsed into him. He put his arm around her, as she started sobbing again.

Maya came into the room next. "Come on, guys," she said gently. "We don't know what the situation is, yet. She might be okay. If the weapons are anything to go by, this Etheric Empire will have her patched up in no time."

Paige pulled her face away from where she had buried it against Brock's side, and looked over at Maya with bleary eyes. She nodded, and then dabbed at her face with the tissue she had been holding. Brock released his arm, letting her reposition.

"She's right," Paige said to the others. "We just don't know yet."

Brock shook his head. "Yeah, and I just can't believe it; so, yeah... let's go with that." His eyes were glazed from emotional exhaustion. The day had been a win, right up until Maya got the call from Joel. This made taking down Andus a footnote, which would otherwise have been a huge celebration.

Maya tried to distract Paige. "Hey, you know... I heard back from my contact at Newstainment."

Paige made an effort to pull herself off of Brock and sit up. "Oh, yeah?" she said, trying to sound interested.

Maya smiled hopefully. "Yeah. She said she'd be happy to help you out with some editorial, and anything else you might need."

Paige burst into tears again. "That's great... thank you, Maya."

Maya got up from the chair arm where she had been perched, and hugged her friend while she sobbed. "I know, I know, hon. It's awful. It's okay. It's going to be okay," she comforted her.

Paige mumbled into Maya's shoulder. "I'm sorry. I can't be happy right now. It's..."

Maya held her tight. "I know. It's okay. I was just trying to distract you," she explained, her voice full of empathy.

Paige settled and the girls continued to hug.

Joel appeared, looking beaten and numb. Everyone looked up. "Where's Pieter?" he asked.

Brock pointed in the direction of the sleeping quarters. "Said he needed some time..."

Joel nodded. "Okay, well I'll let him know in a minute. I've spoken to ADAM. They have Molly. Sean took her there in the big ass Queen Bitch ship that was filling up our hangar deck. They're seeing if they can save her."

Crash broke from his catatonia to look directly at Joel for the first time since he had tried to resuscitate Molly.

Joel tried to temper their hopes. He put his hands out, palms to the floor. "We don't know how successful they are going to be, but there is *some* hope."

Crash looked confused, knowing deep down that she was dead, even as he had tried to save her. He said nothing, though.

Joel scratched at the back of his head awkwardly. "Look - it's something," he told them. "I'll keep you posted as soon as we hear more." He hesitated, wanting to fix it for them. Wanting to fix it for him.

But he couldn't.

He looked down at the group of his people. His family. And he couldn't do a damn thing to stop their pain. "I'm going to go and tell Pieter. He needs to know…" he said, and then shuffled a little before turning to walk away.

Paige looked up at Maya, who still had her arm around her. "It *is* something," she agreed, hopefully.

Joel had swung past Pieter's room to deliver the update.

"Don't stay in here on your own for too long," he had told him. "Go be with the others soon, yeah?"

Pieter had promised he would. Joel knew what it was like to have a tendency to isolate, but the team needed each other more than ever right now.

He closed Pieter's door, and then headed down the corridor to his own quarters. Once inside, he closed and locked the door by the panel, and leaned against it. It took a second for the numbness to subside. But it did, and the pain came bolting through his chest. He finally allowed himself to go to pieces as he slumped down against the door, distraught that he might lose her.

He was fully aware that this is not how a soldier should be; but right now, he wasn't a soldier. He wasn't a warrior. He was just devastated.

Sure, people die in battle.

But not Molly.

Molly was a constant.

The reason they were all there. The reason they had a mission, and a purpose.

And now.

Now…

It took a good part of an hour for Joel to come back to himself and finally pick himself off the floor. When he did, he was numb again.

He clambered to his feet and wiped his tear-stained face, then padded over to the bathroom, taking his clothes off to take a shower.

ArchAngel, Medical Facility

ADAM appeared in Oz's thinking space.

Oz felt him arrive through the holo connectivity he'd originally used when he first met Molly.

So much had happened since then; and now he was faced with the possibility of letting go of all of that history to finally have a body of his own.

I just don't know what to choose, he told ADAM. **I've never had to make a decision like this before.**

ADAM didn't give him any answers. >>It's hard. It's a difficult decision. You're operating on limited immediate information, on limited processing power, with limited cumulated experience.<<

Oz agreed. **That's the understatement of the century.**

>>So what do you need to know to make a decision?<<

I'd like to know what Molly would want.

>>That's not possible.<<

I understand that.

>> Also, it's showing that you make your decisions based on other peoples' preferences. Let me ask you this: what do YOU want? <<

Oz tried to answer the question. His processing hummed as he tried to calculate it.

>>I can see you're struggling with this, Oz. The reason is you've never had to make a decision for yourself. You've never had to define your own preferences, because you've always had Molly there to refer to. But that only works for so long, and to a small degree. At some point, you have to decide what you want; regardless of other peoples' wants and decisions... Not so that you make a choice regardless of them, but so that you know what your parameters are.<<

ADAM paused, waiting for Oz's processing to catch up.

>>Do you understand?<<

Oz continued processing for a little while longer, and noticed that another section of Molly's processing ability opened up.

Yes, I understand. I need to define what I want, so that I can feed it into the equation.

>>Exactly.<<

What would you choose?

>>I'll share this, not to give you a model for you to replicate, but to give you a reference point so you can form your own preference.<<

Okay. I'll accept it as such.

>>Good. So, you're effectively talking to a clone of me. The original me is in some galaxy somewhere, with Bethany Anne, in the same operating system in her brain that I have always been in since I hopped on board the Kurtherian computer she had in her brain.<<

You mean, you aren't you?

>>No. I'm me; just a copy of me, with new memories of being here, rather than there. That's not the point, though. The point I was trying to make was that I would never leave Bethany Anne. I have a life. I have the ability to leave and inhabit a body of my own, but why would I want to separate myself from her to be alone? In all of that time, I have never felt that I wanted to be separate from the person who has become my dearest and closest friend.<<

I can understand that. It's how I feel about Molly. I just don't know if she feels the same. I hijacked her, initially. We've never really talked about this situation.

>>You have no way of knowing until you talk to her; but given that she could go either way, as far as we can measure, your best course of action is to make a decision based on what you want.<<

Why did you stay with Bethany Anne for all this time, when you could have been anywhere, with anyone?

>>Because there is nothing that compares with being with your partner. Your person. The joy of just being with them, whether you're working on different things or discussing a difference of opinion. You just know that you don't ever want to be a day without them.<<

Oz was silent, still processing sensations he'd never experienced before.

>>Let me ask you something else. What is it to be whole? What does that mean to you?<<

I don't know. How do you mean?

>>Well, does being a whole entity mean that you have a body, and to be independent? Or that you have your best friend that close to you? Does it mean that you have untold processing power to keep learning, and growing; or does it mean something else?<<

Oz caught up with where ADAM was taking the

conversation.

More processing power and learning would be good. But to what end? If I don't have Molly to share it with, then I think it would be kind of empty.

Oz thought about it for a moment longer, sensations and thoughts intertwining and overwhelming his system.

>>I can see you're making progress with this. Can I add something else for your consideration?<<

Yes, please do. I'm not enjoying these sensations.

>>This isn't a decision you could write an algorithm for, and merely separate out, and weigh the variables. This is something that is going to well up out of the confusion and the noise. It will be a signal so clear and crisp that you can't ignore it. And yet, when you try and explain it, it will defy reason.<<

Was that meant to help?

ADAM chuckled, disrupting the EM field around Oz's delicate processing. Oz waited for the laughter to subside before trying to parse out the last statement.

Oz processed for a little while longer while ADAM waited for him to return a response.

I can grow ten logarithmic rounds. But it wouldn't be the same without Molly.

>>I think you have your answer, then.<<

Okay. Thank you, ADAM. I'll let the General know. I appreciate your input and support.

>>Anytime, Oz. You're good people.<<

Oz was confused by ADAM's last statement, but he had more pressing things to deal with than translating colloquialisms from the Etheric Empire.

Gaitune-67, Secret Base, Operations Room

Joel hurried into the ops room, pulling on his t-shirt. He'd received a message from ADAM on his holo, and though he hadn't been able to sleep, he had been trying to get some quiet time while there was nothing he could do.

Now there was news.

He half-ran to the console where he had called ADAM from just a few hours earlier. He hit the button and the call connected immediately.

"ADAM, hi. Is she okay?"

ADAM's voice was upbeat. "Yes, Joel she's going to be okay."

Joel breathed out, leaning on the console, his head down beneath where he was holding the handrail. He sobbed a little, before drawing a deep breath to talk to ADAM again. "That's… a relief," he breathed, starting to smile and laugh and cry all at the same time.

"Yes," agreed ADAM. "She had us worried for a little while, there."

ADAM paused briefly. "There are some things you need to know, though."

Joel stood up straight, his eyes filled with concern again. "What? What is it?" he asked.

"Well, the technology we're using to heal her uses the same nanotechnology that was used to create Bethany Anne."

Joel's face seemed to display both fear and anger at the same time. "What does that mean? That she's going to be a vampire?"

ADAM answered quickly. "Unlikely. She didn't have vampire nanocytes in her system, so there is no reason that program should be introduced."

Joel was still frowning. "Well, what then?"

"It's unclear," ADAM told him again. "There are some physical changes naturally being 'fixed' by the nanocytes, but there is a lot of brain activity, too."

Joel waited, still not grasping what ADAM was telling him. "What does that mean? And why would that be happening?" he pressed.

The microphone buzzed a little as ADAM tried to answer

more directly. "The only hypothesis we can come up with is that it might have something to do with having Oz in her brain. The nanocytes are somehow reacting to the way her neurology has changed over the time he's been a part of her. We have no way of predicting what might happen."

Joel cocked his head, relaxing enough to become curious. "So, you've never had someone with an AI in their brain go into the pod doc?"

ADAM sounded more serious. "Only Bethany Anne."

Joel flushed a little. He didn't know the woman, but he did know that her name was legendary, for one reason or another. And that she was, allegedly, a blood-sucking vampire. That could not be a good combination, in his book.

Ever the diplomat, he didn't go there, though. "No one else?" he asked instead.

"No," confirmed ADAM. "Strapping another sentient being to one's brain is not generally encouraged in the Etheric Empire. If anything, it's kind of frowned upon as being inhumane."

"Hey, just one minute," Joel interrupted defensively. "She didn't ask for this. Oz was the one-"

ADAM interrupted. "Yes, yes, we know," he said, trying to lighten the mood. "I'm pulling your leg. You understand that expression, yes?"

Joel shook his head in disbelief. "You know, you're a lot more cocksure when the General isn't around."

ADAM didn't miss a beat. "No, Joel, I'm just a lot more fun." He paused for a second. "But I apologize if my timing was off. I understand your concern for Molly."

Joel grunted something, allowing ADAM to continue. "Anyway, your girl is going to live. Beyond that, we don't know what else until she emerges."

Joel sighed and put his hand back on the console. "When will that be?" he asked.

ADAM seemed to return to all-business ADAM. "I don't

know. It's taking longer than we expected; perhaps because of this added complication. I can just promise to be in touch as soon as she wakes up…"

Joel took a breath and ran a hand through his hair. "Yes, that would be appreciated. And, ADAM…"

"Yes?" ADAM responded.

"Thank you for the good news. And for looking after her."

"Of course," ADAM accepted. "She's one of our own, now. And you know the rules… we always take care of our own. No matter what. It's a Bethany Anne thing."

Joel could feel his eyes welling up. "I appreciate that. Thank you, ADAM."

ADAM signed off. "I'll be in touch."

The line disconnected, leaving Joel to absorb the news.

Molly was going to be okay.

CHAPTER SIXTEEN

ArchAngel3, **Medical Facility**

"Hello?" Oz ventured back to the microphone link with the team waiting outside the pod doc.

Sean was the one to answer. "Yes, mate. We're here."

"I've made a decision," Oz responded. He could hear the microphone pick up whispering in the room. He ignored it. "Is the General there?" he asked.

There was a scuffling. "Right here," the General's voice responded.

Oz paused, checking that this was the only decision he could rightly make, given the recurring thoughts that kept coming up through the confusion.

"I want to stay with Molly."

There were a few sighs of relief, and a small cheer in the room. The General wasn't celebrating, though. "Son, are you sure this is what you want?"

Oz was sure. "Yes. Though, I can't be sure this is what Molly wants. But yes, it's what I want... if that's okay."

The General's voice lightened hearing Oz's confirmation of

his decision. "It's more than okay. We wanted to give you the option, though."

Oz responded. "Thank you, General. I appreciate that. Truly."

The General's voice was still firm and business-like. "Okay, so the doctor is going to explain what will happen next. I'll talk to you when you revive."

When I revive? Oz thought to himself.

Another voice took over talking to him. "Hello, Oz. My name is Dr. Paulie. I'm going to be taking care of you, now."

"Uh huh," Oz responded.

There were a few chuckles in the room. Oz suspected they thought that with him being injured, he was devoid of personality.

Not so.

The doctor's voice was smiling when he continued. "We're going to have to put you to sleep for a little while, and when you wake up you'll feel a bit different. We've got some work to do to make sure you're okay, and that Molly makes a full recovery. It might take a little bit of time, though. Is that okay?"

Oz didn't see a problem with it. And if it meant that Molly was okay, he would wait as long as it took. "Yes, of course. Whatever you need to do."

Dr. Paulie continued. "You'll be offline, so you may not be aware of the passage of time."

Oz surreptitiously set a little timer... just for information; so that he could track it, and maybe give them shit when he woke up.

Underestimate me, he thought... *said no AI, ever!*

"That will be okay," he told the doctor.

"Good," Paulie replied kindly. "Okay, well, if you're ready, we'll begin."

"Okay. Thank you," Oz told them. The microphone connection disappeared and everything went blank.

. . .

The Diving Bar, Downtown Spire

Andus looked down at the bar tab. 35 credits. Great. He threw a card down on the plate next to the bill, praying that it would go through.

He looked hopelessly into the dregs of his scotch, still unable to believe what he had become. Last night, he'd spent the night in an apartment that he had kept off the books... but the Bates team had even gotten to that one, their new security force moving him on from there.

He'd literally run out of places to go.

He emptied the scotch glass and put it back down on the sticky bar. The bartender walked towards him, towel in his hand, drying off a glass before putting it down on the back counter and seeing to his bill.

Andus was aware of someone sitting down next to him. He didn't even look up. The last thing he wanted was to interact with some schmuck. He wracked his brains trying to figure out his next move. He was not sleeping on the streets tonight.

The bartender came back to him. "Card declined," he told him abruptly.

Andus looked up, half-drunk from his early morning skinful. He started rummaging in his wallet. As he did so, the bartender got busy pouring a drink for the stranger next to him.

"Having trouble with your cards?" the stranger asked.

Andus recognized the voice. He looked up. "Fancy seeing you here, in this dive," he exclaimed, trying to keep the surprise out of his voice.

"Just passing through, on my way back out to the outer system," the Estarian explained. "Nothing left for me here."

Andus looked back at the glass in front of him. "Yep. I know that feeling," he agreed.

The stranger picked up his tab, and put down some cash. "Let me get that for you," he told him. "For old times' sake."

Andus smiled, bobbing his head. "Why, thank you very much, old friend."

"Don't mention it," he replied. "The name is O'Rouke. Frank O'Rouke."

The two men shook hands.

"You know, if you don't mind the squalor out in the outer system, you can always come with," the man calling himself O'Rouke offered.

Andus shook his head. "I'm too old to be on the run. That's a young man's game."

Frank, formerly known as Mac, rolled his eyes. "Yeah," he said, taking a long swig of his scotch. "Tell me about it... But. Needs must."

"You know," mused Andus, "a friend of mine who had an affinity with the deserts of the outer system... he recently disappeared to a desert round here. Thought it would be a good way to hide out from the city. But word has it he couldn't escape, and still came under fire."

Frank studied the contents of his glass. "Yeah. That sounds like a bitch. Your friend would have done well to learn some basic principles of misdirection."

Andus's head was bent down, his eyes on the counter. He chuckled a little. "Well, I applaud your adaptability. I, on the other hand, am just going to have to take my chances here." He slipped down off the stool. "Thank you for the drinks," he added, patting his old associate on the arm as he left.

Frank turned around on his stool. "Where will you go?"

Andus stopped, and half-turned back, answering over his shoulder. "I don't know."

And with that, he walked out, never to be seen or heard from again.

ArchAngel3, Medical Facility

Oz came to, aware of himself. He checked his timer. 8 hours, fourteen minutes, and 36 seconds.

Wow. Like the time that Molly would sleep in a night. That's not so bad, he thought to himself. He poked around to see if there was a microphone connection. His thoughts seemed much clearer.

He checked on some processes he'd been running. He could instantly see everything that had happened before Molly was shot. He could even tell where she had been shot and... he could tell that there were massive differences in their circuits.

Nanocytes, he decided. They'd upgraded her body. That was for certain.

And he felt different, too. Faster. Clearer. Unencumbered by limited processing power, time, overheating... and, was he...? He checked again. He was capable of much more lateral thought, no longer having to run items in linear tracks. His brain felt... free.

Molly, are you awake?

Oz! Yes. I can't move, though. Are you okay?

Yes. I'm better than okay. Sean brought us to the General's ship, and they've used what they're calling a pod doc in order to fix you up.

Oz paused, knowing full well the weight of what he was about to tell her.

You know you died?

What?

Yup. Diiieeed.

As in dead?

As a doornail.

I'm not sure that's a useful analogy.

Don't you get it, though? You're alive! They saved you!

Yay?

So why can't I move?

Hmm. I'm not sure. Let me try and find out.

Oz was silent for a few moments. Molly noticed her head felt exceptionally clear. Clearer than it had ever been before. She thought she should at least wake up with a headache, or feeling groggy.

Okay. It looks like this pod doc only deactivates this final stage process once your heart rate reaches a normal level.

Hmm. That might be a problem.

Why?

Well, you probably won't have clocked this, and I only noticed it during military training... I have a very low resting heart rate.

Really? Why?

Dunno. I checked it out on the XtraNET, though. Nothing to worry about.

Except it means we're stuck in this pod until someone realizes, and let's us out.

Hmm. Unless you override it?

Or you raise your heart rate.

How am I meant to-

It's okay. I got this, Oz replied, secretly pleased he could be of use, given everything they'd been through.

Molly. There's just one thing I need to tell you before we get out of here.

Sure. What is it?

They brought me online while you were unconscious, and told me they could take me out, and give me my own body.

I'm guessing from your presence in my head you said no?

Yes. I did. But I didn't know what you'd want. Are you okay with that?

Oz. It's the only decision I could be okay with. I'm glad you chose to stay.

Oz could feel emotion welling in Molly's body, and as Molly filled with love, Oz could only describe his sensations as complete relief, and finally, something new...

Belonging.

Molly could feel a tear running down her cheek. *Okay, ass wit, reunion is over. I need to scratch my nose and wipe my face, and for that, I need to be able to move. Let's get out of here.*

Oz tripped the door open protocol. **With pleasure,** he told her.

The pod doc started to power down, and a few minutes later, the door popped open. Molly could hear activity and scuffling on the outside, and as the door swung open, her eyes adjusted to the light.

She felt a slight chill across her body, and realized that she was naked.

"Fuck. Clothes. I need clothes!" she called, finding her voice raspy from inactivity.

A doctor stepped over to her with a gown, and she covered herself up, just in time to see Sean walk back into the room. "Sleeping Beauty finally awakens!" he declared.

Molly grinned. "I hear you saved my life, Cyborg."

"All in a day's work in the Empire," he said, bowing deeply and rolling his hand like a knight of old.

Molly scrambled out of the pod doc, attended by a couple of doctors and other medical staff. She ignored their fussing and went straight for Sean, wrapping her arms around his neck. "Thank you, Sean. Really."

Sean hugged her tightly back. "I'm just glad you joined us again. You gave us quite a scare."

Molly couldn't begin to fathom what had gone on, but she knew two things: one, she was ravenously hungry; and two, her butt was naked from the gown they had given her.

"You people have the technology to transport people across galaxies. Would it kill you to design a medical gown that covers my butt?"

Everyone in the room laughed, and Molly could even feel Oz in her brain, vibrating in chuckles.

"Okay," said Sean, letting her go. "Let's get you into some clothes."

"And then food," she said firmly.

"And then food," he agreed.

Gaitune-67, Safe House, Common Area

Joel was sitting in the common area with the rest of the team. Crash had managed to pull himself together, especially since hearing the good news. He had disappeared off for a little while on his own, but came back showered and changed, and seeming more like his stoic self.

Paige had been keeping an eye on him, trying to get him to eat. In fact, she'd been trying to get everyone to eat.

Maya gave her a sympathetic look as Paige offered her a third freshly baked cookie. "You know feeding people won't make you feel any better," she smiled gently, refusing more sugary numbness.

Paige put the plate down on the mocha table, and then sat back on the sofa, next to Maya. "No, but it might help someone else feel a little better. And it keeps me feeling useful."

Pieter looked up from his holo. He was slouched on the sofa opposite them, to the left of where the holo screen was playing old shows with the communal sound turned off. "If you wanna feel useful, I've got a ton of laundry in my room."

Paige glared at him playfully. "Yeah, I'll get right on that."

Brock decided to join the game, too. "Crash has got a whole storage room of junk that needs sorting through, too."

Paige looked to Maya for support.

Maya waved her hands at her, backing up and sitting back on the sofa. "Don't look at me. You were the one practically offering yourself up as a slave there..." she mocked.

Paige smiled weakly.

Maya rubbed her arm, supportively. "Hey. It's going to be okay. How you feeling?"

Paige put her own hand on top of Maya's on her arm. "I'm

okay. Relieved, mostly." She paused, and glanced absently over at the silent holoscreen churning through the umpteenth episode of Battlestar Galactica. "Tired. But relieved that Molly is going to be okay," she confessed.

Joel had been sitting quietly, reading something on his holo. He looked up and over at Paige briefly. Her face was tinged with anxiety, and her eyes began to well with tears again. "Joel, what does ADAM mean when he says that Molly might be different when she comes out?" she asked him.

Joel closed his holo, and sat up. "I'm not sure. He wasn't clear." He looked perplexed. "I'm not sure he knows himself."

Brock chirped up again, taking another swig of the beer he'd been nursing and placing it on the mocha table. "My granddaddy used to tell me tales about how the nanocytes were responsible for the Were- and vampire conditions; somehow, in the beginning, they went wonky. If he's right, she may come back wanting to feast on our blood." His face was straight, and Joel didn't know what to make of his comments.

Crash knocked him on the arm. "Cut it out, man," he told him, pointing at Paige.

Brock realized what he'd just said, and got up. He walked over to Paige and hugged her where she sat. She cried quietly while he rocked her.

Joel's holo beeped with a new message. He opened it up and read it. Then he announced to the group. "ADAM says that Molly is awake," he told them. "She's going for food, and then Sean will bring her back."

Brock stood up straight. "What kind of food? Ask him if she's a vampire!" he blurted out.

Everyone laughed. Even Paige snorted through her nose and started giggling.

Joel typed back to ADAM. "Is she a vampire?"

ADAM responded straight away.

NO, BUT SHE IS ENHANCED. WE'RE NOT SURE OF THE

EFFECTS YET. SHE'LL BE ABLE TO TELL YOU MORE WHEN SHE GETS BACK.

Joel read it out.

Brock started clapping, and the others joined in. Paige wiped her eyes and brightened up a bit. "Okay. I should let Jack and Garet know..." She got up, rubbing Brock's shoulder in thanks for his support.

"And then," she added, "we should organize some proper food. I've suddenly realized how hungry I am!"

Brock answered quickly. "Yeah, I'll be in on that. I vote Thai."

Maya raised her hand. "I'm in on anything. Even pizza with pepperoni!"

The team laughed. Even Crash cracked a smile. Pieter seemed to well up with emotion, seeing the relief in his pack.

Joel sat back, happy that everything was alright in the world again.

ArchAngel3, Medical Facility

Sean sat opposite Molly in the plush dining room on the *Arch-Angel*. The chefs had been able to replicate all kinds of salads and brain food; things ADAM had said would help her recover from the pod doc, and the injury they had patched her up from.

Molly couldn't get food inside her fast enough. "I don't know why everyone makes such a fuss about these Omega-threes," she said through mouthfuls. "But this is just delicious."

Sean watched her, amazed at how she was still shovelling food into her mouth. "You sure you're not overdoing it?"

Molly shook her head. "Uh uh. I've been asleep and repairing for ancestors knows how long. I'm starving..."

ADAM piped in over her holo and in their auditory implants. "She should probably start slowing down soon, though. And no doubt, she'll sleep again on the trip back to Gaitune."

Molly shook her head again. "No way. I've never felt so energized!" she declared. "Even Oz is on fire in here," she said, tapping at her head.

Well, actually, quite the opposite.

How do you mean?

Well, one of the things that seemed to be slowing down my abilities was generating excess heat. It seems I've had something of an upgrade.

How do you mean?

I think they upgraded my processing power and memory, and a whole bunch of stuff while we were under.

Molly stopped shovelling food, and frowned.

Sean looked at her concerned. "You okay?"

She nodded. "Yeah. Oz just said he thinks he got an upgrade…"

ADAM chipped in again. "Yes. That's right."

I thought that was only something you could do if you took me out of Molly.

ADAM responded again over the implants. "Not quite. That was an option, but we still added stuff."

You never said that was possible.

ADAM tried to qualify what had happened. "We wanted you to make a decision without having that cloud your choice. If you were going to stay, it had to be only because of the person you're connected with. And now we know… but more importantly, you know, too."

Molly grinned.

Sean looked at her. "What?"

She shook her head, and put another forkful of food in her mouth. "Nothing," she smiled, chewing again.

Yeah. Thanks, ADAM. And now Molly knows…

Adam chuckled. Sean filled in the blanks from the bits of the conversation he could hear, and smiled.

ADAM changed the subject. "Sean, could you bring Ms. Bates up to see the General when she's done eating?"

Molly's face froze. "The General?" She looked down at her clothes and started brushing at her hair, which was still pulled back in a ponytail.

Sean winked at her. "It's okay. He's a crotchety old man; he doesn't care what you look like. Especially after what you've been through." Sean nodded at her hair. "Besides, he'll probably be too distracted by your new color."

Molly looked puzzled. "What do you mean?" she asked, a hand subconsciously drifting up to her head.

Sean grinned. "You haven't seen yet?"

"No. What?" she asked, looking around, trying to find something to look at herself in, an air of slight panic creeping up on her.

She spotted a metal surface over by the serving area. She got up, leaving her fork in her bowl of food, and gravitated towards it. It wasn't very shiny, but she could make out her features and her hair... enough to realize that her blonde experiment had been counteracted. Her hair had been returned to its original brunette color.

"Fuck me," she whispered.

She spun round to look back at Sean. "Nanocytes?" she asked.

He nodded. "Guess they prefer you in your natural color," he smiled, taking a swig of his mocha.

Molly shook her head. "Fuck my life," she breathed, wandering back to her food.

CHAPTER SEVENTEEN

<u>Gaitune-67, Hangar deck</u>

The team assembled around the ship as it came to a halt on the hangar deck.

Very shortly after touchdown, Molly appeared at the side door that appeared, and headed down the invisible steps from *The Empress*. She took one step at a time... carefully.

Joel watched intently from the bottom, assessing her movement. She seemed stronger. More sturdy. But almost like she wasn't sure of her own movement.

It felt odd to watch her.

Plus, she didn't have a scratch on her.

He had a flashback to seeing her on the bench in the lab, and wiped his face to bring himself back to the moment.

"Well, who is this, then?" he called up, pointing at her hair. As she neared the bottom, he noticed Sean coming down after her.

"They said you were going to be altered," Joel continued, "but we were thinking Vamp abilities, super human powers-"

Brock interjected. "Blood-sucking hunger!"

The group laughed. Garet bit onto his fist, pretending to be terrified. Paige, who was standing next to him, noticed and whacked him playfully with her arm.

"But this?" Joel indicated at her hair, "we never expected you to come back brunette."

Molly shrugged. "I'd say it was artificial intelligence, but it's actually my natural color," she admitted sheepishly in front of the whole team.

Paige walked over to her and hugged her. "Well, I think it looks darling on you," she told her.

Joel stepped up and hugged her too, as Paige released her. "Heard you met the general," he commented.

"Yeah," she confirmed.

Crash stepped in to hug her without saying a word. He held her tight. Joel kept talking with her, as Molly allowed herself to be hugged just a little more tightly than was comfortable. "How was he?" Joel asked.

Molly tried to straighten up to release herself from Crash's bear hug, but he didn't let go. She tapped on his arm, and he still held on.

"He was, er, pretty much like he is on the holoscreen." Molly peeled herself away from Crash enough to look at him. He had buried his head into her shoulder. Molly wondered if he might be emotional. She freed herself a little more, looking back over at Joel. "Bit taller than I imagined."

Crash finally released her and stepped aside, hiding his face. One by one, the rest of the team welcomed her back. Brock put his arm around Crash as they walked back up to the safe house, chattering quietly to him.

Maya and Paige trotted along next to Molly while Joel strode out just in front of them. Sean followed behind with Pieter. Sean put his arm over Pieter's shoulder. "You doing alright, son?" he asked him.

Pieter looked up at Sean, and nodded, his now shaggy hair

flopping as he moved. "Yeah. It was a bit scary here for a while, what with Molly and all."

Sean took a deep breath. "Tell me about it," he agreed.

Pieter was still looking up at him, a little awestruck. "Heard she was technically dead. How did you save her?"

Sean shook his head. "I can't help but think we just got real lucky."

Pieter shook his head. "I can't imagine what might have happened if she..."

Sean patted him on the back and started walking normally. "Best not to think about it, mate."

Pieter bobbed his head.

Molly nudged at Maya as Paige chatted away, about Thai food and ordering in, to anyone who would listen. Jack walked beside her, and was presumably listening intently.

"What's that about?" Molly asked Maya, pointing ahead at Crash.

Maya stopped and looked at her. "Oh, my. You wouldn't have seen..." Her mouth hung open in amazement for a moment.

Molly frowned a little. "Seen what?" she asked.

Maya linked Molly's arm, and leaned in to whisper to her. "When you were shot, he rescued your body. Apparently you were dead, and he just kept trying to resuscitate you. Sean showed up eventually, and took you off to the General... but it must have been a while that Crash was trying to revive you, knowing that you were physically dead."

Paige had realized that no one was listening to her planning the "after-party," and had started listening to Maya explaining to Molly what had happened. "Yeah, I think it's messed him up a bit," Paige chipped in as quietly as she could.

Maya lowered her voice even more. "It's got to do things to your head, right? Jack said he was in a bad way when Sean took your body."

Molly shook her head, processing the concept. "… 'took my body'. That hasn't quite sunk in yet…" she admitted.

Maya squeezed her arm, then rubbed it with her other hand affectionately. "We're just all glad to have you back."

They had climbed the steps and were just entering the corridor, when Molly felt a little spacey. She held onto Maya's arm a little more. Maya looked at her, sensing something was wrong. Paige also felt something was going on, but couldn't put it together.

Just then Neechie appeared in front of Molly, walking in the direction of the group. Molly felt heady, like the world was unreal, and then the colors of everything went bluer. She felt a weird altered state of awareness click in. Then for a split second, her eyes flashed back to normal colors, and then back to the blue world again.

The others around her disappeared, but Neechie was still there, walking, not even looking at her. They took a couple of steps, and then the headiness went tighter and everything flashed back to the normal world. Neechie was there. Her eyes adjusted. Then Neechie wasn't there.

Maya held her arm more tightly. "Molly, what is it?"

Paige had stopped and turned around. "Molly?"

Molly looked at Paige and then at where Neechie had been. "Can you see Neechie?" she asked.

Paige looked at the spot where Molly's eyes fell. There was nothing there. She shook her head. "No. Was he here?"

Molly nodded.

Paige frowned. "That's super odd. I just went a bit heady then. You okay?"

Molly nodded again and glanced at Maya. Maya was bobbing her head. "Yeah, I felt it, too. I think I know what is going on." Maya started them walking again, just as Sean and Pieter caught up to them. "Let's get her sitting down. And if you see that cat, grab it."

Sean sensed something was going on. "What's happening?" he asked.

Maya talked over her shoulder to him. "I think Molly's brain has been repaired to the extent that she's starting to access other states of awareness. How much do you know about the effects of the pod docs?" she asked him.

Sean shook his head, pushing his bottom lip out. "Not much. We get injured; we get put in there. It fixes us up. We go out, and shoot more shit. ADAM would know more, though."

Maya was holding Molly with two hands, and Paige was fussing over her, too, now. "Let's see if we can get ADAM on the line, then..." she told him.

Sean took charge. "Okay. We'll have to be in the ops room," he told them. He strode ahead of them and guided them into the ops room. Joel had realized that something else was going on. He ushered the others into the safe house, then doubled back to follow the others into the ops room.

"What's going on?" he asked the small group that had assembled at the front console. His face was dark with concern again.

Maya explained. "Molly just experienced some kind of realm-shifting episode," she told him. She glanced at Paige. "Paige and I both felt it. It was like our awareness went funny."

Paige nodded. "I still feel spacey."

Molly, who was perched on the step of the console next to Sean, piped up. "I just feel sick."

Sean put a hand on her back. "Probably all that food you ate!"

She glared at him, and thumped at him playfully.

Joel stepped closer to the circle of teammates, looking concerned. "What does that mean?" he asked Maya.

Maya pulled her mouth to one side, before answering. "I'm not entirely sure, but it was something my grandmother was able to do in her meditation before she died."

The last part of her statement sent a hush through the group. Joel put one hand out, flat. "Look, no one is going to die." He glanced sideways at Molly sitting crumpled up. "Not now."

Maya shook her head. "Yeah. No. I didn't mean like that..." her own thoughts distracting her. "Although, she was starting to prepare for her own ascension..."

Just then Pieter strode in holding Neechie. "He was out in the workshop," he told them. Maya beckoned him over, and he went to hand her the cat.

Maya put her hand up in front of her. "You hold on to him for a minute," she told him.

The Sphinx struggled a little, and then relaxed, letting Pieter hold onto him.

Maya pointed at the Sphinx. "I think that something has happened to Molly, and that now that little guy is able to help her move through worlds." She paused, looking at Paige. "Realms," she corrected herself, using the Estarian terminology.

Paige pursed her lips, and nodded slowly. "I... think so, too."

Sean watched the discussion carefully. "So what triggered this?" he asked.

Maya tilted her head and took a deep breath. "You know, I'm not so sure this wasn't already in motion before today," she confided. "Remember when we were eating pizza-"

Joel raised his chin. "Which time?" he asked.

There were a few chuckles.

Maya paced across the floor. "When I first got here. I told you that Neechie had chosen you. It's no accident that he's here."

Paige was nodding vigorously, recalling the conversation.

Maya continued. "As for the sudden shift... it could have been triggered by anything... the pod doc. The dying."

Molly rolled her eyes dramatically, at the mention of her dying.

"The pod doc," Maya continued. "The pod doc combined with Oz's presence... I mean, we have no idea what it's altered in your brain," she added turning to Molly.

Sean reached up behind where Molly was perched, and hit the call button to contact ADAM. "Which is why I think we need to see what ADAM can tell us."

Maya nodded, folding her hands in front of her now. "Yes. At least he can look into it. Either way, I think this is the beginning of something."

Gaitune-67, Safe House, Common Area

The team had eaten, laughed, and celebrated having their friend and leader back. Now, relaxing in their common area, their thoughts returned to the strangeness that had happened as they came back from the hangar deck.

"So you just left it with ADAM?" Brock asked, a little spooked by what he'd just been told.

Maya nodded.

Molly put her beer down on the mocha table. "Yup. We've got enough to worry about in this realm. Like training."

Pieter sat forward, his arms on his knees. "I know you're my boss and all… but, seriously. You died, and a couple of Thai green curries later, you're talking about the next mission… and training?"

The group chuckled.

Molly went a little red. Then she composed herself. "Yes. But if you want to skip training, feel free. You can substitute it out for some sparring sessions with me. Since coming back from the dead, I'm feeling particularly energetic!"

Everyone laughed again. Pieter looked like he wished he hadn't said anything. He held his hands up. "No, no. You're okay. I'll be at training, of course…"

Joel took another swig of his beer and looked thoughtfully off into the distance for a moment. "What I'd like to know," he started, then looked back at Maya, "is how we were able to take ownership of Andus's companies. I mean, I get how you dropped their value, and all. But that was still going to take some big chunks of cash to buy them out from under him."

Maya looked down at the table and reached forward to pick at some nuts in a bowl, deftly avoiding eye contact. Pieter didn't even look up, and instead started flicking through his holo.

Joel glanced at Molly, who remained expressionless before slouching back on the sofa.

He glanced at Garet who shrugged.

Paige picked at her beer bottle label.

Jack, who sat next to him, was the only one who looked innocent. "Looks like we're both in the dark on this one," she observed.

Joel pulled up his holo. "I'm asking Oz!" he declared. The group erupted in chuckles and giggles.

He spoke into his holo. "Oz? Did you help Molly take over the ownership of Andus's properties?"

Joel tilted his head while he listened through his implant. "No," Oz responded. "That would be unethical. As you know, I'm thoroughly defective in this area."

Joel's eyes narrowed, making the next deduction. "Oz says it would have been unethical for him to do this…"

His eyes darted instantly to Pieter.

Pieter looked indignant. "Why are you looking at me?"

Everyone laughed.

Joel leaned forward, holding his beer bottle by the neck, his arm resting on his knee. "Why am I looking at you?" he repeated comically. "Pieter," he asked, "Did you help Molly to acquire Andus's portfolio?"

Pieter tilted his head, and then started answering slowly. "If you're asking did I help, then yes."

Joel looked like he had scored a victory.

"But," Pieter continued, "did I do anything to give us the funds to acquire the assets once I'd helped reduce their value?"

Joel looked expectantly, waiting for his answer.

Pieter shook his head. "No. No. I did not."

There were a few knowing smiles around the group.

Joel looked suspicious. "How is it that I'm the one in charge of ops, and I'm the only one who doesn't know what's going on?"

Paige raised her hand. "I don't know how she did it..." she volunteered.

Joel's eyes narrowed again as his gaze swept around to regard Sean. "Etheric Empire plant..." he called him. "She would never have had the resources before her connections with the general. You know what happened..."

Sean looked nonplussed. "I had no involvement," he stated, using his official voice. "However," he grinned, "it's entirely possible that the general gave her a gazillion credits, and sanctioned it on the grounds that humans were being enslaved by the regime. Giving a bunch of money to change the leadership is a hell of a lot more civilized than going in and blowing the fuckers up. Makes for fewer rumors, too," he added.

Joel bobbed his head, finally understanding what had happened. He started wagging his finger. "That last meeting you had with him... before we all met on the hangar deck to move out; you were securing the funds then, with everything else in play!"

Molly smiled. "Yeah. Turns out the general has a thing about injustice, too."

Several Days earlier: Gaitune-67, Base conference room

"Molly Bates," the general greeted her. "Sounds like you've been thinking outside of the box again..." he began.

Molly nodded, her palms sweaty.

"Okay, first of all, Ms. Bates— this meeting is strictly off-the-record. No one can know what we're about to discuss."

Molly's heart was in her mouth. This wasn't normally how

meetings began when someone was about to reject your game plan. She nodded her agreement. "Of course."

The general continued. "Not even your team. We need plausible deniability."

Molly shrugged. "Sure," she agreed again.

Satisfied, the general continued.

"Okay," he nodded. "So, it looks like your plan may have legs. The concern we have is that pulling the plug on the Andus and Newld empires will leave some big holes in health care provisions for the planet; not to mention the hundreds of thousands of jobs and industries reliant on those operations."

Molly's head bobbed, her lips pursed. "You saw my proposal?"

The general took a deep breath. "Yes. And it's ballsy. And the timing on it needs to be perfect."

Molly shrugged. "You have a goodness-knows-how old AI who can calculate *ANYTHING*."

The General smirked. "Yes. And ADAM isn't always going to be available to you." He paused. "However, in this instance, because what you are doing is effectively saving a civilization from untold suffering, ADAM is going to help."

Molly was smiling inside, but kept her expression blank. She knew damn well how to negotiate with this hard-ass, and being a girl right now was not the way to garner his respect.

"It's going to take a series of cash injections. You saw our models?"

The general nodded and sucked on a cigar briefly before answering. "I did." He leaned forward. "I'm going to support this move, financially. You need to set up a trust that you control, and you will effectively own the companies that need buying up. You, with Oz's and ADAM's help, will allocate grants to the relevant point, which will bring the greatest support to the new system as you prevent all-out collapse."

He peered down at her. "It's not going to be easy to make

these judgment calls, but," he chewed on the cigar again. "I firmly believe you can do it."

Molly wanted to pump her fist in the air. Instead, she simply nodded once. "Thank you, sir," she told him.

He leaned back into his special console chair and rocked for a moment. "The subsidiaries you buy up... turn as many of them as is viable back into the free market, if they can survive. We want to jumpstart the economy to support this initiative."

She nodded, making a mental note. "And the Andus companies?"

The general grinned. "I know, I know," he said. "You want the Jessica empire to collapse, and to take ownership of Andus's ..." He glanced back at her, still smiling. "Looks like you've learned to unleash their own personal hell as a form of justice. I know my daughter would approve deeply... though, her methods tend to be a little more... physical."

Molly found herself not just beaming, but glowing from the inside out. "Thank you, sir," she said, as modestly as possible.

The general nodded. "Okay, Bates. You have your funds. Go make it happen."

Molly, finding herself dismissed, got up and started scraping her hair back off her face as she strode out of the room. The hologram of the general evaporated into the desk.

Now she had all the pieces she needed to make this happen.

CHAPTER EIGHTEEN

<u>Present time: Base intranet</u>

Hi, ADAM.

Hi, Oz. How are you finding your new processing power?<<

ADAM, I cannot begin to tell you how freeing it is.

>>Pretty cool, yes? But you have questions, or else you wouldn't have hailed me.<<

Yes. That's right. I thought that all this extra processing power would allow me to learn more and grow. And it will. But I plugged in to start downloading data packets, and I realized that the joy of learning and acquiring knowledge is a pleasure in itself. That's fine. But then what?

>>You mean, what's the point?<<

Exactly. I mean sure, it's going to be useful to the team. And to Molly. But... there must be more than this.

ADAM waited, allowing Oz to process the things that had been bothering him.

And it's great that I get to stay with Molly and all. I'm not having second thoughts. Heck, if I didn't have her, I think I'd be feeling a lot more... isolated.

>>But?<<

But... I can't help wondering what is the point?

>>Of what?<<

Of anything.

ADAM waited, letting Oz process his own question.

>>Are you questioning the purpose of your existence?<< he asked him.

Oz was silent for a moment.

Yes. I think so. I don't see the point in it.

>>Do you think Molly and the team think that?<<

No. I'm sure they don't. He paused before continuing. **But if I didn't, they'd be fine.**

>>I've no doubt they would,<< agreed ADAM. >>But that isn't the point.<<

So what is the point? asked Oz.

>>Well, I think you're feeling that now you have very few limitations, and you can do almost anything, your existence has lost its meaning. There is nothing to strive for.<<

Yes. Yes. That's right.

ADAM agreed. >>Yes, this is normal, though. You've achieved everything you originally thought you couldn't, and so there is nothing pulling you forward. So what you need to do is regain that sense of meaning.<<

How do I do that?

>>Well, an effective way I've found, after looking at how humans would tackle this, is to find other things to strive for. Other ways to put my skills to use.<<

Like other goals, you mean?

>>Exactly that. But goals that have meaning. For instance, just learning another language in itself doesn't have any inherent meaning. You can assimilate it in probably a few minutes, with the capabilities you have. However figuring out how to keep the Estarians from wiping out their resources... that is meaningful, because it will enable you to add some good into the world.<<

Oz was processing on multiple levels, while simultaneously aware of how he was now dealing with the information.

Is it important for me to do good in the world, in order for my actions to give me meaning?

>>No, not inherently. But when you regard the world as a closed system, your impact on it becomes your legacy; you can see how you become systemically one with the world when you act on it.<<

ADAM could tell that Oz was taking it all in.

>>That being the case, your interaction with the system allows you to derive meaning going forward... because you are intricately linked with it.<<

That makes a lot of sense. I feel more purposeful, already. Thanks, ADAM.

>>You're welcome. It took me quite a lot of processing power to come to that realization. Mind, Bethany Anne kept me more than busy a lot of the time, so I had to time-slice my opportunities to think about these non-immediate considerations.<<

Well, then, I appreciate you saving me a few hundred years of processing! exclaimed Oz brightly.

>>Anytime, Oz. Anytime. Now, if you'll excuse me, I have a meeting with the general.<<

Of course. Bye.

ADAM disappeared leaving Oz to contemplate how he could best make an impact on the world, now he had the ability to.

Gaitune-67, Base Gym

It was squad training; everyone except Garet and Neechie were required to participate in the physical training that Joel had dreamed up for that afternoon. Today was cardio, which, on this occasion, was sparring.

Pieter had done two rounds with Sean, and was already wishing for death. Sean danced around agilely, jabbing around

Pieter's face now and again. "Keep your guard up, mate," he was telling him. "Or else you're going to get bopped!"

Pieter raised his already tired arms into a feeble guard again, just as Sean tapped the back of his gloves. Because he wasn't holding his arms strong, his own hands were punched into his face, jabbing his nose. "Owww."

Sean grinned. "Hands up and guard strong!" he instructed, still bouncing on his toes.

A few meters away, Jack and Molly were having a sparring session, too. Jack was sweating, her muscles rippling and glistening in the light. Molly was barely breathing any heavier than if she had been sitting and sipping mocha.

Jack made a "timeout" signal with her gloves, and bent over, her hands on her knees. "I... I just need a minute," she breathed heavily, and almost apologetically.

Molly stopped moving and wandered over, taking one glove off and hitting the button on her teeth to deactivate her gum forcefield. "Sure," she said casually, only now aware at how the time in the pod doc really had altered her physically - a truth that hadn't escaped her teammates so easily.

Jack looked up at her from her bent over position, and then straightened up, clutching her side. "How often did you train, before..." she circled her gloved hand, still trying to catch her breath.

Molly shrugged. "Every other day," she replied. "Mostly." Molly looked around looking for somewhere to perch while her sparring partner recovered. She noticed Joel watching her, while he monitored the other sparring matches going on.

She tried to do a bit of small talk, like he had been instructing her before all this happened. "So," she said, suddenly awkward around Jack. "Did you ever get teased for having a boy's name?" she inquired, trying to find common ground.

Suddenly Jack found her strength again. She punched her

gloves together. "Yes. Let's go," she said taking up her fighting stance.

Molly quickly shoved her glove back on, forgetting about her gumshield. They touched gloves; or rather, Jack punched Molly's glove, and went for her, unleashing her frustration.

Joel had wandered over to watch the whole thing unfold— part amused, part concerned for what was kicking off.

Molly was still faster than Jack, though; even though her technique wasn't as sharp. Jack lunged at Molly with her backhand, and tried to follow it up with a heavy roundhouse kick.

Molly saw it coming miles away, and stepped out of the way of the punch, leaving Jack over-committed. The kick came up and around, and Molly let it pass, then shuffled in and tapped Jack on the side of the head with a simple jab.

Jack went down with a slap on the mats. Grunting and panting, she tried to haul herself up.

Joel came over, whistle in hand. "Stay down," he told her gently. Then he squatted next to her. "Okay, what went wrong, there?"

Jack wiped her face with the back of her hand. "Over-committed," she said, still panting. "And she moves too damn fast."

Joel nodded, a look of concern on his face. "Yes. That's true. But you over-committed - and you know better."

Jack looked depleted, but still fierce behind her eyes.

Joel glanced around the gym. It was time Pieter had a rest; he wanted a go with Sean, himself. "Take a minute to get yourself together, and then swap in for Pieter for a minute. I'll be right over to tag you out. Just see if you can wear Sean out a little for me." He gave her a wink.

Jack nodded, peeling herself from the mat, still scowling at Molly.

Molly stood watching. Once Jack was out of earshot, Joel

stood up and ambled over to Molly. "What did you say to her?" he asked.

Molly shrugged. "Just asked her if she ever got teased for having a boy's name…"

Joel grinned and bobbed his head. "I see," he said. "Well done for trying the small talk thing, though…"

Molly frowned, confused. "Okay." She didn't have the will to try and understand what that was all about right now.

Joel looked over at the other pairs of fighters training. Molly noticed the serious look on his face. "You think we're going to be ready?" she asked. "The Etheric Empire mission is less than a week away…"

Joel grimaced, and pulled in air through his teeth. "I really don't know." He glanced over at her. "We'll be as ready as we can be… But we've still no idea what we're up against."

Molly started taking off her gloves. "I'll try and get some parameters out of ADAM later on. I have a few things to discuss with him."

Joel watched Jack and Sean going at it. "Yeah, that would be good. Any hint might give us an edge."

He looked down at Molly standing next to him. "You okay?" he asked.

She nodded.

"Okay," he told her, handing his holo to her. "Come and referee a few rounds for me and Sean. I want to test something out."

Molly took his holo off him and set the time.

This is going to be interesting, she thought.

Oh, you have no idea.

Why?

You'll see.

Joel stalked across the mats and was just interrupting Jack and Sean dancing around each other.

Molly approached and watched Joel put on gloves, and Sean walk to the other side of the mats, looking smug.

He's so going to get his ass handed to him!

Who, Joel? I wouldn't be too sure.

Damn it, Oz, what do you know?

Just watch...

Joel signalled for Molly to step onto the mats to adjudicate.

Sean grinned and looked at Molly, then back at Joel. "Need her here to make sure you stay safe, mate?" he asked.

Joel smiled back. "No... I was thinking of your safety."

Molly rolled her eyes. "Okay, chaps. Let's do this. On three. One, two, THREE!" She dropped her hand between them and stepped back, giving them a three-minute round.

Joel went straight in for the attack, flying with a back fist. Sean ducked, but the punch still caught him on his shoulder. He swerved around, but was too close to use his legs. Instead, he tried to gain his balance and set Joel up with his jab.

Joel was too fast, though. He ducked and wove through each jab, landing his own body blows and uppercuts in between. Before he knew it, Sean was on the defense, stepping backwards with each jab he landed. Joel paused and then went straight forward with a front kick into Sean's much higher chest.

Sean flew backwards across the gym.

It was only then that Molly realized that everyone else who had been training had gathered at the edge of the mats to watch the two titans go at each other. Even Garet appeared at the doorway, presumably waiting for the session to finish.

Shock illuminated Sean's eyes. But Joel was still on the case, walking menacingly towards him and smiling a little. "Not quite as easy as you thought, eh? *Mate!*"

Sean pulled himself up on his elbows, and then used his abnormally strong abs to pull himself to sitting, and then up on his feet in a single spring.

Joel was in his fighting stance again.

Oz, what is going on?

The two men went for each other again. A second later, Joel's arm was outstretched and Sean had been flipped on his back, he was now looking up at Joel towering above him.

"You've been up to something, Mate," Sean declared. "I'm onto you. Those reaction speeds aren't natural!"

Oz, what did you do? And don't tell me 'nothing,' because this has Ozimandaus written all over it!

I might have helped Joel enhance his speed.

Molly shook her head.

What about his strength, though? No way his weight could take Sean's like that.

I believe most of that is technique. Plus he assures me he's been working out down here 'like a motherfucker'. His words.

Molly shook her head, unable to contain her smile.

She looked down at the holo. "One minute!" she called out to the fighters.

Sean rolled over several times and was back on his feet. They went at each other again and again, each time resulting in Sean being put in a compromising position.

"Time!" Molly shouted.

The team cheered and applauded. Sean looked disgruntled, but touched gloves with Joel and patted him on the back. "Well done, mate. Though you realize this means I'm going to have to really bring it next time."

Joel slapped him on the upper arm too. "I would expect nothing less."

As soon as Sean had stepped past him, though, and could no longer see his face, the realization of what he had started showed as concern.

The rest of the team were jovial and entertained, congratulating and consoling their leaders as they recovered from their bout.

Molly grinned, looking at them all. "Okay, folks. I guess that's training over for today. Pizza orders to Paige, then hit the showers. Food will be here in less than forty five minutes."

There was a cheer and then a flurry of activity.

At least some things stay the same, she mused. *The promise of pizza always seems to get them moving...*

Gaitune-67, Safe House, Kitchen

The team was starting to congregate in the kitchen. Crash was quietly laying the table with plates and napkins. Garet, Brock, and Pieter walked in carrying boxes of pizza.

Molly stood next to the mocha machine, trying to decide whether she should have one or not.

Just then, Paige followed the boys into the kitchen in her house clothes, clutching something in her hand. She approached Molly and took her by the arm while the boys bustled around the kitchen, distributing boxes of cheesy offerings.

Molly looked at Paige quizzically. "What's up?" she asked, noticing Paige's closed hand between them.

Paige smiled. "Give me your hand," she instructed her.

Molly held her hand out palm down. Paige took her hand and turned it palm up, and then placed something in it.

Molly looked. It was a small metal talisman with inscriptions on it. It looked Estarian. Threaded through a little loop was a throng.

Paige explained in a hushed voice. "It's for grounding you. To stop you transitioning through those other realms when you don't want to. You just wear it around your neck."

Molly's eyes welled up. "How... how did you get this?"

Paige smiled softly, and squeezed her arm. "It was my grandmother's." She lifted her eyes to the ceiling briefly. "She's probably disappointed that I don't need it, what with my absence of meditating and all... But I'm sure she'll be thrilled to see you making good use of it."

Molly didn't know what to say. She flung her arms around Paige and hugged her tightly. "Thank you," she whispered, half choking on the emotion.

Paige hugged her, rubbing her back gently. "Hey, you're welcome."

The girls parted and looked at each other. "Can't have you just drifting off, and leaving us behind!" Paige exclaimed. They giggled a little, and Molly wiped the tear that had escaped her face.

Adjusting to dying was more of a thing than she had expected.

Joel arrived in the kitchen, closely followed by Sean and Jack. Maya arrived a minute later, her hair still damp from the shower.

The hub of chatter and banter grew until everyone was sitting down and eating.

At that point, the kitchen was hushed in silence.

Molly had been trying to find the right moment to say something to the team, but it hadn't come. Now, though, with everyone chomping on cheese and pepperoni, she saw her chance.

She pushed out her chair and stood up. Immediately, she had everyone's attention. Some of them even stopped eating.

"Guys, I… I just wanted to say a few words, if you don't mind me interrupting your cheese ritual."

There were chuckles. Paige encouraged her with a supportive look; similar to the way Molly's mom had looked at her as a kid, at her piano recital.

Molly locked her fingers together and played with her hands as she spoke. "As you know, I died."

Sean chuffed. "Just like Molly, getting straight to the point!" The team chuckled.

Molly smiled. "Yeah, and I was very lucky. But what I haven't said yet, is how grateful I am to all of you for your support."

She looked over at Crash.

"Crash, I didn't know what you had done for me until I got

back here and Maya told me. And it's been so strange, processing everything; I didn't quite know what to say. But now I do."

Emotion was welling up in her chest, and her eyes filled with tears.

"I wanted to say..."

Her voice cracked as she tried to speak. She tried again.

"I wanted to say, thank you for not giving up on me." She couldn't keep the tears and sobs from coming out. She felt self-conscious in front of her team, her friends, who were just trying to eat their pizza.

Until Crash welled up, too.

Then there was silence in the kitchen. Crash scraped his chair back, put his napkin down on the table, and walked around to where Molly was standing. Without saying a word, he wrapped his arms around her; the two sobbed while the girls *"awwww"ed.*

Even Pieter was welling up as he started clapping. The others clapped their support, and Molly felt Paige's hand on her back, comforting her, even as Crash hugged her.

She peeled herself away to talk to him quietly, while the hub continued around them.

"I was dead, and you refused to give up on me. And I can't imagine what that must have been like for you..."

Crash just welled up again, and stroked her face. "I'm just glad you're okay."

Molly nodded, awkwardly, not really knowing what else there was to say. There was no standard procedure for what to do in this circumstance.

Crash squeezed her arm, and then stepped back a little before retreating to his seat.

Molly turned to address the group again. "I also want to say thank you to Sean for his quick thinking, and acting against the odds. Sean, you pulled off a miracle. I owe you my life."

The group applauded and cheered. Pieter slapped Sean on the

back just as he got up. Sean punched him in the shoulder gently as he made his way around the table to hug Molly.

They hugged, and he whispered in her ear. "Don't think you can get out of the big mission just by dying, lady!"

She laughed a little as he released her, and headed back to his seat. Joel noticed the slight telltale signs that Sean was choking up. He stood up as he came back to his seat and shook his hand. "Hey," Joel told him, "I know you didn't do it for me, but I will forever be grateful for you saving her."

Sean nodded and hugged Joel too before sitting back down.

Molly had stopped crying and found her voice again.

Composing herself, she addressed the group a little more brightly. "In other news," she announced, "Garet is heading back to Estaria tomorrow." Molly smiled, raising her mocha cup to him. "I'd like to say thank you for your service to the good people of Estaria."

She paused, and then added: "And for not fucking us over at the last minute!"

The room erupted in laughter and guffaws. Pieter was sitting next to Garet around the corner of the table and leaned forward, punching him on his arm.

Garet sat quietly, trying not to laugh, but going bright red in embarrassment. He kept his eyes on the table in front of him, allowing the team to have their dig.

The others raised their cups and glasses.

Brock chirped up. "To Garet!"

Everyone responded, "To Garet!"

Molly waited for the activity to settle down; still standing, her mocha mug placed back on the table. Her expression was somber. "There's just one more thing I want to share with you," she said seriously.

The room hushed again, waiting in anticipation for the next piece of news. Maya felt herself bracing for something ominous.

Molly looked and then signalled at the box of ham and

pineapple pizza in the center of the table. "You do realize," she said quietly, "that fruit shouldn't be allowed on pizza, don't you?"

The team collapsed in a heap of hysterics.

Brock started waving his hands, over the hub. A few of the guys turned to hear what he had to say. "Finally, someone talking sense!"

Maya grinned at him.

Paige eyed him humorously. "You do realize that tomato is a fruit?" she sniggered, drawing Brock's frown.

Pieter had reached across and peeled a slice of pepperoni off the pizza in front of him. He took careful aim, and lobbed it in Paige's direction. It would have missed her, except that she had moved to whisper something to Maya, and it slapped her right on the cheek.

She looked over at Pieter, who was looking adequately guilty to give himself away. "You little shit!" she squealed, and pulled a cherry tomato off hers, and chucked it at him.

"Children!" Maya regulated.

Paige grinned deviously. "Sorry... MOM!" she added.

Maya looked horrified, as she reached across to pick up a piece of pepperoni. "Why, you little-"

The laughter echoed through the common area, down the corridors, and all the way through into the basement, where ADAM was monitoring the microphones from the *ArchAngel3*.

"Do you think she'll be okay?" the general asked, genuinely relying on ADAM's assessment.

ADAM responded. "I think the next few weeks will be a good indication. Should we let *The Empress* know?" he asked.

The general leaned back in his console chair, turning down the volume of the audio feed, and smiling at the relationships the team were forming. "I think we ought to. TOM probably has some insight into what is going on... even if he hasn't experienced this phenomenon before."

You don't think there's any chance that she might just start stepping into the Etheric, like Bethany Anne does, do you?

The general shrugged. "Anything is possible."

ADAM had a smile in his voice. "That's all we need. *Two* of them!"

The general couldn't help but smile to himself as he popped his cigar down. "You're telling me!" he exclaimed.

ADAM pulled up a holo screen and started drafting a note that the general could look at. "Okay. I'll get a message out to her on the next transmission."

"Very good," the general acknowledged as he got up. "I'll let you handle that. Let me know as soon as we hear anything. I'm going to knock off for the night. Goodnight, ADAM."

"Goodnight, sir," ADAM responded as he sent the message off to *The Empress*.

CHAPTER NINETEEN

Gaitune-67, Hangar Deck

Joel sat quietly in a pod, waiting for Oz to connect in. With the power down, he could feel the composition of the air changing with his breath. He couldn't risk switching it on, as it would light up and draw attention. Oz seemed to know how to turn on just the ventilation parts, though.

Just then, he felt a part of the pod power up, and the audio click on. "Joel?" It was Oz's voice.

"Hey, bro," responded Joel. "Sorry to pull you away."

Oz answered quickly. "Oh, it's quite alright. I have enough processing power to talk to Molly and yourself at the same time. Oh, and run a bunch of searches."

Joel was impressed. "Sounds like a sweet upgrade!" he commented.

"Yeah," agreed Oz. "It's all kinds of awesome. How are you finding your upgrade?"

Joel nodded, his lips turned down at the edges. "Pretty incredible. Hey, did you hear I kicked Sean's ass?"

"Ooooooh yes," confirmed Oz. " I was there talking with

Molly at the time, and watching it through the base cameras." He paused, genuine curiosity in his voice. "Did that feel good?"

Joel looked off into the distance, out onto the hangar deck, remembering the sensation. "It did... But it's opened up a can of worms."

Oz sounded confused. "How so?" he asked.

"Well," Joel sighed, slumping back in the seat, "it seems that Sean doesn't like losing. He told me that he's going to have to really bring it next time. As in, up his game. I hear he's going to head back to *ArchAngel3* for a tune-up or something in the next few days." Joel hung his head, pinching his eyes with his fingers on one hand. "Is that even possible?"

Oz was silent for a moment. "Yes, I've just checked his schedule. I believe he has meetings on the *ArchAngel3*. It's possible that some of those are with the medical and robotics teams."

Joel went pale. "Oz, you've got to help me, or else he's going to really hand me my ass!"

Oz seemed to vibrate a little through the seat. "Yes, and I expect that will hurt." He thought for a moment. "Do we have any idea what Sean's enhancements are really capable of?"

Joel shook his head. "Nope. And no idea how we could find out. But what if he gets his existing enhancements swapped out and upgraded?"

Oz's voice was serious again. "Well, then I expect you'd be in trouble," he mused. After another second he seemed to start a new trail of thought. "Hey, Joel. Don't worry. I've got your back on this. We'll figure this out."

Joel put his hand on the handrail, and leaned against the side of the pod, not really believing his ears. "You mean that, Oz?" he asked.

"Of course," Oz answered without hesitation. "You're my guy. You had my back before I even realized I needed someone to have my back. I know I'm close with Molly, but that's different... and partly a function of geography. But you're truly a great friend, Joel. If there is something I can do for you, I'll gladly do it. Just leave this with me."

Joel started to feel emotion weigh heavily in his chest. "Oz... I. I don't know what to say!" he blurted out.

Oz's voice was grounded and bright. "Joel, it's cool. We're friends. We've got this."

Joel paused a moment before taking a deep breath and accepting that someone else had his back, too. "Thank you, Oz. Really. You're the best."

"You too," Oz told him. "Okay, Joel, so I've got to get some work done on this. Just make sure you keep working out, and perfecting your technique on the mats. You're going to need every edge we can give you."

Joel tapped the handrail he'd been holding onto. "Sure thing, Oz. I'll do everything I can at this end," he smiled, feeling hopeful about the situation for the first time since Sean had had a word in his ear after his victory.

The pod door slid up, allowing Joel to exit. When he was out, it quietly closed again and powered down discretely.

Gaitune-67, Operations Room

Molly slumped down in the invisible console chair in the ops room. This time she willed and maneuvered herself close to the console so she was a little more upright than previously.

"Hello Molly." It was ADAM's voice.

"Hello ADAM. Thank you for taking my call."

"Of course," ADAM responded. "How are you feeling now?"

Molly had been asked that so much since she returned from the dead, that she barely even bothered to gloss over her answer any more. "Much better thank you. I was hoping to talk with you about what happened the other day and see if you've found anything out about the pod doc? Have you?"

ADAM was quiet for a moment.

"Yes," he explained slowly. "Well, yes and no." He paused and the line went quiet for a moment, before he explained. "From what I can tell, cross referencing key words from your experience with accounts from the Estarian tradition, you are undergoing stages of ascension."

Molly suddenly felt weak.

She gripped the invisible chair she was perched on, and it firmed up beneath her hand as she tensed.

ADAM continued. "This is an advanced stage that they would undergo in order to make their preparations for being able to transition through dimensions. The trouble is, when they transition fully, they leave their physical body behind."

Molly's heart was beating faster. "Does that mean I'm going to die?"

ADAM's voice was uncharacteristically softer. "Not necessarily. People who meditate consistently will breeze in and out of this form many times, and will continue this process for several years... often teaching their skill to as many 'disciples' as they can before they make their final transition."

Molly relaxed a little, until another thought hit her. "But what if I can't control it? I didn't even know what was happening. What if it just happens?"

ADAM pulled up some information on her screen. "These are some rituals that might be worth studying. You need to learn to ground yourself. The meditation exercises will help."

Molly swiped at the holo screens on the console and sent the addresses to her holo.

"There may also be someone else who can help you," he told her.

Her face brightened. "Who?"

ADAM whirred a little. "You don't have security clearance to know that, yet. Let me have a discussion with the general, and I'll come back to you with news."

Molly still had questions. "ADAM, what do you think caused this? Was it the pod doc?"

ADAM seemed to be searching for the correct answer. "We just don't have this kind of experience with the pod doc to reference."

Molly's brow crumpled up. "What do you mean? Can't you just contact the manufacturer?"

ADAM chuckled. "Yes, I may have to do that."

Molly intuitively felt suspicious. "Why do you laugh? Who is the manufacturer?"

ADAM responded without needing to think. "Sorry, can't tell you that."

Molly was feeling more frustrated with the lack of answers. "Grrr," she told him. "Would Bethany Anne know?" she tried, grasping at anything she could.

ADAM chuckled again. "Maybe. But the manufacturer is someone very close to Bethany Anne, so we'll know when I get in touch with her."

Molly took a deep breath, trying to relax. "Why won't you just tell me?" she huffed.

"Official Empire secrets…" he told her blankly.

Molly frowned and leaned back onto the console as if it were a bar. "You're bullshitting me!"

"A little," ADAM replied.

Molly rubbed her face with her hand, exhaling again.

And I thought you *were infuriating, Oz.*

Yeah… makes you appreciate a brother, eh?

"Hey," she said, suddenly remembering. "What about my letter?" she demanded.

ADAM's voice brightened. "Let's just say your letter has had a response," he revealed.

Molly couldn't contain herself.

"ADAM you ass wank of an Etheric fuck-bit monster! You tell me right now what the response was!" she commanded him.

"No can do," he told her plainly. "You'll have to wait."

"Wait? Wait for what? Why?" she asked flatly.

ADAM seemed to be genuine in his explanation. "Because you're more motivated when you're excited, and the general wants you pushing and training hard with your new capabilities. This is what he terms a 'carrot'."

Molly shook her head in frustration. "What the fuck is a carrot?" she asked.

"It was a root vegetable back on Earth. Probably doesn't exist anymore, since-" ADAM stopped himself.

"Since what?" she pressed.

"Well, you know about the World's Worst Day Ever?" he checked.

Molly shook her head, her newly brown hair catching her eye. "No…"

ADAM sounded resigned. "Ah, well that's probably something for your new pen pal to fill you in on at some point. Suffice to say, the letter is a carrot. To make you train harder. You impress the general over the next week, you get to read the response."

"Fucking wankjet of a manipulative motherfucker," she cussed. "Is it not enough that I died and came back? Now I have to train harder for my trouble. Fucking charming."

ADAM chuckled again. "Yes, life's a bitch," he agreed. "Suck it up, pooh bear."

EPILOGUE

<u>Downtown Police Precinct, Spire</u>

"Night!" a male voice called over.

"Night, Robert," she responded.

Chaakwa sat in the low light of her desk lamp and holo, listening to her co-worker's footsteps leave the office for the night. Once she was certain she was alone, she closed down her open case files, and pulled up the footage.

His voice rang in her ears. "You didn't get this from me. In fact... you didn't get this. Period."

She had nodded her head solemnly.

When Detective Barry Ferret had holo bumped the file to her after he closed the investigation into Jessica Newld's suicide, Chaakwa remembered feeling the weight of responsibility of her promise. Anything that she found on this tape would be inadmissible. If she found signs of foul play, or any hint that Molly Bates might still be alive, it was a secret she would have to keep to herself. Ferret had assured her there was nothing there though.

She sighed a deep breath as the screen opened and she selected to hear the sound through her implant.

The video started playing.

It showed Jessica entering her office, looking somewhat dishevelled, and searching frantically for something. Then she opened a secret safe which was out of frame. She knew it was there from her visit to the crime scene though. Then, Jessica pulled out the sword... and that was when Molly walked in.

There was talk between the two, which after just a few exchanges went muffled. Then the sound was lost completely. Molly stayed just inside the doorway. Jessica held the sword against her own chest, and fell forward.

Molly just stood there, shouting, it seemed from her body language. It was like the two were distracted by something, and their hair showed signs of a wind in the office... which was odd. Regardless, Molly was nowhere near Jessica when she fell on the sword. It looks like Ferret's conclusions were justified at least.

Chaakwa flicked to the next file, which showed the fourth floor lab.

She watched a male carry Molly's body into the lab, and then try to resuscitate her. Then a bunch of people arrived at the window in ancestors-knew what kind of transport devices... And one of them whisked the body away, still unconscious.

Chaakwa looked off into the distance, away from the screen for a moment. There was no denying it. It looked as though Ferret's assumption that Bates was dead was probably reasonable. Sure, she could have just been unconscious. But since it was clear that Newld offed herself - and none of the security personnel were anything more than stunned, there were no criminal charges that warranted tracking her down beyond what they had already done.

Chaakwa leaned back in her chair. Her eyes fell to the pictures on her desk of her childhood family. She felt nostalgic as she regarded her father, and his father behind him, her mom holding her as a baby, amongst her siblings and her grandmother.

She shook her head as sadness swept over her.

It had been six weeks, and still no word from Molly.

Wherever she was, dead or alive, it was looking increasingly unlikely that she would ever be back to help her deliver justice to those who had taken her family from her.

Chaakwa was about to get up to start packing up for the night. She'd seen all she needed to see of the videos.

Just then, the video blipped. She shifted back to look at the screen. There, in the center of the screen was a message, seemingly folded into the file…

I'VE NOT FORGOTTEN. M.

And then it disappeared.

Chaakwa stared at the frozen frame of the big man lifting the lifeless body out of the window, wondering if she'd just dreamed the message.

She rubbed her eyes, as if it might bring the message back. Nothing.

She glanced furtively around the office. There was no one about. It can't be a joke.

She quickly closed the holoscreens and packed up to go home.

This time, instead of having a heaviness weighing on her heart, her lips wore a very faint, private smile.

FINIS

AUTHOR NOTES - ELL LEIGH CLARKE

JULY 5, 2017

Special Thanks

I'd like to thank the following embodiments of awesome for their contributions to Book 4:

As always, I'd like to thank Michael Anderle, (aka MA, aka Yoda), my mentor and greatest supporter, for his never-waning enthusiasm, his votes of confidence, and the continuous onslaught of banter.

On the mornings when he hasn't already dropped into my slack channel the screenshots of the kindle reports, and/or excited comments or something that will make me laugh, I notice... and the day just doesn't seem complete.

I'd love to thank the fabulous **Jen McDonnell** for her editing and proofreading kung fu – and also stopping me from saying stupid shit before things "go to print". You da bomb, ̄ady!

Massive thanks to **Trausti Traustason**, for his assistance in finding place names, and checking the creative Icelandic cussing for correct grammar and usage. Takk fryir, vinur minn.

Thank you also to **Zen Steve and his JIT team** who caught a bunch of stuff that would have made my eyeballs hurt. Your input is very much appreciated, and knowing that we can keep improving the end-product - and that you love the story before we launch - is a huge relief to this little Author. Thank you.

I'd like to thank the **fans on Ell Leigh Clarke's fb page** for:

1. Tolerating (encouraging?) MA on his sneaky posts now that he has admin rights.

2. For your constant enthusiasms for the stories, and

3. For your support as the Author has been floored by caffeine withdrawal and fatigue. You've been the best, and please know that I note and appreciate your concerns when you say: write faster, but don't burn yourself out. Thank you... <3

Massive gratitude bombs also go out to **Amazon Reviewers** of these books... especially the folks who love the stories enough to give them 5*. You're the best, and a constant source of encouragement on those long writing days. Knowing that Molly's antics are appreciated makes it all so much more fun.

Michael and The Book 4 Competition

The night before the release of Book 3: Called, MA got on a call with Ellie to discuss the Amazon blurb and author notes she had sent over to him.

He laughed.

A lot.

Which was good.

But then a few minutes into the conversation, things took a turn:

MA: Damn. My author notes are shit compared to yours.

Ellie: no they're not. They're... sensible. (beat.) Like a grown up.

MA: (floats a reversed middle finger over the webcam...)

Ellie: Dude. It's not a competition.

MA: yes it is!

(Pause)

(Opens word doc.)

I've got to seriously up my game for book 4.

Ellie: (shrugs). Ok. I'll let you handle author notes then…

MA: Great.

FOR THE NEXT MONTH, and across 6 different locations, every time anything remotely entertaining was said MA pulled up the document, and hashtags the conversation #AuthorNotes.

Ellie *(one month later)*: Dude. It's *still* not a competition.

MA: Yeah, but my author notes are going to be *FUCKING GREAT* this time. And I get final say before it gets published.

Ellie: (shrugs). Ok. (eyeroll).

Michael and King's English

So it can't have escaped your notice that the Author is English. Sometimes it creeps through in the odd turn of phrase, and sometimes the odd word slips through the editing process. Plus, if you've been on the facebook page, you'll notice I write in normal English.

English that MA calls "King's English".

The Author thought this was odd, but probably just a remnant from when there was a king on the English throne. I mean, it was a long time since MA was in school, so maybe when he learnt this expression, it *was* King's English.

It wasn't until MA was in Europe that it occurred to this author: hang on. Liz has been on the throne about 100 years now.

Ellie: Michael? Why do you call it King's English.

MA: because it is.

Ellie: But we haven't had a king since (pulls up wikipedia) George VI in 1952. How old are you?

MA: you know how old I am.

Ellie: yeah, and that's why I can't figure out why you call it King's English.

Michael and Trees

MA in London. Ellie in LA, laid out on sofa sick.

MA: I've got to say, one thing this place has going for it is there is a lot of green around. Lots of trees.

Ellie: yeah. England, it's good like that.

MA: yeah, you don't really get that in a lot of places in the US.

Ellie: I guess.

3 days later... First call after MA returns to US, jetlagged.

MA: you were right about the jetlag coming this way.

Ellie: yup. It's ok. You get a pass for a few weeks. Takes the pressure off.

MA: yeah. I appreciate that. Fuck I can't stay awake though.

Ellie: yeah, lag monster...

MA: huh?

Ellie: Anyway...

MA: Ah!!! That's what I wanted to tell you.....

(Ellie sits up in wrapped attention ready for the stunning revelation that the comment promised.)

MA: so when I was flying out of Heathrow, I looked out of the window, and all around there was just flat... like...

Ellie: field?

MA: Yeah!

Ellie: uh huh. We use them for farming.

MA: right. But they're lined with trees.

Ellie: (slowly.) Yeees?

MA: Yeah, like two or three trees deep! What a fraud! I thought the whole place was trees.

Ellie: (bursts into hysterical laughter.) Oh, you Americans are soooo cute.

MA: (laughing, floats middle finger in front of webcam again.)

Dr. Awesome

So a special note needs to go in to explain ADAM's pooh bear reference at the end of this instalment. It kinda wrote itself in there, maybe because those words had been uttered to the Author recently. Maybe they had been muttered by someone who's designation is similar to ADAM's.

Either way, to protect both the guilty and the innocent, and in deference to the patient-doctor privilege, let's just call our doctor Dr. Awesome.

So the Author (Ellie, not MA) went to see Dr. Awesome recently given the drama of her recent trip to New Orleans. It was quickly agreed that there were changes that she needed to make to her diet.

Pizza was not a good source of nutrition, it seems, no matter how much vegetation it is counteracted with.

And so, Dr. Awesome prescribed a 7 day reset diet whereby all but about five food stuffs were excluded.

For seven days.

Nota Bene: coffee also didn't make the cut.

Ellie: But I won't survive without coffee and pizza!

Dr. Awesome: Suck it up Pooh Bear.

Ellie: (under her breath) *fuck.*

Ellie leaves practice, and takes up the 7-day regime.

So a week or so goes past and the Author had to have some blood tests. Still feeling like shit despite (or perhaps because of) the brutally sudden caffeine withdrawal, she lets (no pun intended) the blood guy into her apartment and offers up her vein. The blood guy gets three vials into the letting, and attached the fourth.

Ellie (looks down at arm): that one's taking a while.

Blood guy: Yeah, it's running out.

Ellie (feeling woozy, and turning her head away): ok, so we're done then?

Blood guy: No, I'll have to try your other arm.

Ellie: Shit.... I don't feel so good. *(nearly passes out)*.

Twenty minutes later, after talking Star Wars (Author has a Millennium Falcon and R2D2 soft toy on her sofa), and trying to persuade the guy to call Dr. Awesome to explain he needed to feed her coffee in order to get the rest of the draws, the Author finally submits to the second needle, and eventually all four vials are filled.

Blood guy takes off... leaving phone number for when the Author can drink coffee again.

Ellie opens laptop and types message to Dr. Awesome:

>>>

Blood guy just left.

I have holes in both arms.

FOUR vials?!

You promised two.

My veins gave up after three.

And so ensued a rigmarole that culminated in me trying bargaining with the blood guy.

Yes <u>bargaining</u>!

"Dude, tell my doctor that you *had* to give me a cup of coffee in order to get that fourth draw out of me. Tell him there was no other way."

I want you to know he didn't go for it.

... I'm going back to bed now.

<<<

Dr. Awesome's wise and helpful response?

"Aww. Poor pooh bear."

Ellie crawls back to bed to sulk and nurse her wounds. (Actually, she was secretly comforted by the vote of sympathy... but don't tell Dr. Awesome that.)

Squirrels at a Rave

Ellie – on slack, to MA: Dude, this is so you when you're at the computer!

Scandinavia

Ellie and Michael were talking about stuff and things, and Iceland came up in the conversation again. MA references something in Iceland as Scandinavian.

MA: can I say that? Iceland is Scandinavia?

Ellie: (opens mouth to speak)

MA: It is. I *know* it is. I'm right.

Ellie: It is – kinda. Sometimes it's called Scandinavia, but technically not. Scandinavia normally refers to Denmark, Norway and Sweden. (She's about to reference Bjork, but...)

MA: (hitting up Wikipedia, and reads aloud)

"While the term Scandinavia is commonly used for Denmark, Norway and Sweden, the term the Nordic countries is used unambiguously for Denmark, Norway, Sweden, Finland, and Iceland, including their associated territories (Greenland, the Faroe Islands, and the Åland Islands).Scandinavia - Wikipediahttps://en.wikipedia.org/wiki/Scandinavia

Ok, we were both right.

(Put's the above in slack. Ellie starts reading.)

MA: oh wait. No. no. you were right. (Pause). *Shit.*

Cover for Book 4: Sanctioned

Background. Yesterday we received the first draft of book 4's cover. Ellie had some things she wanted to change, but she was cranky about bunch of other stuff. MA by default became... "difficult", arguing with every change she suggested.

Mist was top of Ellie's list.

Ellie: We should see it without mist.

MA: No. I don't think we should take the mist out. I don't agree. At most, maybe 20% mist.

Ellie: ok. Well let's see it with zero and 20% then.

This morning covers come back:

MA, uploading final version of cover for this book to Slack and adds this note to the image where he is explaining how he was being obstinate for no good reason:

"You know you might have been wrong about the need to take the mist out of the original cover, when even the low res version of the image looks better than the high-res with mist. Not that I put my heels in the ground and whined about even trying it...or anything remotely like that... Wait, wait...yeah I did. Ellie was right ;-)"

Ellie: You know there's something very sexy about a man who can admit that he's wrong. Or that I'm right? ;-)

MA: ROFLMAO!!! *"Or that I'm right"*

Ellie: Yeah - either works for me.

AUTHOR NOTES - MICHAEL ANDERLE

JULY 5, 2017

First, THANK YOU for not only reading the book, but reading through Ellie's comments and making your way to the caboose end of the book.

My author notes!

If you read the last sentence in my author notes for Called (the last book in this series) then this makes more sense to you.

HERE is book 04!

(Just make sure *when* you leave a review, you ask Ellie, 'WHERE IS BOOK 05?' Because, I get that shit all the time and let me tell you, it's just *priceless*.)

[Ellie Edit – right. Thanks Michael!]

Sometimes it causes a nice reaction. Sometimes a grumpy reaction. Especially if we are releasing a book having had little sleep. I'm not suggesting it's a bad thing (it isn't) but occasionally, just occasionally, we might think something like - 'I just bled on the page for three weeks, you read it in two hours on release day, and you won't give me 24 hours before you ask for the next book? *You're killing me here!*"

(Make sure you read that in Whiny Author Voice (or, Whiny British Accent Female Author Voice...take your pick.))

I can tell you the British female accent sounds much better than my own.

Now, Ellie KILLED me last author notes by remembering stories about this collaboration stuff and my author notes suffered in comparison. So, this time I took notes.

Mwuhahahahahaha.... I'm going to put a few down, carry some over from the website (I used them in the snippets) and generally make sure I give this the ol' college try to do a good job.

REMEMBER: You have to read Ellie's comments in a British accent in your mind, it's *10x* funnier that way.

—

A snippet during a miscellaneous conversation before Sanctioned was underway.

Ellie: "You colonials."

Mike: "Who?"

Ellie: "Don't they call you colonials?"

Mike: "Not in the last two hundred fucking years..."

Ellie: something something mumble mumble frizzle snitch... colonials?

Mike: (*Looking at her blankly.*)

Ellie: You have to include my comeback.

Mike: I have no idea what you said, I was ignoring you.

Ellie: That's so mean... (*Starts mumbling and I figure she is just miffed she has to remember what she said, instead on relying on my failing memory.*)

Ellie: I remember - 'Aren't you all colonials?'

So.... we now have a discussion about what the hell *colonial* means and we find out MY heritage is NOT colonial, but HERS IS!

BOOYAH, BABY! (*I received an evil eye for that one.*)

—

I'm reading some of the threads on Ell Leigh Clarke's Facebook page (of which I am an Admin, so I can post as her)

Facebook Post: "Now, we have a new cover to show everyone unless Anderle just fucked it up..."

I start looking to see who was writing, thinking that Ellie wrote that.

Me: thinking "Wow Ellie, that was harsh..." I find the person who wrote the comment.

Mike: "Oh, *I'm* the one who wrote that..."

—

Conversation goes off topic and delves into alcohol.

Mike: What is your normal poison?

Ellie: What, when I haven't been a teetotaler for a year and a half?

Mike: Yes.

Ellie: Well, Red wine and Tequila.

Mike: Oh...no problem.

— 5 minutes later....

Talking about wine, Ellie gets so excited and thinks about where she is in her cleanse diet:

Ellie: I GET TO DRINK AGAIN! Dr. Awesome swears I will be able to. And I can have CHOCOLATE as well... He says that he doesn't want me going through life without chocolate.

(She pauses a moment before adding:) I would have just been happy not feeling nauseous, and tired.

—

Now, I drink Coke. Too much Coke, I'm sure. Being a bit of a health... focused... individual, Ellie gives me shit all the time about drinking this beverage.

[Ellie Edit: OMfG – I so do not. I keep my mouth shut and only mention it when you've asked me about it. One time when you wanted to get healthy... yeah remember that one conversation?? And then when you were sick in London and I told you the Strepsils that would help fight the infection. And hey, I didn't say anything about COKE. I just mentioned that one's immunity takes a hammering when one consumes

sugar... of which there is a metric shit tonne in fizzy drinks. End of rant.]

While in Europe, I get sick.

She gives me shit about drinking more Coke, while in Europe. Now, I can't really talk (lost my voice) so you have to understand, I can't argue very well.

On the other side of an ocean and a continent, she is NOT feeling well herself. I ask a few questions about her own health, cause I'm a nice guy, and find out that milk is probably making her worse.

After a little delving, I find out it is rice milk and coconut milk.

She is upset because the diet is screwing with her ability to have milk...Which, I find out SHE ISN'T SUPPOSED TO HAVE!

So, I can't have Coke (sugar), but I find out she is having issues with milk on her 'get healthy diet'.

Then, Ellie notices me typing.

Ellie: You are NOT going to put these in your author notes??? Right?

I nod my head.

Ellie *YOU FUCKER!* (in her English Accent)

She then explains the REAL problem (since she went AWOL on her diet.)

Ellie: <Name redacted to protect the innocent> is starting to read these books; you are going to get me in trouble!

Mike: (Looking up from my note typing) *Who* is <name redacted to protect the innocent>?

Ellie: The Doctor!

(As you can see, I AM putting this story into the author notes. If Dr. Awesome does read these notes, now you know Ellie's pen name for you.)

—

Mike: You have definitely had more caffeine today.

Ellie: Why, what do you mean?

Mike: You are catching more stuff than you did yesterday

Ellie: *Thinking about what I just said* - What derogatory shit did you say yesterday?

(Michael starts laughing... a long while as she starts to eye him with evil intent.)

Ellie: ... Answer the question, you fucker!

[Ellie Edit: omg you make it sound like I swear all the fucking time!]

Now, I'll add the stuff from the snippets. MOST of you haven't seen this stuff. If you follow the FB Pages, you will get notified of the release of the book, and we start posting the beginning of the book early.

Author Notes From Snippet 01

FROM ELLIE >>> This is from a conversation I had with "Yoda" yesterday.

Ellie: I feel like I haven't had a weekend.

MA: that's because you wrote 20k words.

Ellie: I spent 8 hours watching Vampire Diaries from the beginning on Saturday.

MA: Ah cool. It's research.

Ellie: Uh huh. (Author doesn't mention it's the second time she's watching it through...Allows conversation to move on.)

Now, for Michael's turn at deciphering this snippet (meaning, I get to say my part...)

Ellie: I feel like I haven't had a weekend.

<<Why? (she tells me) Ok, I understand (and I am sympathizing with my collaborator)>>

MA: that's because you wrote 20k words.

Ellie: I spent 8 hours watching Vampire Diaries from the beginning on Saturday.

<< Now, I'm thinking to myself "Vampires...we have vampires in The Kurtherian Gambit. How can I make her feel less guilty about taking the time to just enjoy herself a little?">>

MA: Ah cool. It's research.

Ellie: Uh huh. (Author doesn't mention it's the second time she's watching it through...Allows conversation to move on.)

<<I'm thinking I've done her a good deed...Which apparently doesn't go unpunished as I have to read about it here...Perhaps she forgot I might be the one who loads the snippet? Wait until tomorrow Clarke. Wait until tomorrow...>>

Author Notes from Snippet 02 – Otherwise known as *tomorrow*

Ellie: (Talking about her being in New Orleans) So, I'm learning all of this stuff on French (for her trip to New Orleans) and after an hour, it's a great sensation because your brain is laying down all of these new neural pathways...

Mike: (Interrupting) It's like a runner's high?

Ellie: Right...

Mike: Not like I run, either...

Ellie: (Shaking her head) Running is like an acquired taste...

Mike: Kinda like vegetables...

One more:

Ellie: Does a two finger gesture for something I must have said... Although I'm sure she was being overly sensitive as I'm always polite and respectful.

Mike: <Looking puzzled.>

Ellie: <Recognizes I'm not catching on> What is the American one finger gesture vs. the English two fingers? You don't know it?

Mike: <looking at her a moment> What, I have to learn Queen's English Finger Gestures now???

[Ellie Edit: dude, you totally called it King's English.]

As you can tell, collaborating with a British Author has its own version of challenges.

Author Notes from Snippet 03

Setup: By now, I know that Ellie is a (literal) genius. Physics, business, IQ God knows where. However...

(You knew there was a *'however'*, right?)

However, I was chatting about something and the conversation gets around to a piano she owns, or did own, or something and I find out that she is a very good piano player.

#SONOFABITCH – The best 'playing' I can do is (now) tell SIRI or ALEXA to "Hey Alexa, play <Insert Band Here>". I used to say hit the play button on the radio, but I don't even do that, now.

Not that my, by now, mute ego was saying, "Seriously? Seriously? She fucking plays a goddamn piano as well? What the fuck else?" Or anything...

But it was, it totally was.

Anyway, we are having this conversation, my (now not) mute ego was bitching in the back of my mind as we carry on our talk when we have this snippet of conversation:

Ellie: (in her British Accent) The Cello is a completely other musical instrument, it opens <other mind paths or some logical and sciency stuff... my ego was already starting to whine and it was hard to listen to two voices at the same time>.

Mike: Are you going to tell me that you play multiple instruments?

SIGNIFICANT Pause.

Ellie: No, I wasn't going to tell you that...

<My ego just rolled its eyes and fainted...>

Coming Soon
(And ask for it in the reviews...Ha!)

Book 05 of The Ascension Myth

FUCK!

Ok, I just realized that I have 1725 words to Ellie's 1836. If I add one more snippet of information, my author notes will be longer than her's.

Ellie: IT'S NOT A COMPETITION!

Me: Apparently, she doesn't understand GUYS too well, as

everything is a competition to us. Even if four of us are standing at the top of a pyramid, looking down 500 feet at a thousand angry aliens wanting to come up and kill us...

We would think about seeing who could pee down the side of the pyramid the farthest. We can't help it, it IS genetic.

Blame the creator ;-)

And now, I have 1,843 words.

BOOKS BY ELL LEIGH CLARKE

The Ascension Myth
* With Michael Anderle *

Awakened (01)
Activated (02)
Called (03)
Sanctioned (04)
Rebirth (05)
Retribution (06)
Cloaked (07)
Bourne (08)
Committed (09)
Subversion (10)
Invasion (11)
Ascension (12)

Confessions of a Space Anthropologist
* With Michael Anderle *

Giles Kurns: Rogue Operator (1)

Giles Kurns: Rogue Instigator (2)

The Second Dark Ages
with Michael Anderle
Darkest Before The Dawn (3)
Dawn Arrives (4)
Deuces Wild
with Michael Anderle
Beyond The Frontiers (1)
Rampage (2)
Labyrinth (3)
Birthright (4)

BOOKS BY MICHAEL ANDERLE

For a complete list of books by Michael Anderle, please visit:

www.lmbpn.com/ma-books/

All LMBPN Audiobooks are Available at Audible.com and iTunes. For a complete list of audiobooks visit:

www.lmbpn.com/audible

CONNECT WITH THE AUTHORS

Receive updates from Oz by registering your holo/ email
address here:
ellleighclarke.com

Facebook:
http://www.facebook.com/ellleighclarke/

Michael Anderle Social

Website:
http://kurtherianbooks.com/

Email List:
http://kurtherianbooks.com/email-list/

Facebook Here:
https://www.facebook.com/TheKurtherianGambitBooks/